THE BREEDLING & THE TRICKSTER

THE ELEMENT ODYSSEYS: BOOK TWO

BY

KIMBERLEE ANN BASTIAN

WISE
CREATIVE + PUBLISHING
Ink

ISBN 13: 978-1-63489-088-5
eISBN: 978-1-63489-089-2

Library of Congress Catalog Number: 2017950132
First Printing: 2017

Cover and interior design by Steven Meyer-Rassow.

Wise Ink Creative Publishing
837 Glenwood Ave.
Minneapolis, MN 55405
www.wiseinkpub.com

To my Desert Phoenix:

Your friendship means more than any price or word will allow.

I cherish the day we met and hold you in the highest esteem.

Thank you for helping me keep my wings,

for being a moment I shall gladly pay forward.

Inger, you are my hero.

Dedicated in loving memory

to my Blue Powerpuff Sister, Dawn Michelle "Bruss" Handorf,

and my niece Jordan Michelle Bastian.

This adventure is for you!

"A man who has been through bitter experiences and traveled far enjoys even his sufferings after a time."
~ Homer, the *Odyssey*

From the Library of the Tales Teller
A Trickster's Origin

*S*tingy Jack stood at the crossroads just outside Blarney's Pub, exhilarated at the prospect of finding someone to match his deviant wit. He had grown tired of the simple-minded penny-pinching, the occasional parlor trick, the grifting, and the thieving of riches only to squander them. He wanted a challenge, and Blarney's Pub was an establishment known for its detestable clientele. He entered the smell-infested, rowdy establishment just before sunset, faking a drunken walk as he approached the bar. He scanned the room to get a feel for the place, underwhelmed by his choices. Many of the pub's regulars were already filling the atmosphere with colorful language. There were a handful of scruffy derelicts and a few wandering pirates as well as a troop of gypsies sitting in the back corner. He noted the unscrupulous owner watching him with curious intent from behind the bar, and he quickly sized him up. The owner was not worth his time, too easy a mark, but the man at the far end of the bar who kept to the shadows was a promising prospect. Stingy Jack swiftly sat down upon an empty stool at the bar just in earshot of the conversation taking place.

"What will it be fer me benefactor tonight?" asked the owner, his Irish brogue strained in his voice as though it belonged to a man long past his life expectancy.

"The usual," spoke the man's hissing voice. His long, thick black hair flowed over the top of his shoulders.

"And what be yer poison, me young lad?" asked the owner, turning his attention toward Stingy Jack.

"I be havin' what he's havin'," replied Stingy Jack, cracking a smirk as he turned toward the man in black. He pushed back his unkempt strawberry-blond hair, exposing his cold cerulean eyes to the stranger. He had found his mark.

The man in black grinned, his pale face bright in the dim and his fiery red eyes piercing with intensity as he leaned into the bar, bunching the sleeves of his tailored coat.

"Hark, me fine young lad, what brings ye all the way out here to the boondocks?" asked the man in black.

"Here ye be, Hades," said the owner, delivering the man in black his drink before going about his business.

"Forthrightly, sir, I was lookin' to swindle a few of them gypsies, but I find little sport in it anymore. That is when I was distracted by yer stature," said Stingy Jack, producing a playful expression, his words filled with flattery.

"Tell me, young lad, why swindle gypsies when ye can have anything ye want?" asked Hades, delighted by the kinship he felt toward Stingy Jack's soul.

"I be listenin', sir," said Stingy Jack.

"What if I could give ye yer true heart's desire?" asked Hades. "I be the Devil, young Jacky, and I would much like fer ye to take me offer."

Stingy Jack's pleasant demeanor faded, replaced with a look of bewilderment. "I'm not one easily tricked, sir," he said, and then straightened. "But I'd be inclined to believe ye. A demonstration of power, perhaps."

Hades let out a laugh. "Surely, young Jacky," he said. "Pardon me, I forgot who I was speaking to. It is quite rare to come across a lad with yer talents."

Stingy Jack did not find the Devil's attempt at flattery sincere, and in that moment he decided to outsmart the man, Devil or not. "I tell ye what, sir, ye turn yerself into a coin to pay fer me drink and then maybe I'll believe ye."

At this, Hades ceased his laughter and took a swig of his ale. "A coin it shall be to cover the ale," he said, and in the blink of an eye, a glistening coin lay on top of the bar.

No one noticed the man vanish, all too drunk to care, but Stingy Jack had seen it. And he now had the Devil at a rare disadvantage. He picked up the coin and examined it for a moment. He rolled it through his rough fingers, his grin wide. Stingy Jack took the coin in a clasped fist and placed it in his tattered coat pocket, next to a silver cross. He then helped himself to the Devil's pint of ale, chugging the remaining liquid down his gullet before slamming the glass onto the counter. Feeling refreshed, Stingy Jack left without paying for his drink and set out into the muggy night air.

Rain soon began to pour as he walked into the street and then headed north onto Elderberry Road toward the village of Winchester. Over the whistle of the heavy wind and the pelting droplets on the cobblestones, Stingy Jack heard a furious voice, cursing in his pocket.

"Jacky, let me out!" shouted Hades.

"I'm sorry, can ye not change back?" teased Stingy Jack, his laughter carrying on the back of the wind. "The trickster of tricksters be fooled by a mortal." He pulled his tattered coat tighter around his flesh in a feeble attempt to keep the cold rain at bay.

"*Name yer price, mortal,*" hissed Hades.

Stingy Jack stopped in the middle of the road and thought for a spell. "I have heard tales of yer deals, Devil, gatherin' souls like some tax collector. So, to earn yer freedom, me price is me soul. I wish ye to leave me be fer one year and if I should die befer then, ye cannot claim me soul."

Hades began to fill Stingy Jack's pocket with laughter—such a small price to pay for his freedom. "A year it is, lad, and I swear on me fire, yer soul shall not be touched by me if ye die befer a year's time when next we meet."

"On yer word," said Stingy Jack; he removed the coin from his pocket, flipping it onto the cobblestones.

The coin shuddered and, in a flash, Hades returned to the form of the man in black. He straightened his now wrinkled clothes, his fiery eyes burning with discomfort, though it was not due to his confinement, but rather the sizzle of his skin as drops of cool rain hit exposed flesh. He motioned toward the mortal trickster and placed his pale, long fingers on the young man's chest.

"Trick me once shame on ye, trick me twice shame on me," hissed Hades. He let his mark sear against the mortal's heart. "When we meet again, young Jacky, twenty-one ye shall be, and next time I shan't be so forgivin'," he promised and vanished without a trace.

Stingy Jack stood in the road, paralyzed by the ache in his chest. He placed a hand over his heart and felt the heat radiate from beneath his clothes. "Turnabout's fair play, Devil," he sneered into the night. Stingy Jack waited until the Devil's fire had cooled on his skin before heading to the village of Winchester, where he managed to perform an impressive count of two hundred and thirty-six acts of trickery.

Element II: The Midwest, 1934

Change in the Wind

Buck huddled in the alley across from McGregor's Tavern. The flying ash of the Black Blizzard whipped through the air, forcing him to squint. He watched the street intently, hardly able to make out the glow of the corner streetlamp but remaining vigilant. He wrapped his beige corduroy jacket over his cobalt shirt, gifts he had used to replace the two-hundred-year-old clothes he had been wearing for the last three days in Chicago.

He shook off the ash gathering on his shoulders and shivered as a gust cut into the alley. He closed his eyes as the muffled call of the stockyard horn blasted through the loud storm, hoping he would not have to wait much longer for his charge to arrive. He looked about the street again, just to be certain, but aside from the darkness and swirling flakes, he could not see past his own feet. He retreated a few steps back into the alley to shield himself from view.

"REOW!"

Buck jumped and spun around. His eyes dropped to the ground; at his feet sat a reddish-brown tabby cat, cradling its tail between its front paws.

"Master Chameleon?" stammered Buck, alarmed by the Euxian spy's appearance. "I—um—what are you doing here?" Buck lifted his eyes to the street again, paranoid. "Are you alone?"

The cat hissed as the fur on its back puffed and bristled.

"A thousand pardons." Buck gave an apologetic bow, his eyes returning to the cat. "Had I known you were there I would have been more cautious."

"It is quite all right, Master Breedling," said the cat. "I should not have snuck up on you like this—though, for your sake, it seems a lesson well taught."

"So it would seem," said Buck with a touch of melancholy. He knelt down to be closer to the feline.

"Losing the grace of the Fates has taken its toll on you," said the cat. "Your inherent abilities it seems no longer come naturally, so you will have to adapt and pay closer attention, be more mindful of your surroundings. At least for the time being, as this sort of thing has never occurred before—a Breedling breaking its chains of obedience, I mean. It is possible your instincts may return in time."

Buck disregarded the Chameleon's attempt to be optimistic, but noted its wisdom. After their last encounter, he had not parted on the best terms with the Fates' spy. The cat and the Tales Teller, the historian of Euxinus, had imposed their expectations upon him and mentioned that he was not conducting himself in a suitable manner to achieve his mission. His task had been to find a mortal—the Child Damek, the name referred to in the Apothecary's correspondence—for he possessed the ability to bestow upon him new magic to reaffirm his tether to the Eden Wanderer, the immortal soul of flesh, who, it was foretold, would help usher the return of the Lost Creators. Buck had disregarded their assessment of his actions, and despite being right—well, to some extent—it had not been for lack of trying.

"Please, Master Chameleon," repeated Buck. "Why are you here?"

"To commend you, naturally," said the cat, sitting proudly.

Buck frowned. "Say what you will, but I do not find Charlie abandoning me something worth celebrating." Only a few hours had lapsed since his friend, Charlie Reese, had fled the city, leaving him in the care of Father Damek Van Lewen. It had never been his intention to involve the mortal orphan, but his entrance into the realm of Eden had been under the direst of circumstances. He had appeared amongst the blaze of Charlie's burning orphanage depleted of his strength. Unable to save himself from the raging inferno, Charlie saved him. It had come at a hefty price for the mortal, who lost his cousin during their escape, the only family he had had left. Buck had done what he could to keep Charlie oblivious to the reality of his supernatural world, but in doing so, his efforts only backfired and his past began to take interest in his friend. To Charlie's credit, he was well capable of understanding such forces and was well on the path to becoming an enlightened mortal, but Buck's hesitation had ultimately driven his friend away, for the mortal could not trust him.

The cat tilted its small head, studying the Breedling's displeasure. "Master Breedling, it is all for the best. The mortal is safer outside the affairs of Euxinus."

"You know as well as I that it is too late for that," said Buck, clutching his fists into his chest. The wind spiraled around him, trying to penetrate the fabric of his jacket. "Charlie beat Hades at his own game, and I am afraid the Master of Hell will not let the mortal's insult stand."

"Why did you not speak of this before?" asked the cat.

"I told you," said Buck, perturbed. "The spell the Tales Teller had cast upon Charlie did not fulfill its intended purpose, for instead of compelling him to lead me straight to Damek, he sought out Hades."

"I recall you shouting something to the effect," said the Chameleon, referring to the Breedling's outburst in the alley the last time they spoke. "You told him the truth then?"

"It was not as though I had another choice," said Buck. "He was my only link to Damek."

"Well, that is all over now, and the Child Damek has fulfilled his bargain with the Eldest," said the Chameleon. "What is done cannot be undone, and I did not come here for a quarrel, but rather, to warn you."

"Warn me?" Buck's hand slid into his pocket and his fingers closed around the harmonica. "Warn me of what?"

"Your new charge." The cat sat back on its hindquarters and curled its tail around its paws. "Stingy Jack is unlike any mortal soul you have encountered. Darkness and regret shroud his past, which has somehow allowed him to possess the same twisted wickedness of Creator Hades. He has more passion for trickery than doing what is right and knows when he is being played a fool, which is why it makes him hard to love. And aside from his mother, Stingy Jack has only ever loved one other soul."

"I know all this," said Buck, less concerned about the Trickster than with finding Charlie to ensure he was still alive and unharmed.

"Then be sure you remember," said the cat as worry crossed its face.

"Is there something else?" asked Buck.

"As you know, if the Trickster is going to stand witness for the soul of his mortal love—the Shepherdess Iona Covington—by way of the Court, he must demonstrate his worth by completing three selfless deeds of compassion: one for a stranger, another for someone he knows, and one for the unknown. With that said, the only way to keep his actions pure is to not speak of the challenge.

You cannot tell him, Master Breedling."

"I understand," said Buck.

"You sound so sure of yourself," the cat said with a hint of sarcasm. "And what will you say to him?"

Buck furrowed his brow, the question alerting his instincts. "He is owed the truth," he said.

"All of it?" challenged the Chameleon. "Will you tell him how important he is to our cause to see the Lost Creators returned?"

"Of course I will," said Buck. "Stingy Jack must understand what he is if he is to fulfill the promise of his coming."

"And will you tell him how his Shepherdess died?"

"What do you know of Iona's death?" Buck rocked back on his heels.

"I know only that you were there," replied the cat.

Buck gaped as his thoughts reeled. The night Iona Covington died, he had watched it happen—well, not exactly. He had held the twenty-year-old maiden's hand, offering what little comfort he could as she lay dying, despite being ill-prepared. He had left shortly after learning the secret she was harboring, abandoning her to the stormy elements and a lonely death. Buck shuddered at the thought of the memory, but more so at the events that followed. After being escorted back to Euxinus, he stood before his masters, who waited impatiently for him to present his final report. But what he had discovered, what Iona had revealed to him about the Lost Creators, he had kept to himself.

"Of course," meowed the cat, stealing Buck from his reverie. "Whatever secret you may have learned from the ill-fated Shepherdess, be cautious with it, Master Breedling. Hades' demon generals are scouting in Eden, some even in this city. Why, the jaguar, General Tezcat, nearly spotted me on my way to meet you. It is also wise to be watchful of Hades' sister, the Mistress of Heaven. Despite Everlyse's constant stance of indifference on the matter of the Trickster, word has spread amongst the lower ranks of her angels, and I have no doubt she will be well informed by the start of the Shepherdess's trial. Keep your eyes on the sky, Master Breedling, for the birds hover, and be wary of the Eden Wickers. There may not be many of the deformed mortals left, but their cursed venom is still a threat to you and will be most detrimental to your charge."

Without further instruction, the cat bowed and brushed past Buck toward the street.

"Wait!" Buck maneuvered himself to his feet and loosened his hold on his jacket. He turned to the Chameleon and readjusted his hands to keep the ash from sneaking under his shirt. He glanced down at the sidewalk, barely able to see the glow of the cat's pink eyes.

"What about Charlie?" he asked.

The cat considered the question. The Apothecary's misjudgment of the mortal had already ensured Charlie's involvement and, given the Breedling's testimony on what transpired between the mortal and Hades, it was easy to understand why the Master of Hell desired to claim the mortal's soul.

"Master Chameleon, please," said Buck, his mind following the same thought as the Fates' spy.

The cat sneezed as a flake tickled its nose. "Master Breedling, you know there is nothing I can do."

"But there has to be something," exclaimed Buck. "The veil will not keep him hidden for long, and with Hades' mark already branding his soul—"

"The mortal bears the mark of the Scarlet Phoenix?" The cat twitched its whiskers. "My pardons, but there is nothing to be done. Hades shall claim his prize in due course."

"But—" began Buck, then held his tongue.

The wind lulled, exposing him and the Chameleon to the street. He looked across the way, now able to see the cursive letters of the tavern sign hanging above the windowless door. He scanned the street to be sure no one was in earshot and then returned his gaze to the cat.

"Master Chameleon, as a Master of Eden, Charlie must be protected."

"A Master of Eden?" The cat flattened its ears. "Master Breedling, you know as well as I do that no mortal can claim Mastery in Eden."

"Then how am I standing here waiting for the likes of Stingy Jack?" challenged Buck. "You know a soulcatcher must be tethered to its charge."

"Of course," said the Chameleon. "The Child Damek bound your will."

"Yes, well, Damek may have said the words, but whatever magic the Apothecary had used to strike his bargain with Father Van Lewen when he was a child, it was superseded the moment Charlie saved me. Had Charlie not granted Damek his proxy, I would not be standing here," said Buck. "Charles Reese is my master."

The Chameleon hesitated. Then it was true, Charles Reese had become more than an accidental piece of eight in the Apothecary's plan of seven protectors. The mortal had managed to gain power far beyond what the Fate's spy was willing to admit to the Breedling. It needed to deliver this news to the Apothecary and the council straight away.

"Then as you say, Master Breedling," said the Chameleon, "I will inform the Eldest of this news, but I must urge you now to focus. Creator Hades will use his hatred for Stingy Jack to ensure the Trickster does not rise to the mantle of witness. Remember, your tether to Stingy Jack only goes so far back and forward in time. Lose him, and you will surely lose the Shepherdess. Do not let the thought of Charles Reese chink your armor, and for your sake, I pray you keep your attention on your charge. You have until you have reached the Ferryman to secure his worth."

The feline bowed.

Buck returned the gesture and watched as the cat scampered into the darkness. The wind picked up again and shrouded him with a cloak of invisibility. Buck lifted his eyes back to the street as a crew of Irishmen filed into McGregor's Tavern. He tried not to think of Charlie or the danger he was in, trusting the Apothecary would send a guardian to watch over him. Instead, he put all his focus on his charge, the Eden Wanderer.

The Trickster known as Stingy Jack.

The Strange Fellow

The hour was late when Mr. McGregor bid his hardworking regulars a restful night. Many of them wished to continue into the early morning, but the old bartender cut them off and sent them home. He booted the last of them out around midnight, and as he began to lock up, Mr. McGregor noticed a dark silhouette in the corner of the room.

The bartender approached the back table and recognized the messy strawberry-blond head lying next to the empty whiskey bottle. The strange fellow's head was pressed against his outstretched arm, the sleeve of his tattered coat pulled back to reveal a curious brand on his pale skin. Mr. McGregor ran a hand through his graying hair, puzzled. The symbol was an ancient Gaelic rune, if memory served, one he had not seen since his youth. He exhaled heavily, remembering the insignia on a leather pouch of silver his mother had found on the doorstep of their home back in Ireland before his family had fled to America. He had asked her about it once, inquiring what it meant, and all she had told him was *sail*, which he later learned was associated with the willow tree.

Mr. McGregor dropped his hand to his side, conflicted about rousing the young man, but his own fatigue demanded it was time to close and so he gave the drunkard a rough shake. The stranger responded by snorting loudly, but he remained unconscious and mumbled as a drop of drool fell from the corner of his mouth. Guarded, Mr. McGregor leaned in closer to listen.

"Two florins do fine. Climb the tree to get the fruit. I be the only one done it twice."

Mr. McGregor could not make out what the young man was saying, and he stirred slightly, letting something from his pocket fall to the floor. Mr. McGregor picked up the purse and inspected its contents. He pulled out a lighter, a burned-down candle, and a hollowed out rotten turnip decorated like a jack-o'-lantern. He held the shriveled vegetable, studying the ominous carved face, and wondered what would compel a man to hold onto such an object. Its two misshaped pentagon eyes stared darkly at him, its droopy smile boasting a hidden secret. Mr. McGregor glanced back at the young man, who, to his horror, was looking back at him. The stranger's keen expression fully aware of the potential theft taking place.

Mr. McGregor returned the trinkets to the purse and positioned it on the table in front of its owner.

The young man responded by pulling down the sleeve of his tattered coat, concealing his brand. He placed his hand in his pocket to retrieve a gold coin, which he set on the table.

Eyeing the shiny metal, Mr. McGregor snatched it up with a sinful swell of greed and placed it in his pocket before his unpredictable guest could change his mind.

The pale fellow smirked as he collected his purse and rose with swiftness from his seat, almost too quickly for someone who had consumed so much alcohol. He swept his hair out of his face and engaged the bartender.

"Thank ye fer yer hospitality, sir," he said, tipping an imaginary hat. "May fortune smile upon ye, lest the Devil get ye first."

Mr. McGregor stood gobsmacked as he watched his guest saunter to the door. For the first time, the young man had uttered more than his liquor order and, on top of it, thanked him. Something was different about tonight, and though he knew better than to invite any of his patrons to stay, Mr. McGregor was willing to make an exception. His curiosity fueled his hunger to learn more about the Irishman, for what a story it would be to tell his regulars tomorrow.

"Young man," called Mr. McGregor, as he grabbed the empty bottle and moved back toward the bar. "Ye need a place to rest fer the night?"

The strange fellow stopped at the door but did not readily respond. "Do ye light the watch candle befer bed?" he asked.

Mr. McGregor's expression changed to one of puzzlement at the unusual question. "No one lights candles in the street anymore—well, at least not around these parts." He let out a soft chuckle.

"Very well, I accept yer invitation. However, I must be gone befer the morn', lest the Black Blizzard continues."

"Ye are an odd mick," said Mr. McGregor as he rounded the bar and dropped the whiskey bottle into the barrel near the sink. He then moved to the center of the counter with his back once again to the mirror. The pale young man joined him on the empty stool across from him, his forearms on the counter. Mr. McGregor considered his guest a little longer and had a mind to ask for a name, but he refrained, uncertain if he wished to exchange such intimacies.

"Would ye care fer another drink befer we turn in?"

The stranger hesitated and then replied with a silent nod.

Mr. McGregor picked up the used glasses and relocated them

to the sink. He then snatched two tumblers and the bottle of gin. He was confident his guest would not object to the choice of liquor. He opened the bottle, filled half of each glass, and then pulled up a stool. Awkward silence followed.

"So, Mr. McGregor," said the young Irishman. "I assume ye be the owner of this here establishment."

"Right ye are," said Mr. McGregor, raising his glass. A spark of pride filled his aged face, even though his weary eyes told a different, harder story.

"I been meaning to ask about those old folktales yer regulars tell every night, and I was wondering if ye won't mind telling me one."

"Was there something particular ye wished to hear?" Mr. McGregor put his glass back on the counter with equal curiosity.

"Can ye tell me what happened to warrant them scars on yer hands?" The stranger motioned his eyes toward the bartender's hands.

"What—oh, these..." Mr. McGregor rotated his hands to get a better look at his scars. The fragmented white marks clashed with the pigment of his skin, reminding him of a traumatic childhood experience.

"If ye can't talk about it..."

"Huh? Oh, no, the story ain't long, just one I haven't thought of in quite some time. Most of the time I don't even see the scars." Mr. McGregor took a large gulp of his gin to build his courage. The liquor stung his esophagus and brain equally, reminding him why he detested the foul drink.

"Is that a yes?"

"Certainly, certainly," agreed Mr. McGregor. "But first there is one thing I'd like to ask. Your brand, the willow."

"I don't speak about it," said the strange fellow, a growl of agitation in his voice. "Not to anyone."

"My mistake," said Mr. McGregor, second-guessing his invitation to let the stranger stay. He looked at his hands again. "Let's see," he began. "I got these as a lad back in Ireland when me parents worked on a potato farm. I had been pickin' berries on the south side of the fields, waitin' fer them to end their long day of work. I do not recall so much of the day itself. However, I do find meself cravin' the sharp taste of barberries come springtime."

Mr. McGregor paused as his taste buds formed an immediate hankering for the fruit of his homeland. He swallowed back the greedy saliva and continued.

"Now, as me maw used to tell me, near sundown a group of hounds crossed the horizon of the field chasin' a potato thief. I kept to meself, but the scallywag spotted me and took off in me direction. I had no choice but to jig into the berry bushes to avoid an encounter with the bloodhounds. I crawled in backwards, keeping me body low, but it did not stop the thorns from ripping at me skin. I heard the thief swear as he ran on by, the hounds keepin' right behind. I remained in me hidin' spot until the howls faded o'er the next hill. As the sun sank, I crawled out of the bushes, grabbin' thorny branches to pull meself out."

The young man smirked at the remark and refilled the bartender's glass.

Mr. McGregor chugged half the drink and proceeded to make an obnoxious face to depict the sting of the liquor before resuming his tale. "As twilight fell, I slowly made me way to the main road towards me village. Me hands were marked with thin streams of blood, some deeper than others. I was tired, and somewhere along the way I collapsed alongside the road from me exhaustion." Mr. McGregor's voice fell quiet and he chugged down the rest of his liquor. "From what I can remember, I opened me eyes briefly to a sight I had never seen befer nor since."

"What did ye see?" the young man asked, pouring another drink for his host.

Mr. McGregor blinked. The drowsy weight of liquor was catching up with him, his tolerance not what it used to be. He glanced at the stranger a bit muddled, losing his place in the story. Mr. McGregor widened his gaze in order to shake the sleepiness.

"Please finish," encouraged his guest.

"I swear on me maw's grave, I saw a ball of light float in the air. It moved towards me, until it hovered over me battered body, as if deciding whether or not to help me. And just like that, I was lifted from the ground. I passed out afterward and awoke just as the light was laying me on the stoop of me house."

Mr. McGregor drifted off into his memories, releasing a hiccup. A rather large yawn followed, before he lowered his head to the bar.

The young fellow removed the contents from his purse and set the candle in the rotten turnip. He lit the burned-out wick, and a soft glow illuminated the dreary tavern. He returned the lighter to the purse and the purse to his tattered coat.

"You were a light thing," he said in a low voice. He took hold of his small lantern and turned to leave, but the bartender grabbed his wrist.

Mr. McGregor glanced up at the young man, certain he knew his face—that after all these years, it was still the same. With tired eyes and a soft voice, as if he were seven years old once more, he asked, "Are ye an angel?"

The stranger stared at the bartender. "No," he replied. "As I would have told ye then, I'm nothing but a wayward spirit."

"But ye saved me," objected Mr. McGregor.

The young man shrugged. "I had a moment of weakness."

Mr. McGregor loosened his grip as a few tears of disappointment dripped from his eyes. He laid his head back on the bar and passed out.

* * *

Jack lingered and lifted his eyes to his reflection in the grand mirror, taking silent counsel with himself. He felt a pesky sense of guilt and wondered if the bartender would have understood the truth. It was not in his nature to care; maybe it had been once, when he was young and innocent, before his mother's horrific death, but the hardships of the world had shaped him into a despicable man, both callous and unyielding. He had swindled and cheated, been party to the deaths of countless souls, but never stained his own hand with murder. He had been the cause of great misery and misfortune for so long that he knew no other way to exist. At least not until his beloved Shepherdess had stood up to his wickedness.

"Yer a right cad, Jack," he said to his reflection. The Mirror Jack smirked wickedly at him, a mere vision of what he knew to be true of the trickster inside him. A constant reminder of the noble and the wicked always vying for control. In those pivotal moments, he felt most akin to the duality of Dr. Jekyll and Mr. Hyde.

The bartender's light snores broke the stillness of the tavern and soon mingled with a somber melody dancing about the room. Jack scanned the shadowed corners but could not find the source of the sound. He came back to the mirror only to see an added reflection. Behind him stood a tall, slender man with a harmonica pressed against his lips. He swiveled on the stool and found the man dressed in a suit with leather shoes, long black hair, and red eyes.

The man in black stared as he lowered the instrument, revealing a reptilian smirk on his pallid face. "Pleasant evening, Jack," he greeted with a presentable bow.

Jack snarled. He knew he should not have lingered so long.

"Tut, tut—oh, Jacky, what a pitiful display you've become."

"Hades, I ain't in the mood for a sparring match," said Jack, unprepared to face off against his rival.

"You cut me to the quick," mocked Hades, delight breaking across his face. "My intent is not to coerce you. I'm only here for the show, to see you at your lowest. It's bloody ingenious really. To save the man as a child, only to swindle from him now and undo your act of compassion. It pleases me to see Iona's influence has lost a great deal of its hold on you."

"Shut yer foul mouth, ye vile serpent!" Jack clenched his fists.

The Devil had pegged him right. He had thought about stealing, maybe even smashing all the empty bottles on the floor and removing the bartender's shoes, leaving him stranded behind his bar. But now that he had an audience, he lost the taste for it. Besides, it was the mention of Iona's name that had gotten the rise out of him, for what the villain had said was true. Iona's influence had been waning, and his deeds were reverting to old habits. Like an invasive vine, Jack's inner trickster wrapped around his feelings for Iona, suffocating them. He stewed for a moment, allowing the pain of her absence to give his rival satisfaction at striking his weakness.

Hades crowed at Jack's struggle. "Come now, Jacky, the Shepherdess has been dead for two hundred years. There's no need to carry a torch for the dead."

Jack grabbed the gin bottle and chucked it at Hades, only to watch it pass through empty air and shatter against the wall, shards of glass splintering about the room. The tavern fell still in the wake of the crash, save for the little snores of Mr. McGregor. Jack turned back toward the sleeping bartender and the grand mirror before glancing at his reflection. He had let it go too far, allowed Hades the upper hand. He needed to calm himself—he needed the trickster within to shut out his feelings for Iona—if he had any chance of defending himself.

"There, there, poor lamb," taunted Hades.

Jack closed his eyes and surrendered, allowing the trickster to take full control. He heard Hades stir, and as he opened his eyes, he found the Devil standing behind Mr. McGregor's slumped body, his long fingers pressed against the bartender's back.

"Now what say you, Jack? Should we steal his liquor, burn the building to the ground, slit his throat?" coaxed Hades.

Jack created a tight fist in his coat pocket and wrapped his fingers around his silver cross as a precaution. His face writhed with choler and fought against the words that would feed Hades victory. He could no longer straddle the duality of his soul, and just as his mouth opened, the trickster slammed Iona's door shut. Jack's body shuddered, and he withdrew his hand from his pocket. Darkness flashed across his face, morphing his expression. His brows sharpened and his cerulean blue eyes exuded a cunning stare. He locked his focus on his rival, determined to beat him once again with his wit.

"I won't kill this man, Hades," said Jack, and added sharply, "I'm not some common murderer who dirties his own hands like ye. I'm an orchestrater of death."

"You try my patience, wandering soul," hissed Hades, placing his fingers on the counter, squaring with Jack.

"And I shall continue to test yer resolve, Devil," said Jack. "Until I break yer threshold."

"You know nothing of my tolerance, Stingy Jack," hissed

Hades. "Be mindful of that, for with just one press of my hand against your flesh, I could rip you from this realm."

"Then do it. Send me to Hell!" challenged Jack, bringing his nose within an inch of Hades' face. He stared at the Devil, taunting him to end it, to make good on his threat. But then a flicker of realization sparked across Hades' eyes and, for a second, pure truth surfaced. "Ye can't," voiced Jack, half-surprised, half-intrigued. "After all this time," he continued, "even with me withdrawal of our deal, ye couldn't pull me down into yer pit even if ye wanted to."

Silence plagued the space between them until Jack burst into laughter.

Hades snapped his fingers and in an instant vanished from sight.

Jack saw the Devil's reflection glare at him. In response, he whirled around at the ready for a physical confrontation, but the Devil merely pulled himself in close and brought his lips to his ear, the villain's warm breath tickling his skin.

"Do not think yourself special, Stingy Jack," said Hades with malice in his voice. "I know your heart and your soul. You're as wretched as they come and no matter your penchant for good deeds, you will never again see the likes of your beloved Iona. I shall see to it. Just to spite you, I will possess the Shepherdess's mortal soul. And she shall endure the worst suffering that can be inflicted on someone as pure of heart as she."

Jack felt his body stiffen in response to Hades' threat, but outwardly, he managed to hold his indifferent expression. "Do not lie to me, Hades," he said. "Or do ye forget Iona Covington lies out of yer reach?"

It was Hades' turn to laugh. "Aww, Jack, you may think me a liar, but you know nothing," he said with a delighted grin. "Your lady has never been far from my reach. And you would know that if you opened your eyes. There are far more things in this world than you and I, forces which you have failed to comprehend even after all your years of wandering."

"Try me," challenged Jack, in an empty attempt to bait the Devil into giving away his secrets, for he detested being impotent in front of his rival. But Hades, for once, did not fall into his trap. Instead, the Devil stepped away, his grin celebrating his victory.

Hades pulled on his suit coat and rolled his shoulders. "'Til next we meet, Trickster." He sauntered to the door while whistling a creepy melody, one Jack knew all too well:

"He was a lad who did it twice,

shamed the devil by a roll of the dice.

His luck ran out the day he died

and was left in Eden—no tears were cried.

Who was this lad who cheated fiery torture and eternal bliss?

Who was this lad who wanders now full of villainy and regret?

He goes by the name of Stingy Jack,

an unsavory character; an unsavory chap.

With turnip in hand to light his way through the darkest black."

Hades opened the door, letting the dusty wind into the tavern. He gave Jack a final bow adieu and disappeared into the storm, the door slamming behind him.

Exhausted by the Devil's banter, Jack collapsed on the stool, the strength of the trickster ebbing. "Stingy Jack," he breathed into the empty tavern, letting the villainous sound of his name blanket the room. What had Hades meant by his threat? Surely Iona's soul was long at rest in the pearly clouds of heaven. Jack spun, grabbed his empty glass, and pitched it at the grand mirror. The impact shattered the glass and left a sprawling spider-web crack in the oxidized reflection. Jack stared at the fragments of his image, seeing the layers of his personality. To rid himself of the sight, he threw the other glass at the mirror, its impact multiplying the fractures.

Jack reached beneath the counter, stole one of the half-consumed whiskey bottles, and hopped off the stool. He kicked his foot back, forcing a cascade of tumbling wood to clatter to the floor. He moseyed for the door, bent on leaving, but just as he closed his fingers around its handle, a prick of unease nipped his conscience. Jack glanced over his shoulder, back at the man he had found as a child. He released the brass and grabbed his strawberry-blond hair, conflicted. His eyes fell once again on the aging man's scars, which were visibly stark in the faint glow of his turnip lantern. The sight of his totem relaxed him, and he returned to the bar to retrieve it.

Jack collected the lantern and then paused, listening once again to the little snores of the bartender. The tavern returned to its quiet atmosphere, settling the frantic commotion he had stirred. Without lifting his eyes to the mirror, Jack got the sense of the destruction in the room and sighed. He set the whiskey bottle on the counter and reached into his pocket. He removed a handful of coins from the pocket of his tattered coat and placed them next to the bartender's outstretched hand, intent on paying for the mess, but as Jack reached for the bottle again, his hand diverted back to the coins and stuffed them once again in his pocket. Then he snatched the bottle and, without another backward glance, wandered to the door, exiting the tavern into the chaos of the Black Blizzard.

The Devil's Plot

Buck watched Hades exit McGregor's Tavern before disappearing around the corner of the block. Minutes later, Stingy Jack came out onto the sidewalk with his signature turnip lantern in hand, its eerie glow sending a ripple of light through the black. He watched the Trickster cross the street, heading toward the section of the city Charlie had called the Back of the Yards. He felt compelled to follow directly, but he wanted to know what evil scheme the Master of Hell was plotting. He knew the Devil well enough to know the fiery deity was well versed on the laws governing trials in Euxinus, particularly in regards to witnesses. If the Devil was working to sabotage Stingy Jack's chances at standing witness for Iona, then he needed to know about it.

Buck inched out of the confines of the alley, unaware that overhead, two red-winged blackbirds were surveying him. He darted across the street and pressed his body against McGregor's Tavern before creeping along the brick to the edge of the building. He peered around the corner and crouched down to make himself small and undetectable. He buried his chin in his knees and let the wind push against his body. Buck leaned into the building to secure his balance and waited until the bluster lulled. The howl died to a soft wheeze as the ash floated back into the dark sky. Buck lifted his head, his eyes dazzled by the additional light illuminating the street corner up the block. Under the lamppost, a pair of pale yellow eyes appeared as a soft growl sliced through the air and filled the void of the empty street. A great black cat crept toward Hades.

Buck held his breath, terrified by the creature's presence, for he had not laid eyes upon the demon general since well before his imprisonment. *Tezcat*, he mouthed, unable to even whisper the name of the leader of Hell's Demon Octet. The melanistic jaguar stood alert as its eyes scanned every dark crevice. With its powerful nose, the great cat sniffed the air for spies, but with the strength of the wind, it was unable to determine a foe. The jaguar looked up at its master and sat back on its hind legs.

"Did you succeed, Master?" growled Tezcat.

Hades did not acknowledge his demon general. Instead, he lit a ball of scarlet fire in his palm and extinguished it as a warning. Judging by the vexation on the Devil's face, his run in with the Trickster had proven unsuccessful.

The jaguar flattened its ears, knowing better than to test its master's rage, especially in matters pertaining to Stingy Jack.

Hades dug his nails into his palm, the frustration mounting on his pallid face. He had been certain he could have convinced Stingy Jack to fall for his temptation, to kill the mortal bartender and defile his soul. But it appeared the pestering influence of the Shepherdess still held enough sway to neutralize his adversary's extreme trickery. Then again, he had never been able to push Stingy Jack to such lengths, and now he was running out of time. Hades gritted his teeth and lowered his eyes toward his general.

The jaguar acknowledged its master with a swipe of its whiplike tail.

Hades broke open his fist. The degradation of Stingy Jack's soul would have to wait.

"What news of my sister, Everlyse?" asked Hades.

"The Mistress of Heaven has dispatched her cherubs to locate the Trickster and the Breedling," replied the jaguar.

"Then word has reached her faster than I had anticipated," said Hades.

"But she makes no motion to strike," confirmed the jaguar. "Instead, your spies have reported that Everlyse's Beloved Twins, the red-winged blackbirds Alyce and Lyes, have been tracking Stingy Jack for several days now, the Breedling too. And yet no heavenly army flies to intervene."

Hades' face flared with vexation as fire burst to life in his palm again. He had suspected for some time now his passive sister was maneuvering her angels to gather information on his movements. His fiery gaze scanned every high point along the street in search of the red-winged blackbirds, but he saw no sign of the passerines.

The demon general followed its master's gaze and sniffed the air again, but was unable to find the familiar bird scent. It growled, wanting nothing more than to sink its teeth into the two cherubs and hand over their lifeless carcasses as tribute.

"It is believed, Master," Tezcat continued, "Alyce and Lyes are not following the orders of the Mistress of Heaven but, rather, another. It is possible one of Everlyse's high generals gave such a command." The jaguar sneezed as it inhaled a few flakes of ash.

"Perhaps," said Hades.

"What are your orders, Master?" growled the jaguar.

"Find the mortal, Charles Reese," said Hades, his voice full of loathing. He returned his attention to the great cat, shifting his anger from his sister to the image of a young man with brown hair, tanned skin, and toffee eyes. "If I fail to twist Stingy Jack's soul before the Breedling extracts him from Eden, then Charles Reese will be all I have left to get the answer I seek."

"The whereabouts of the Lost Creators," said Tezcat.

"That Breedling knows where they are or at least knows Iona carries such a secret," said Hades. "The Fates should never have entrusted such a charge to a mere soulcatcher. However, the obedient Breedling could never have fallen for any other reason. He needs Stingy Jack to save her and he needs her to lead him to my lost siblings."

"Shall I alert the other generals?"

Hades stroked the creature's velvety fur in response. "That will not be necessary," he declared. "I wish to leave this matter to your sharp senses. Tell the others to keep an eye on my sister's angels and if she looks to truly enter this game, I want to be told."

"As you wish," growled the jaguar.

"Oh, and Tezcat," chirruped Hades, as his bony fingers gripped the great cat's scruff. "Do not disappoint me. The mortal is my only leverage to force that insufferable Breedling into telling me where my siblings are hiding. Bring him to me as you like, but I want him alive. Do you understand?"

Tezcat made no verbal reply, but rather acknowledged the command with a nod before padding back into the darkness.

Buck felt his innards twist with worry, his heart pounding in his ears. Tezcat's tracking skills were by far the acutest of any demon in Hades' horde, and undoubtedly the general would have no problem finding Charlie, especially since he bore the Master of Hell's mark. A sudden urge rose within him, begging him to abandon Stingy Jack, forget his promise to save Iona, and instead find his young master. Buck clasped a hand over his mouth but was not quick enough to prevent an anxious whimper from escaping his lips. He saw Hades' eyes flash in his direction, and he pulled his head out of sight. His body thrummed and his fingertips went numb. He focused on Hades' aura and felt it draw closer, and closer, and closer still. He darted for the door of the tavern and hid himself behind it.

Buck left a sliver of a crack and saw Hades come into view, his deathly figure a haunting sight. He could barely breathe as Hades retrieved the familiar cherry-wood harmonica from the inside pocket of his suit. He watched the Devil examine the crest of the Scarlet Phoenix, his expression falling into a sort of melancholy, as though Hades longed for the days of his once fiery image.

"Ah, General Rachel," said Hades, as a large masked raccoon skittered from the shadows.

"You called, Master Hades," cooed the raccoon.

"Follow Stingy Jack," said Hades, without fully acknowledging his demon general. "And by any means, do what is necessary to force his hand."

"Then it will not be long now, Master," said the raccoon.

"Indeed," said Hades, as he brushed his thumb across the emblem. "It has been far too long for my siblings to remain in hiding." He curled his fingers around the instrument. "And once I have found them, I will use them to take hold of Eden before burning it to ash. Then I will dethrone that treacherous trinity, the Fates, and restore my siblings and me to our ancestral home. The Elements will rule Euxinus once more."

"An inspired plan," said the raccoon. "I will do as commanded."

"Time is fleeting," said Hades.

The wind responded with a reassuring gust as though to agree.

"Be mindful of my sister's angels," added Hades.

The raccoon bowed and scurried off into the darkened streets.

Hades stood statuesque for a mere second before he pressed his lips to the warm silver of his instrument and began to play an ominous tune befitting his character as he disappeared.

Buck slammed the door shut, overwhelmed, and slid to the floor. He took a deep breath, hoping the Chameleon was already in Euxinus delivering his message to the Apothecary. If there were any way of protecting Charlie, his mentor would know. Buck stared into the tavern, the smell of liquor and mold filling his nostrils. In the dim atmosphere, he spotted the specks of glass twinkling on the floor. He glanced across the room to the bar, where a man's head rested on the counter, his body slumped over. It was then that he noticed the dual spider-webs in the mirror and in a panic rushed to the bar.

"For the love of the Golden Faun, please do not be dead," he muttered, giving the old man a shake.

Mr. McGregor snorted and mumbled under his breath.

Buck let out a sigh of relief, relaxing his stance. It was as Hades had said; Stingy Jack had not brought any harm to the mortal. For had the Devil succeeded, the villain would have what he wanted—the Trickster's love and the whereabouts to the Lost Creators. Buck eyed the mirror again, staring at his reflection. It was much better than the one from a few days ago when he had hardly recognized himself. The natural color of his ivory skin gave him a porcelain doll look, now that the redness in his emerald eyes had subsided. Buck looked past his reflection, concentrating on the images of what had happened only moments ago, first between the bartender and Stingy Jack and then with Hades. As the images faded, Buck looked at the scars on the bartender's hands. He examined them, revealing their age.

"By the stars," he breathed. "It seems the power of the Shepherdess was on our side, Mr. McGregor."

The bartender snorted in response.

Buck pushed away from the counter and headed for the door.

He exited the tavern to a welcome pause of black flakes. The supernatural elements were finally dispersing from the city. The glow from the lamppost brightened the deserted street, casting eerie shadows along the pavement. Buck scrutinized each one before he let himself breathe. He looked to the west, aware that Stingy Jack had already followed the train tracks north and was waiting for the midday locomotive, which currently idled in the train yard.

Buck stuffed his hands into his pockets, his right one brushing against a piece of paper and the cool sheen of a harmonica. His heart sank at the thought of Charlie and he clasped the instrument. A sudden pain clamped his chest, and he felt an unyielding sense of shame gut him, leaving a hollowed void. He could not quite explain it, but he understood it had something to do with Charlie.

"By the powers of Earth and Sea," he said aloud, somehow hoping the wind would carry his words to Charlie, "may protection find you, my friend, and keep you safe." Buck let go of the harmonica and tugged on the collar of his jacket, shaking off a pile of ash. He stepped out into the street and ran for the train yard.

From the Library of the Tales Teller

Porcelain Prey

Stingy Jack sat underneath the umbrella shade of a weeping willow tree, his back pressed against its trunk. Laying on his chest was Iona Covington, his beloved shepherdess. He rested his chin atop her head and breathed her in, the smell of amaretto and honey filling his nostrils. He ran his fingers through strands of her cherry-colored hair and listened as she hummed a familiar lullaby he had long since forgotten the words to. He loved her with every ounce of himself that his trickery had not been able to corrupt, which was not much, but somehow it was enough. She was the only one who saw him for more than what his hardships had made him become.

Iona Covington saw in him what he could have been and what he could still be.

She had first noticed him in the village market one morning, stealing food from several of the vendors. She had thought nothing of it, but upon the second day, she took to watching him more closely. She had followed him for days, bearing witness to several other acts of thievery, an elaborate scheme of coercion, cheating, and at least one scandal involving a lady's virtue. Upon the sixth day of stalking him, she witnessed him pass a destitute child without regard. Outraged by his heartlessness, she ran after him and in that moment, Iona Covington convinced the wandering trickster to give the rest of his bread to the child.

"There is hope fer ye yet, Master Jack," she had said with praise in her voice.

Iona nuzzled against Stingy Jack's cool embrace, the stillness of his heartbeat no longer a secret to her but a secret she kept. He had told her enough for her to know he had died years ago and was cursed by his own foolishness. Her strong arms rested at his waist, their bodies nestled in the grass. She wore a cerulean dress that matched his eyes, the laced sleeves covering her freckled butter skin. The skirt furled in the breeze as she lifted her head before pulling herself away, as she always did when she asked her love to tell her stories of his life.

"Ye must have stories to tell," she said, her voice sweet and airy. "Adventures, women."

"Naw, of those I have none," said Stingy Jack. "There only be one worth speaking of, and she be the one in me lap." His lips broke into a smile to throw her off, but Iona was cleverer than that, for she always knew when he was lying.

"Oh, come now. Havin' lived as long as ye have, never aging, to be twenty-one ferever, ye must have found the favor of someone."

Stingy Jack simply shook his head, knowing better than to kiss and tell, even to someone lacking jealousy.

Iona stared at him and formed a pout, forcing her eyes to swell.

"Honestly," said Stingy Jack, exasperated. "Ye simply won't let up." He moved his head slightly, causing a few locks of his strawberry-blond hair to fall over his eyes.

Iona pulled the strands back into place. She smiled at him. "Of course not, me love. I need to know I'm the only one fer ye," she teased.

Stingy Jack took Iona's hand and kissed it. "If that be the reason ye ask, then let it be known there be no lass in all the world that could ever take the place of me beatin' heart. Save fer the one who has stolen what remains of it." He kissed her hand again. "I'm yers, me lady."

Iona's cheeks flushed, and she kissed him. She pulled him into her and did not let go until she needed to take a breath. She let out a gasp as he cradled her face in his cold hands.

"Are ye well?" asked Stingy Jack.

"Ye need not worry," she breathed.

"Breathe, me angel."

Iona giggled and took Stingy Jack's hands in hers. "Do not be foolish, me love, mortals cannot be angels," she said. "We do not carry wings on our backs. Besides, an angel cannot love ye like I."

At the sound of her words, Stingy Jack broke away, feeling unworthy of her, ruining the moment.

"What?" It was a silly question, for Iona knew the look on his face all too well, but the word escaped her lips before she could refrain. "Ye still think yerself unworthy of such love," she continued, "but that is why ye deserve it the most, because ye know ye have been wrong in yer ways. Even the lowest of creatures must be loved by someone, or what hope is there fer redemption?"

"Iona..."

"No," said Iona. "Ye shall not deter me, Jack. I'm not afraid to say I choose ye, fer I love ye. Because there is still hope ye can find yer way back to the light."

Stingy Jack looked into her eyes. One was hazel with a starburst of yellow around her pupil and the other was brown. He placed a mask of defeat on his face, for there was no point in arguing, and pressed his forehead to hers.

"*Then if ye be not an angel, ye be a saint,*" *he said, in a whisper.* "*What could I have possibly done to deserve ye?*"

Iona brushed her hand across his cheek and rose on her knees to make herself taller than him. "*Ye were born with a good heart, and that is all that is needed.*" *She drew his head close to her chest, reassuring him she meant every word. He could hear her heart beat at a fluttering speed and did not envy the sound of her life. He wrapped his arms around her as she tilted her head to kiss him tenderly on the forehead.*

They lost themselves in each other as the rising sun evaporated what remained of the morning dew. A bluster whipped across the pastureland, stirring the sheep into frantic retreat. Iona withdrew from the tender moment and got to her feet, ready to go after them, but Stingy Jack reached for her arm.

"*Jack,*" *she said crossly, but when she looked at his expression, lines had creased his brow.*

They stood in silence and watched as broken clouds banked together in the makings of a storm. On the wind, laughter danced around them. Stingy Jack scanned the pasture, clenching his fists, anticipating the appearance of the owner of the disembodied voice. He felt Iona's hands lightly on his back, and it sent piercing terror through him.

"*Show yerself!*" *demanded Stingy Jack, trying to hide the worry in his voice.*

The laughter slowly centralized itself behind the tree and gave way to the familiar rasp of Hades' voice.

"*Well, well,*" *hissed the Devil, stepping into view, dressed in his usual black suit, his long black hair braided, dangling like a piece of rope over his shoulder.* "*I thought surely the rumors could not be true. That Stingy Jack, my Jack, could not be in love. But it appears I was wrong to doubt such whispers.*" *His fiery eyes* flickered as they observed the porcelain beauty nestled between his rival and the willow.

"Leave her out of this!" shouted Stingy Jack, as he took Iona by the arm and pulled her away from Hades. He spun her around behind his back, ensuring the Devil would have to go through him to get to her.

Iona peered over Stingy Jack's shoulder to take in the sight of Hades. She felt the heat of his presence on her skin and stood motionless as it began to burn. Tears swelled in her eyes, a few rolling down her cheeks. She let out a hesitant gasp as Stingy Jack realized what was happening and quickly turned around. He pulled her into an embrace and buried her head in the protection of his arms and chest.

"Don't look at him," he whispered.

Hades laughed as he circled the lovers. "Oh, Jacky, I had no idea ye were getting so bored with our game," he said with a sneer. "To be honest, after fifteen years of the same old thing, I'll admit, I was as well. But now, ye have increased the stakes. Fer this is a prize worth taking. Although, I must confess, I would never have thought ye capable of such a feat, bringing such innocence into the middle of our vendetta. I applaud yer treachery, sir, and bow to yer mastery."

Hades paused to present a mocking bow before fully confronting his adversary. "Now, what shall we do with her? Burn her, drown her, leave her tied to this willow?"

"I said, leave her out of this," growled Stingy Jack. His defensive anger stirred the trickster from its muted slumber.

Hades frowned, disappointed in the Trickster's dismissive behavior. How dare he replace their rivalry with love. His frown curled and unpleasant thoughts resumed. He would see them both rid of the lass, but he would first dangle her in front of

Stingy Jack before separating her soul from her body. Finally, he had the advantage needed to best his nemesis.

"Oh, no, Jacky," taunted Hades. "What fun we shall have together, the three of us."

Stingy Jack pressed Iona up against the rough bark of the willow.

"Jack," whispered Iona, her voice trembling.

"It shall be all right," he whispered back. "When I let ye go, don't move from this spot, understood? No matter what happens."

Iona gave a nod into his chest and loosened her grip on his shirt. She lifted her head to look at him, but he would not allow her to see his anger nor the sinister expression mounting on his face, and he swiftly turned away from her. He dug his feet into the damp ground and lunged at Hades, tackling him to the grass.

"Give me yer best shot, Jacky," baited Hades.

Stingy Jack took his clenched fist and drove it into Hades' face. His boiling anger took hold of him, and for a moment, he lost himself. The trickster within surfaced, stifling all thoughts of Iona and his love for her. He thrashed at the Devil, unable to remember why, except for the raw emotion of contempt. The contact of his knuckles against Hades' flesh sizzled, clashing ice with fire. He let out an enraged scream, dispelling all sound. He drew upward, ready to barrel the full force of his strength against his enemy, but midway he stopped.

"Jack."

Stingy Jack's body shuddered at the tender sound of his name, Iona's voice shimmering through his blind rage, and he remembered himself, remembered her. He began to lower his fist, giving Hades the opportunity to strike back, but the Devil merely stared, mystified by the abrupt transformation. Stingy Jack lifted himself off the ground and took a step back. He kept his gaze on the Devil, ignoring whatever horror might exist on Iona's face. He slid his hand into his pocket and watched as Hades gained his feet, the Devil's fiery eyes following his movement.

"Ah, yes," hissed Hades, recalling the blessed relic in the Trickster's possession. "Use yer weapon if ye can, send me back to Hell."

"With pleasure," said Stingy Jack through gritted teeth.

Hades grinned and lifted his hand in response.

Reading the Devil's next move before he made it, Stingy Jack instinctively turned toward Iona and shoved her toward the tree. His intention was to move her away from Hades' reach, but instead of backing into the trunk of the willow, she slammed into Hades.

Iona held in a scream, subdued by biting her lower lip. She braced her body with her arms as Hades' gangly arms embraced her. She felt the heat radiate from his touch as though at any moment they would both burst into flames. She stared as though helpless, her terror manifesting on Stingy Jack's face. She felt Hades' cheek brush against hers, and though she winced from his warm touch, she made no attempt to break away. She wanted him close because she did not want the Devil to see it coming.

"I shall make ye regret falling in love with him," hissed Hades.

"And I shall make ye regret twistin' his soul," said Iona.

It only took a fraction of a second for her to pull her face away and brandish the silver cross against the Devil's skin.

Hades cried in agony as the sheen of the relic burned white hot. It was a sensation he had felt before, and instead of fighting, he let the punishment continue, if only to make the feeling last. The pain cut deep, weakening the fire within him. Once his body became dead weight, Iona squirmed from his embrace and staggered away. Hades panted, his pallid face even more ghostly *than before. He pressed his bony fingers against his neck. The flesh was tender and flaky. He peeled a piece and saw the ugly black char. He lifted his eyes to Stingy Jack.*

"Ye will regret this," said Hades, his threat made weak by his lack of breath. And before his rival could snap a retort, he vanished.

The sun reemerged as the banked storm clouds separated and the sheep returned to commence their grazing.

Stingy Jack looked at Iona, her body shaking violently. She dropped the cross in the grass and then collapsed to her knees, tears swelling in her dazed eyes. He moved toward her slowly and with the utmost caution, uncertain if the Devil had been able to ensnare her with some sort of spell. He picked up the cross and placed it back in his pocket; his sleight of hand had worked. He crouched down in front of her, placing his hand over the redness of her cheek, not realizing the coolness of his touch would be tantamount to pouring water over warm coals. Iona whimpered and shied away. Stingy Jack placed his knees on the ground and sat back on his heels. He opened his mouth but decided it was better to wait for her to acknowledge him. To give her time to process what they had done—what she had done.

"What sort of creature lets itself be tortured in such a manner?" she said, more rhetorically to the grass than to her love.

"A masochistic one," said Stingy Jack.

Iona shot him an incredulous look.

"No, yer right," said Stingy Jack. "Hades is too self-preserving to allow such an insult of injury last so long."

Iona looked away again. "Why is he so angry? What does he want?" she asked, thinking aloud. "Why does he hate ye so much?" This time she looked at him, expecting an answer.

It was Stingy Jack's turn to shy away.

"Tell me," she insisted, her gaze enraged by the presence of Hades' touch.

Stingy Jack sighed, a sense of shame taking hold of him. This was not a side of himself he had wished her to see. It had been foolish to think his moment of bliss could have lasted, that she would be untarnished by his past. It was a moment of self-loathing that would haunt him always. He squared his position and looked at her, finding an uncharacteristic contempt in her expression.

"It's because he couldn't have me," he said, and proceeded to tell her the parts of his life's story he had managed thus far to keep from her. He spoke briefly about his mother, what little he could remember. What he had to do in order to survive after her death, how it had changed him. He spoke of his first meeting with Hades and how he had tricked him. He confessed what tricking the Devil a second time had cost and what had happened to the Village of Lentil. He shared with her the truth about his fractured soul, the guilt he was starting to feel after feeling nothing for so long. He spoke of all the horrible things he had done in the year before his death.

"And then I was caught and thrown in the stockade, where I remained for three days until I died and became what you see, a wandering soul made of flesh, though I don't entirely know how," he continued. "I tricked the Devil and lived to speak of it, not once but twice. Heaven disregards me and Hades remains true to his word and doesn't pull me into Hell. He could renege on our bargain at any time, but I think he delights more in our unending duel. For fifteen years I have succumbed to his wishes, I have acted my part, at least until . . ." He paused. "Until ye came up to me in the street and challenged me to be something more. I don't know how ye found it or even saw it, but that voice I had

buried underneath all my treacherous deeds spoke once more."
He shifted, preparing himself for her judgment. "I wish ye not to
send me away, but I shall go if ye wish it, and prefer if ye do, fer
I've not the will to do it on me own. Hades will make good on
his word and return to see to the ruin of us and the claiming of
yer soul."

"Then let him come," said Iona, her words shocking him.

"But—"

Iona drew forward and pressed her finger against his lips.
"I will hear no more," she said. "The Devil does not rule me. I
choose me own path in this life and I choose ye, Jack. Ye seek to
protect me from yer past, and I seek to protect yer future." She
lowered her hand and placed it over his silent heart. "Know this,
Jack: I will never send ye away, turn me back on ye, nor forsake
ye. I am yers and ye be mine, now and beyond the meaning of
time."

Stingy Jack leaned into her and kissed her with a ferocity he
never thought possible. The words of her vow sank deep into
the core of his broken soul, embedding itself in firm foundation.
The last stronghold untouched by his villainy. He would do
anything to protect her, but what escaped him was that she in
turn would do the same for him. And as the storm clouds began
to put themselves back together, he would soon discover the true
strength of Iona's resolve.

FREIGHT HOPPERS

Jack sat in the underbrush beneath a half-dead willow amongst a cluster of trees guarding the railroad tracks. He yawned as the dying wind of the Black Blizzard bid him farewell, a sure sign Hades had left the Windy City. The sounds of Chicago still lingered in the air, but they had grown into soft hums the further north he had traveled.

He stretched his arms overhead, his fingers crawling up the bark of his hard pillow. The lively branches of the willow tree hung low, shading him with a cool blanket. He welcomed the smells of spring grass and new earth and watched the insects march about the colony of weeds and flowers. He laid his arms back in his lap and listened to the pleasant tune of a red-winged blackbird perched overhead while he surveyed the landscape, his thoughts still focused on his Shepherdess.

Jack lowered his gaze to the brand on his forearm and rubbed his fingers across the scarred flesh. She was never far from his thoughts, but he could not recall it ever being this strong, as though she were truly reaching out to him from beyond the grave. He felt her care and reassurance even now, the sound of her voice penetrating his memory, possessing some unspoken magic. She had always seemed to know how to tame the flames the hardships

48

of life had forged. The only one to see past his indiscretions. The only one able to tap into whatever sliver of humanity he had left. Jack took the final swig from the whiskey he had stolen from McGregor's Tavern and chucked the bottle at the railroad tracks. The shattering impact disturbed the bird, who took flight. Jack watched it soar toward the cloudless sky, lamenting its departure, for it left him to his self-loathing.

The train whistle filled the country air as puffs of smoke loomed over the tracks in the distance; the midday locomotive was right on schedule.

Jack prepared to jump on the train, crouching low at first to keep out of the engineer's line of sight. He felt the steady vibrations of the approaching iron horse, the call of the horn sounding a second time. The black engine barreled forward, a magnificent display of the industrial revolution. The horn whistled as the engine roared past Jack's hiding place, followed by a great number of the cars housing livestock, the brays of cattle muted by the cacophony of the locomotive. Several flatcars carrying logs or steel rods followed swiftly behind, along with a few tankers. Bringing up the rear, a handful of brown and red boxcars sped past, most of which were closed.

Jack waited for one of the last red cars and sprang to his feet. He ran alongside the train, its speed not nearly as fast as he had thought, which was convenient. Any faster and he might not have been able to keep up. Jack reached for the large bar next to the open door and grabbed it. He swung his feet up onto the boxcar, but they slipped. His body dropped, his feet dangling beneath him, gravity threatening to make an example of him. His arm locked as his fingers began to loosen their grip. Jack closed his eyes and anticipated the fall. It would be a quick death—well, if he could actually die. Mortality had become an impossible dream for him, but it would not stop the pain—no, that would be real. The wounds his body would suffer would be horrific, but his skin and bones would mend, branding him with scars—and what were a few more scars?

Jack's feet scraped against the sharp granite rocks, one managing to scratch his ankle, but not enough to draw blood. His fingers pried themselves apart from the handle, ready to release. Jack tried to imagine falling into a pile of leaves or into water, hoping to trick his mind, even though it seldom ever worked. His knees hit the rocks as his fingers slipped their grasp, but before his body made impact, it jerked violently, halting his descent.

Jack lifted his chin and found a mule of a man holding onto his arm. The man's dark skin clashed with his own and his grip acted as a vice around his bones. With little effort, the man hoisted him inside and slid him on his stomach across the dusty floor until the toes of his shoes rested securely on metal before releasing him. Jack lay warily before lifting his head to meet the mule's dark eyes. The man reminded him a great deal of what he imagined the steel-driver John Henry would look like in person. The colored man gave him a nod as if to say, *You're welcome*, even though the deep crevices in his cheeks gave his face a mean look. Jack acknowledged the gesture with one of his own, silently thanking the man for his assistance. Satisfied, John Henry rejoined a group of men similar in color and stature.

Jack pushed off the floor and propped his back against the corner of the door, giving his body a moment to recover from the shock. He took to listening to the conversations nearest him, the rich, baritone voices of the colored men booming over the rattle of the train. He then surveyed more of the car, disappointed it was so full of hoppers. To his left, a troop of scrawny white folk, dressed in ragged clothes, sat nestled amongst a mountain of hay, their expressions lazy and withdrawn.

"Hobos," mumbled Jack. His dealings with simple-minded folk never seemed to end on the best of terms.

Jack turned his gaze outside the boxcar again, a cool breeze instantly nipping at his nose. He listened carefully to the gait of the iron horse, using its rhythm to distract himself from the voices around him. He did not want to give himself any reason to let the trickster take hold of him again, but if the last two centuries had taught him anything, it was that the tactic only worked for so long. His stomach lurched as the trickery impulses stirred and he began to contemplate methods of deception he wanted to use on the hoopleheads. It was then he noticed a pair of emerald eyes staring at him with curious interest. He stared back, registering an odd kinship with the teenager. Jack watched him come out of his hiding place and pull out a piece of dull metal. The teenager stood in the middle of the boxcar, not bothering to remove the strands of hay stuck to the corduroy of his clothes, and began to play a haunting lullaby with his harmonica.

The somber voice of the instrument captured the attention of the freight hoppers as some of them began to hum. Jack felt his skin crawl as the music continued and anticipated the young lad changing into Hades at any moment. The trickster stirred again, ready to take action at a moment's notice, but in his head, Iona's voice managed to calm him.

It be well, Jack, her voice rang with reassurance. *Trust me— I'm right here beside ye and shall catch ye if ye falter.*

Jack expelled a deep breath, uncertain of her advice. He was in a confined space with enough people to engage. There was nothing about his current situation that was well. How could she not see the danger around him? Jack's frantic thoughts crashed into each other, reminding himself her voice was merely in his head, for his Shepherdess was dead. He tried to curtail the words of his love and do as he intended and release the trickster from its cage, but he was distracted by the smooth vocals of John Henry. The dark man's confessionary lament took Jack unawares and he gave into the safety of the notes, entrusting himself to the care of music makers. When John Henry finished, the assembly raised their hands in the air in a silent *praise the Lord* sort of way. The teenager played another measure or so before a petite woman with a swollen eye stepped forward to tell her story. Her voice was mousey, much like her thin presence, but her words wove a tapestry of family and loss. She recounted the scattering of her family, a beating that left her with only one good eye, and how, more than anything, she wished to find her child. It was a mother's lament and all present grew solemn as they thought of the mothers they would never see again.

"If you speak to me," she said, "address me thus, for Mara be my name. For I have grown bitter through the years and have been dealt with unfavorably. I cannot say what hope still remains, if any I do possess, and I'm afraid I'll pass like the dust of the plains before I see my darling *sladkaya* again."

Mara returned to her seat, relinquishing her turn to a baby-faced boy with wispy black hair and cool eyes that made him appear older than the age of ten, for in them such misery was displayed, mingled with what was left of his innocence. She acknowledged the boy by his name, Orrin, and as he began to sing, a peculiar wave filled the boxcar, his angelic voice soothing everyone's despair and lifting their burdens, if only for a moment. Orrin sang about a friend he knew, who had taken him under his wing and had been a hero. He recounted how his friend defeated two monsters, Frankenstein and the Bogeyman—a tall tale if ever there was one.

The teenager abruptly stopped playing; his eyes wide and fixed on Orrin, as though he knew some truth to the story. His ivory skin paled and he opened his mouth to speak, but Orrin walked across the boxcar toward Jack and offered his hand. Everyone looked on, acknowledging the exchange, but Jack brushed off Orrin's invitation, much to the youngster's dismay, and returned to his place next to Mara.

Jack scanned the dismal faces staring at him, and felt a knot ball in his gut. He had no desire to confess his misfortunes to complete strangers, but when his eyes came back to the teenager, there was a challenging way about the harmonica player that was not present in any of the others. It sent a chill down his spine and he could not tell if his challenger was friend or foe—or if the teenager was mortal at all. He had dealt enough with Hades over the centuries to notice the subtle nuances in the Master of Hell's features that gave him an otherworldly presence, separating him from mortals, but this teenager, who *coincidently* knew how to play the harmonica, was a mystery to him.

Tell our tale, Jack, came Iona's voice. *Sing, Jack, of how ye loved and lost, and now wander far.*

Under his skin, Jack felt his core warming, threatening to unleash anger rather than sorrow. He did not want to trust her words, fearful it was a foul ploy the trickster within was whispering in order to reassert its control of him.

Be content, me love, her voice whispered.

Jack's shoulders dropped, lowering his defenses, exposing what little humanity he had left. He unclenched his fists and presented himself as a shell of a man. He opened his mouth, and the tenor words of his singing voice passed from his pale lips like bitter milk. He confessed to the open air his woes of pain and regret. He sang about Iona, though he did not say her name.

How it would have been better to have denied himself her love and driven her away than to have had her die. But his love would not let him go, even after the Devil threatened to take her for his own. Jack admitted Iona had sought to set him free, but in her attempt, she paid the price and was slain, though by whose hand he knew not.

"How cursed, how damned the bastard ye see," he sang. "Fer truth be told the hardship I bear was placed there by me."

The harmonica ceased and the boxcar fell eerily silent. The wind teased strands of Jack's hair as judgment beat against him. He turned inward and scanned the worn faces once again, this time each one staring at him, their expressions trying to determine if he was a liar. For why would anyone admit such an awful tale? One by one, they resumed their conversations without any regard for his confession.

Jack felt his vulnerability vanish, replaced by a venomous desire. *They do not honor ye fer telling yer tale,* whispered the trickster. *They mock ye fer showing yer pain. They see ye as weak. Ye hate them, Jacky—and what do we do to things we hate?*

"We teach them a lesson," said Jack to no one in particular as the train began to slow. His expression showed a devious grin as pure mischief brightened his face. This time, Jack did nothing to fight his inner demon. He scanned the boxcar, judging the two groups of freight hoppers. Pitting them against each other would be marvelous sport, especially with the threat of the train police. The Bulls would be out in full force searching the idling locomotive for hoppers, with bloodhounds and guns ready.

The train jerked and the gears screeched to a complete stop. Everyone in the boxcar shifted abruptly, and panic erupted in worried voices. Jack straightened his tattered coat and pressed his hands down the front of his shirt. He prepared his words as he stepped toward the group of colored men, but the lad with the harmonica stood right in his path.

"Out of me way," sneered Jack, sidestepping to the left, but he was countered by the teenager. "Are ye deaf? I said, out of me way."

"I cannot," said the teenager. "Whatever you are planning, you must stop. There is no need for you to make a scene."

Jack furrowed his brow, perturbed. Nobody told him what to do—nobody. "Beat it, pipsqueak," he said, and feigned his intention before stepping around the harmonica player, addressing the colored men with vibrant gusto. "Gentlemen," he stated, focusing his attention on John Henry. "The name's Jack," he added for good measure.

Jack noted the man's skeptical caution and gave the man a fake but convincing smile of friendship. John Henry took hold of his hand and shook it firmly, sending him a message not to cross him. Jack's grin widened, even though he was unimpressed with the man's brute strength, and he eventually weaseled his fingers out of the mule's grip.

"I know it ain't none of me business," he said, "but I've been through a similar situation befer. A mate of mine and I were on a stopped train like this outside the city of Indy. We had no choice but to make a break fer it across an open field in order to escape the beating clubs of the Bulls."

"Yaw mean fer us to make a run fer it?" voiced one of the hobos, sliding down the haystack.

"Whatever you do, don't listen to him," objected the harmonica player, his voice filling the boxcar, stealing the spotlight.

Jack's body stiffened as an annoyed grimace plastered his face. He quickly caught himself and changed his expression before he could lose face. "Excuse me," he said, and unceremoniously wrenched the teenaged lad by the arm, bunching the fabric of his jacket. He led him aside to the empty corner of the boxcar as the two groups went back to their frantic debates. He threw the lad against the metal walls.

"Ye do well to stay out of a man's business, boy-o," he said.

"Jack—" started the harmonica player.

"Don't say me name, I didn't introduce meself to ye, mate," said Jack.

"Buck," said the harmonica player.

"Like I said, Buck, we ain't familiars," he added. "Now if ye'll shut yer trap, I've—"

"What, got a plan to pit the two groups against each other?"

Jack smirked. "Not a bad idea," he said, imagining the unbalanced carnage. He turned to address the freight hoppers, but the lad persisted in holding his attention.

"Stingy Jack!"

Jack whirled and brought his face close to the teenager's nose, startling him. "How do ye know that name?" he growled.

"I know a great deal about you," said Buck.

"Ha!" mocked Jack, reaching into his pocket for his silver cross. "Enough of this! I don't know how ye did it, Hades, but come out from behind that disguise."

"Jack, I am not Hades," said Buck, his eyes radiating with truth.

Jack slid his hand from his pocket and slammed it against the wall without having retrieved his weapon. The bang rattled the boxcar, resonating a loud sound directly into the lad's ear.

"Ye speak lies, Devil."

"No, Jack, I . . ." stuttered the lad as a barrage of shouting voices and howls began to bombard the air outside the boxcar.

The commotion inside ceased and a sickening fear replaced the tension. Jack glanced over his shoulder at John Henry, his hushed baritone voice addressing the other men around him.

"I know what the mick said," exclaimed John Henry.

"And we should just take our chances," challenged one of the colored men as he tightened a rope around his waist to prevent his trousers from falling off his hips.

John Henry wiped sweat from his lined brow. "We are better off running for our lives, as we have always done, than sitting here and waiting. The beating we receive will be no less severe. And at least this way we've got a fighting chance."

Jack watched the other men nod in agreement, despite the weariness on their faces. It was all they needed to be convinced and within seconds, the men collected what few belongings they had, stuffing gloves in pockets, putting their hats on their heads, rolling up blankets to fasten them with rope around their shoulders. In pairs, they jumped off the train and ran into the cover of the trees. Immediately, the hounds bayed, their paws pounding the earth as they ran to intercept the escapees. Jack pushed away from the wall and went to the opening of the boxcar to watch the scene unfold. His eyes caught sight of several large dogs as they cut two of the men down, their growls mixed with screams as their teeth no doubt found flesh.

Jack sensed the hobos gathering behind him, their stares cutting past him, looking on in terror at the fate that soon awaited them. Five more large hounds charged up from the rear of the train and split up, circling John Henry and two others. The men moved back to back, their hands out in front of them to keep the hounds at bay, but it did little to protect them. With a few stealthy movements, the hounds pounced, tackling the men into the underbrush.

There was a soft whimper next to Jack and he rotated his

head to find the angelic boy standing next to the woman with the swollen eye.

"Mara," he heard him say with worry in his voice, his fingers gripping the woman's skirt.

Mara straightened, rolling her shoulders back, doing her best to make herself taller, but next to Jack, she was still a petite thing. She lowered her chin with a stiff neck, her unwavering expression firmed by confidence.

"It'll be all right, Orrin," she said, readjusting her salmon-colored blouse.

"Ye shouldn't lie to the kid," said Jack. "Just because he's a child, it won't stop the hounds."

Mara looked at Jack with her good eye and took a step toward him. She raised her hand and slapped Jack across the face. His head turned a little to the right, and everyone still present on the train gasped. Jack brought his face back, and the woman gave him another slap. He waited a moment before looking back at her, and when he did, he stared into the woman's good eye. Without difficulty, he found the heart of her fear and knew her bravery was a shallow act of self-preservation.

"You are as you said," she spoke. The words were shaky in her throat. "You're a wicked creature."

Jack drew his face closer to hers, catching the woman off guard. She stumbled back to avoid his closeness, nearly tripping over the boy behind her. Mara moved to strike him again, but Jack countered by grabbing her wrist.

"Sticks and stones, me lady," he said. He opened his mouth to say more, but he caught sight of the harmonica lad.

"Let her go, Jack," said Buck, his voice surprisingly commanding. "If you want answers, then you will let her go."

Jack snarled. "Answers to what?" he asked, unmoved.

"Iona Covington," said Buck.

Jack immediately released the woman.

Mara rotated her hand as she withdrew her gaze, opening herself up to an attack, but Jack made no attempt to take the bait, the trickster within him too subdued to move.

"Come, Orrin," she said, taking the angelic boy by the hand, and joined the rest of the hobos as they evacuated the boxcar.

Jack did not care to watch them go, his attention on Buck, but on the edge of his peripheral vision, he caught a glimpse of disappointment on Orrin's face. He lifted his gaze an inch, to meet the boy's piercing eyes, which stabbed through the fragmented parts of his soul in an attempt to reach his buried humanity. Mara, however, interrupted his effort as she called to him to jump. Orrin withdrew and fell into the arms of the woman with the swollen eye and together they disappeared from sight.

Veritas

"Jack," said Buck, taking a step toward him.

"No," said Jack, snapping to attention. "I won't be fooled by ye, Hades. I won't let ye win."

"Jack, I am not the Devil," said Buck. "I am here to help, nothing more."

"Malarkey," said Jack. "There ain't be a creature, man or beast, who would seek to find favor with me."

"Then it is a good thing that I am neither of those things," said Buck.

Jack's eyes widened, his earlier suspicion confirmed. Whatever this lad was, like Hades, he only gave off the appearance of a mortal. And yet, unlike the Devil, the harmonica-playing teenager possessed a spark of humanity. There was something familiar about him, as though they had crossed paths before, and on a more recent encounter. He studied his features carefully and pieced the image together: the slumped bundle in the alley of Ziemba's Speakeasy who had been defended by a young man—Charlie, if memory served—whom he had given advice to, telling him there was nowhere far enough to run from the likes of Hades.

"If ye ain't be Hades," said Jack, "then what are ye? Some kind of demon?"

"I am no such thing," said Buck, taking offense.

"Well, ye ain't mortal."

"What I am, Jack, is a Breedling, an immortal soulcatcher, with no soul of my own," said Buck. "I hail from the realm of Euxinus, the parallel twin to your Eden and the origin of all things. I am as you see me, the outward shell of a fifteen-year-old mortal, but I have existed for thousands of years. I was created this way by my former masters, to allow me and others of my kin to walk amongst mortals unnoticed."

"And these masters of yers—" started Jack.

"The Fates," interjected Buck. "An insufferable trinity I had the misfortune of serving for the entirety of my existence until most recently."

"Fell, did ye?" said Jack in an accusatory tone, his thoughts recalling stories about fallen angels.

"In a manner of speaking, I suppose." Buck shrugged.

Jack lifted a skeptical brow.

"You do not believe me," said Buck, easing some saliva down his dry throat. "As a creature of uniqueness yourself, Jack, I would have suspected you more capable of embracing such possibility."

"I take no such liberty, Breedling," Jack barked. "Hades has made it pointedly clear to me that he and I aren't the only two beings to wander amongst the mortals." He folded his arms across his chest, unconvinced that the teenage creature was telling him the truth. "What I do find odd, however, is that he spoke these words to me only a few hours ago, and just like that, here ye be, proof of his claim. Almost as though he sent ye himself."

Buck closed the distance between them. "I would never serve the Master of Hell!" he shouted. "I am not here on his behalf or on anyone else's but my own. I am here because of Iona Covington, because her soul is in danger."

Your lady has never been far from my reach.

Jack shuddered, recalling Hades' taunting words, his guarded stance relaxing. He turned away from the Breedling's challenge and sat upon one of the lower bales of hay.

"I come bearing nothing but the truth," said Buck, turning to reengage the Trickster.

"Then speak yer truth, Breedling, and let me be the judge of yer sincerity," said Jack, despondent by the thought of Iona's soul in danger.

"If only it were that simple," said Buck. "In order to acknowledge the truth of your love's peril, you need to understand how important you are first."

"Me?" said Jack, caught off guard.

"Yes, you," said Buck. "You see, in Euxinus long ago, before the creation of mortals, there was a promise made that proclaimed the arrival of the Eden Wanderer, which would mark the return of the Lost Creators, and that this being would be the key to finding them."

"The Lost Creators?"

"Hades' lost siblings," said Buck.

"Siblings?" said Jack, rising to his feet. "Ye mean to tell me that vile serpent has family?"

"Three, to be exact," said Buck. "Everlyse—his sister, the Mistress of Heaven—and their lost siblings the Black Tortoise and the Golden Faun. Ever since the Fates exiled the four of them from Euxinus, Hades and Everlyse have been in a heated rivalry. It has escalated since the creation of mortals, the two deities at odds, marking mortal souls to increase their depleted divinity." Buck paused to catch his breath. "As you may suspect, these marked souls are carried to Heaven and Hell by angels and demons. Breedlings, like myself, are charged with the retrieval of those souls that go unclaimed, known as amid souls, and ferry them to Euxinus. It is there that amid souls are paraded on trial to determine deity ownership or—in rare cases, if a witness can be procured—granted a reprieve."

"And ye believe Iona is one of these amid souls?" asked Jack, flirting with the possibility that Hades' taunts actually carried weight.

"As certain as I am that Hades will do what he must to stop you from saving her," said Buck.

Jack felt inclined to respond, but steps on top of the boxcar silenced him. He lifted his gaze, following what sounded like large paws rather than boots. He felt an uneasy flicker of fear course through him and opened his mouth to ask the Breedling what it was, but Buck pulled on his arm, forcing him to lean over, and clasped a hand over his lips. He looked at him out of the corner of his eye.

"Hellhound," Buck mouthed.

The footfalls stopped directly overhead and everything became void of sound as if time itself stopped. It was a standoff, although Jack was unclear what the creature above was hunting. Had Hades sent it after him when he left Chicago? Was it following the Breedling? Or with all the commotion had it been drawn to the blood and screams? Jack felt the impulse to flee. Saliva gathered at the corner of his mouth, wetting the Breedling's hand, but he refused to release him. Minutes went by, until at last the snapping of twigs broke the silence, followed by a murderous howl. The Hellhound changed direction and thundered its way toward the front of the locomotive.

"Buck, ye can let go," mumbled Jack as time resumed.

It took the Breedling another moment to agree, but he eventually released him, and watched as he wiped his hand on his pants, his face distorted with a hint of disgust.

A rumble tickled in Jack's chest, and he began to laugh.

"You find that amusing, do you?" said Buck, taken aback by the humor in the Trickster's voice.

"Oh, quite," said Jack. "This whole thing is a farce. I mean, ye really had me going there."

"I do not follow," said Buck, sensing his breakthrough was merely an illusion.

"Hellhounds," said Jack. "Demons, angels, lost creators, the Fates. Please, do ye take me fer a fool?"

"Of course not," said Buck, missing the sarcasm in the Trickster's voice. "You are more than that."

"Ye mean the Eden Wanderer," said Jack.

Buck nodded.

Jack released another laugh, but the serious glare he received from the Breedling stifled the rest. He looked away and moved toward the open door, leaning against its frame. His eyes searched the wooded landscape, but were unable to find any of the freight hoppers, the Bulls, or their hounds. Nor was there sign of the hellhound, though he was not sure what one looked like. Instead, he spotted a large raccoon scurrying into the underbrush. He lifted his gaze to the sky, the sun passing the prime of day, and in one of the treetops, he watched a red-winged blackbird land upon a high branch and then take flight after its brief chirps received a response.

"You can stand as her witness, Jack," said Buck. "Prove to the court Iona still has a strong tether to Eden."

"And what will that prove?" asked Jack, shifting his gaze back to the Breedling. "How will that stop Hades or his sister Everlyse from claiming her soul?"

"Because, as I said, it will grant her a reprieve—a rarity for amid souls, but once granted, it will allow her to return to Eden, return to you."

Jack dropped his arms and lunged at the Breedling, who in

turn retreated to the opposite end of the boxcar. Fire danced in his eyes and fury took hold of him. He reached for Buck's neck and without mercy closed his fingers around it. His forceful strides barreled them toward the empty corner of the boxcar, pinning Buck against the unforgiving metal. Buck struggled to loosen the Trickster's hand, but his rage made it unmovable.

"Don't play games with me, Breedling," sneered Jack and hoisted his victim from the floor, his civil sensibility suspended. "I be the master of trickery."

Buck wheezed as he tried to speak, but the Trickster's grasp cut off his voice. "But—" was all he managed.

"The dead can't come back," said Jack, his anger prime to commit an act of murder. Recognizing this, Jack released Buck immediately, dropping him into a heap on the floor. He staggered back, mortified by his action, his left arm shaking from his malicious attack. His jitters worsened by the whistle of the engine blasting into the late afternoon. The train shuddered and the wheels beneath the boxcar began their forward motion.

Buck lifted his head and positioned himself against the wall, his hands massaging his neck as he tried to swallow. "Jack," he said hoarsely. "Jack, you must believe what I am telling you is the truth. Iona needs you."

Jack stared down at the teenager, again nearly forgetting himself, but there was a question lurking on his tongue. "Tell me, Breedling," he said with a sneer. "What's in it fer ye? What is yer end game?"

"I have no endgame," said Buck, forgetting the Chameleon's warning about the Trickster's intuition.

"Lie," challenged Jack, his eyes narrowing.

"She . . ." began Buck, with a cough.

"Out with it," shouted Jack, making an intimidating advance.

Buck composed himself and breathed. "Iona knows the whereabouts of the Lost Creators," he blurted. "Well, at least one of them." Buck climbed his hands up the wall and on shaking legs matched the Trickster's stance. "That is why it is imperative we save her. Imagine what Hades might do to her if he knew she held such a secret. The torture would be no less severe than if Everlyse performed it," he added, without confirming the Master of Hell was already aware Iona carried the secret.

"Stop!" shouted Jack, pressing his palms over his ears and shaking his head.

"As you wish," said Buck, and he lost the battle with his legs. He slid to the floor, closing his eyes for a brief moment, and when he reopened them, he saw Jack sitting once again on a bale of hay, his face in his hands.

Jack inhaled a prolonged breath. He heard her voice off in the distance, calling to him, trying to get through to him, but he ignored her. The trickster clawed at his insides, ready to finish what it had started and dispatch the creature without mercy, but he wrestled it into submission. He mediated the duality of his personality and muzzled both halves in order to process everything the Breedling told him, revisiting every taunt Hades had initiated. Despite all the information or questions he now had, one thing rang clear in his head—Iona could come back to him. Jack lowered his hands into his lap and found the Breedling waiting on him, his ivory skin a sickly shade of green. He felt a sudden pang of remorse, but did not outwardly acknowledge it. He did not trust him, not entirely, even if his Shepherdess urged him.

"Tell me, Buck," said Jack. "Why keep the Lost Creators from Hades and his sister?"

The Breedling offered a smile. "Aside from the obvious threat to Iona, the Lost Creators are the rightful rulers—or caretakers, if you will—of Eden. If Hades or Everlyse are able to find them, in their weakened states, the Black Tortoise and the Golden Faun can be controlled." Buck paused. To say there would be all-out war seemed too melodramatic because truthfully there would be only a massacre. "But that, Jack, is not our primary concern." Buck managed to gain his feet and gingerly walked over to the Trickster. "My charge first and foremost is to you, Stingy Jack, the Trickster, the Eden Wanderer. I am to see you safely to Euxinus, where you will stand as witness for the amid soul Iona Covington. Together we can save her tenfold. From those who would do her harm and from the secret she bears. And though I may say you are the key, Jack, the choice is yours."

Jack lifted himself, standing taller than the creature before him. He cleared his throat. "It appears, Buck, Breedling of Euxinus, we have an accord." He extended his hand.

Buck took it without pause, and they said no more on the matter.

Jack assembled his turnip lantern and hid it in a small crevice, its light casting a ghostly glow in the boxcar. He rested his head, exhausted by the day and the internal battle between his two halves. He closed his eyes and thought of Iona, her gracious smile comforting his dreams.

Buck climbed onto the bales and found a spot big enough for him to fit. He curled his knees to his chest and propped the side of his head against a bale. He heard the wheeze in his voice until he fell asleep without fear of returning to his prison cell, thanks to his promise from Charlie.

"Yes, Buck, you can stay," Charlie whispered. "Stay as long as you like."

MILWAUKIE

The sound of Charlie screaming his name violently tore Buck from his rest. The image of his mortal master surrounded by Hades' demon generals faded as he looked about, disoriented, until his eyes adjusted to the darkness around him, revealing he was still inside the boxcar. The sounds of a city began to fill his ears, and he noticed the lack of movement: the train had stopped. He looked down at Jack, who was still asleep, the glow from his lantern vigilant in its nightly charge. The Trickster's body sprawled across several bales, his left arm buried under his head. Out in front of him, his right arm stretched, propped up on a higher bale, while his left cheek dug into the hay. The position reminded him of how Charlie had slept on Grocer Pawlak's couch. Buck gripped strands of hay, his fear threatening to undo him.

"Unpleasant dreams, Master Breedling?"

Buck jumped with a screech, his movement tossing hay everywhere. He turned quickly to berate the owner of the soft voice, but when he gazed upon the Tales Teller, an uneasy sense of concern filled him. The Fates' historian was in a dismal state, her typical translucent skin an unusual ghostly shade of gray, her catlike ears folded back against her head, and her whiskers frowning. A brown cloak covered her humanoid body, which was an uncharacteristic color for a member of the Euxian council.

"Madam Teller," he whispered, too afraid to announce her presence any louder. "What? What are you doing here?" He paused, suddenly fearful his nightmare had been real. He shifted in order to properly face her. "Is it Charlie? Is he well? Has the Apothecary sent him protection?"

"Slow down, Master Breedling," she replied warily. "I have neither spoken to Master Chameleon nor the Eldest since you stormed out of the alley after your mortal companion."

"Charlie is not merely my companion, Madam Teller," said Buck, prepared to tell her about their connection, but it seemed she already knew. Her fragile smile was evidence of it. "Please, Madam Teller, tell me what has happened. How is it you appear in such a tragic state?"

"Curiosity is to blame," said the Tales Teller with a heavy sigh.

"Curiosity of what?" asked Buck.

"Not what," said the Tales Teller, "but whom." She lowered her glowing cat eyes to the Trickster.

"Jack?" said Buck, glancing at his charge. "What of him?"

"I have read every account, every deed, every interaction with Hades," said the Tales Teller. "I have learned all there is to know about Stingy Jack, but not Jack."

"I don't understand," said Buck, returning his gaze to her, but she was not there. "Madam Teller," he whispered.

The brushing sound of a heavy cloth answered his call.

"Madam Teller, what are you doing?" he asked, inching his way to the floor, and watched as the Tales Teller placed her hands around Jack's head. She whispered an incantation multiple times, but whatever she was trying to do was not working.

"Huh," she sighed and withdrew. "It was worth a try."

"What?" asked Buck. "What did you do?"

"This time, I can assure you I did nothing," said the Tales Teller and hid her hands in the folds of her cloak. "I was merely trying to find the stories I'm missing in my library. Not the ones of Jack and Iona, but of the ones further back, the ones that tell of Jack's beginning. Of all the mortal souls ever to exist, he is the only one that has three origins. The Eden Wanderer; the Trickster, Stingy Jack; and Jack. The first two I know, but Jack remains a mystery to me."

"You mean Iona's Jack?" said Buck.

"Iona's Jack is the core of his whole existence, and before he became hers, that Jack belonged to someone else."

"His mother?" asked Buck.

"Perhaps," said the Tales Teller, skepticism in her voice.

"What then?" asked Buck.

To this inquiry, the Tales Teller did not answer. She simply stared inquisitively at the Trickster, for it was rare she got the chance to decipher a mystery.

"The angels did this to you," said Buck, finally formulating the reason for her disheveled appearance. "You tried to speak with his mother."

"Of that, I did try," she said with weighted words. "As you know, Master Breedling, I am the only Euxian amongst the Fates' creations granted access to the trove of souls in Heaven and Hell. In no uncertain terms I was denied passage beyond the snowy gates by Everlyse's high general, who, after accosting me, informed me Jack's mother is not in Heaven. I found this knowledge disconcerting, given what I know about the woman; however, given the circumstance of her death, I supposed I had miscalculated."

"No," said Buck, keenly aware as to where the Euxian historian had gone next.

The Tales Teller quirked the corner of her mouth. "I'm sure the Chameleon will be of the same mind when I tell him," she said. "But I did. I ventured to Hell's vaults, and a lower class demon told me, again, in no uncertain terms that if she were in Hell then Master Hades would have long ago persuaded the Trickster to take his standing offer."

"Impossible," said Buck, flabbergasted.

"Impossible, you say," said the Tales Teller. "I am afraid that word no longer carries its true meaning, Master Breedling, for now, all things are possible."

"Well, then, that would mean Jack's mother is an amid soul," said Buck.

"You would be right to think so, but I checked every charge the Fates bestowed on every Breedling in the last two hundred years, and there was no order for the retrieval of the Trickster's mother."

"So that is why you came here, because you could not find his mother. To what end?" asked Buck.

"To help you," said the Tales Teller, her skin brightening with a faint yellowish glow, showcasing the silver blemishes, the injuries to her skin. "It is one thing to convince the Trickster to follow you into the great unknown; it is another to make certain he completes the necessary challenges of a worthy witness. I thought that if I could unlock the origin of his soul, no battle would be waged within, that his true identity, the thing that makes him most unique, would take hold. But it appears I have failed in my endeavor. Instead"—she knelt in front of Buck to meet his gaze, her pointed ears perking up—"you must remind him of his only connection to that part of himself."

"Iona," said Buck.

"Yes," said the Tales Teller. "Be sure to ask him about her. Let him remember her fondly and tell you stories about what she was like, the first time they met, the moments of time they stole. Avoid any mention of Hades if you can; keep your focus solely on her and his love for her. Hopefully that will be enough to give the goodness in him a chance to act selflessly."

"I will ask," replied Buck, falling into the old habit of taking orders. "And . . ." He trailed off, not wanting to ask the question.

Again the Tales Teller offered a knowing smile, glad she was able to pass over any further explanation of Jack's mother. She and the members of the council needed him focused.

"And what of your way home," she finished his inquiry.

"Euxinus is not my home," mumbled Buck.

"As you say, Master Breedling," she said. "For that, you must make your way to the Land of Ten Thousand Lakes." She placed her thumbs against his temples.

Buck closed his eyes, and in the darkness a map appeared, showing him the way. It was a formality she performed often in the Fates' palace after a Breedling was charged with the retrieval of an unclaimed amid soul and would provide a keen sense of direction in locating a charge. Buck tried to recall the last time the Tales Teller had given him such instruction, but for some reason it was escaping him.

Buck blinked as she pulled him toward her, then kissed him on the forehead.

"Blessings on your journey, Master Breedling," she said. "Remember, your charge must complete his challenge, so you may have to create the opportunity for him. Without his knowing, of course. It will be in his hands to do the rest."

"But is that not manipulative?" asked Buck, the unease mounting on his face.

"Sweet Bartholomew, not if it is done correctly," she said. The

Tales Teller attempted to touch his cheek, but the Breedling pulled away, refusing to acknowledge his given name. She dropped her hand and sighed. "Be mindful of your time. You only have at best three Eden days to deliver Stingy Jack to the Ferryman, but as you know, time is a tricky thing. If you cannot find it in you to be more than the obedient soulcatcher then all will be undone."

Buck watched as the Tales Teller vanished before him, allowing his gaze to look beyond the belly of the iron horse. Morning's first light broke across the sky as several whistles wailed, their collective sounds ringing through his body. He tickled his ears with his fingers, and once the residual ring faded, it gave way to familiar city sounds, although the orchestrated rhythm was different from the City in the Garden. Metal collided in quarter notes and the hum of factories played a continuous drone. He looked to the skyline, where a red-spired clock tower overlooked the congested train yard. He sighed, overwhelmed by the sight— another modern city he knew nothing about and, this time, no Charlie to help him navigate through the streets. If he was going to create an opportunity for Jack to act selflessly, they would have to do it before crossing into the Land of Ten Thousand Lakes.

"Milwaukee," said Jack, stepping alongside the Breedling and breathing in the air. "Ah, nothing like the smell of malted hops mixed with a hint of cocoa."

"You know this city?" asked Buck.

"Of course, mate, it be one of me favorites in the American Midwest," said Jack as he stretched his arms over his head. "Best damn brewing city in the world—well, now that the cursed Prohibition is over. It's been awhile since me last visit, nearly twelve years if memory serves."

"Well then, why not give me a show?" said Buck, his voice a little too anxious. "I mean—" He felt his stomach tighten and then gurgle. He recognized it as a hunger pang, realizing it had been an entire day since he had eaten any food. *You don't eat, you die, simple as that.* He recalled Charlie saying these words after he had tried to refuse a cup of soup. His young master had been quite adamant about the mortal practice of gathering sustenance, and it seemed he would have to continue it if he wished to appease his changed form.

"Are you hungry?" he asked, jumping out of the boxcar and onto the dusty ground of the train yard.

"Buck, are ye daft?" said Jack. "What about all that prattle about Iona needing help? Or was that merely a lie?"

"No, of course not," said Buck, desperately getting his thoughts in order. He needed to be smart about this. He stared at Jack, mapping out their route ahead, but he was unable to move forward far enough in time. He was blind to the dangers afoot, but he knew if they ventured out into the city, there would be opportunity for Jack to begin his tasks. Buck sensed a flicker of discontent push back at him from the Trickster and blinked.

"Mind telling me what that was all about?" asked Jack.

"Merely looking ahead," said Buck, treading closer to a lie than the truth, but just enough to pique Jack's interest.

"Ye can do that?" said Jack.

"There are many things I can do," said Buck, not directly answering the question. "For instance," he added, pulling the harmonica from his pocket, "I can play this mouth harp after only hearing it played once. Using that same ability I was able to beat a goliath at a game of pool."

"So ye can adapt. That don't prove ye can do anything special," said Jack, folding his arms.

"Fair enough," said Buck, putting the harmonica back into his coat.

"And what of the future?" asked Jack.

Buck bit the inside of his lip and thought carefully about his next words. "I cannot see the future, Jack, but I have a sense that our journey will not be hindered by our stop here," he said, with every ounce of confidence he could muster, though he could not be sure of his own words. "Stopping here for a bite to eat will do no harm nor will it be the worst idea, for where we are headed, Euxinus has no nourishment for the body, even an immortal one."

Buck waited as Jack scrutinized his expression. He created a mask, a fragile one at best, worried the Trickster would see through his ruse. But after a moment, Jack leapt from the boxcar.

"I could go with some grub, meself," said Jack. "Me belly has been starved for a few days and could use more than drowning it with liquor. I know of an eatery nearby, just a stroll across the yard, past some warehouses over yonder," he pointed. "Then east on St. Paul Avenue a few blocks, up Fourth a tick, down a block and then up Fifth. We can be there in twenty minutes and then back on the next train to . . ." He looked down at Buck. "Where is it we even need to go in order to get into Euxinus?"

"The Land of Ten Thousand Lakes," said Buck.

"Ye mean Minnesota?" said Jack. "Seems like an odd place."

"Well, that is where we will need to go," said Buck, starting to walk in the direction Jack had pointed in an attempt to prevent the Trickster from asking more questions about how they were going to get to Euxinus.

"Oi," shouted Jack. "Where ye be going?"

"To the eatery," said Buck, picking up his pace a tick. "You said it would take twenty minutes. The faster we move, the quicker we return."

Jack ran after Buck, catching his stride.

They exited the train yard without trouble from any of the rail workers, which according to Jack was a stroke of luck, before they hit the streets of Milwaukee.

Distraction

"Tell me about Iona," said Buck casually as they walked past a group of men loitering in front of the John Pritzlaff Hardware Warehouse—the white-painted letters on the nearly windowless brick building hard to miss.

Jack did not answer right away, distracted by the heated discussion between the men, for there was rumor of a strike brewing in Minneapolis.

Buck had no idea what any of it meant, but he gathered from the worried intensity in the voices slowly drifting out of earshot that it was nothing good.

"What do ye wish to know?" asked Jack.

"What was she like?" asked Buck.

"I called her me angel, but she would scoff at me use of the word, and from what ye said about Everlyse, I'm inclined to agree with her."

Buck bit his lip, for this was the type of reaction he needed to avoid.

"Aside from that," Jack continued, "Iona Covington was the kindest soul I have ever known. She had a sense of empathy unparalleled in any mortal. When someone in the village was ill or injured she cared fer them. When tempers prevailed over cooler heads, she settled arguments. When death took those most dear, she was a source of comfort. She almost sounds like a dream, fer how could anyone be so pure? But she was. Her heart was limitless. It had to be, fer how else could she have seen right through me?"

"Sounds like she tended to more than just her flock of sheep," said Buck.

"Ah, yes," said Jack. "To anyone else that herd would have looked like nothing more than dumb animals whose sole purpose was to provide wool and meat. But to Iona, her flock was as precious as flesh and blood. What little family she had. I remember a week or so after our first meeting, one of the lambs had fallen into the stream and was swept away by the current. With no regard fer herself, she ran ahead and waded across rocky shallows to catch the thing, but the speed of the animal knocked her off her feet and the two of them drifted fer miles downstream."

"Were you with her?" asked Buck, crossing St. Paul Avenue, the smells of soap and sawdust mingling with the coal barren odor of Freight House No. 7.

"I was on me way to meet her in the lowlands but had not yet arrived."

"Then who saved her?" asked Buck.

Jack smiled with a rare glow—a reserved expression used only for her. "She did," he said, with a hint of stardust in his eye. "Iona Covington was well capable of taking care of herself. Although," he added, with a lighthearted chuckle, "she did get one hell of a cold after that. Was laid up fer two days with a fever." Jack paused to recall his beauty bundled in wool blankets to keep her warm as he nursed her back to health with spoonfuls of stew. "Speaking of rescues," said Jack, "ye never told me how we're to get to Euxinus."

"By way of passage, naturally," said Buck, not realizing Jack was about to steer the conversation from his intended course.

"Speak with some sense, Buck," said Jack. "I know nothing of such things."

"Right," said Buck. "If we are to get to Euxinus, we must pass through an Eden Scar, a hidden gateway that allows Breedlings to return home from Eden. There are many throughout the realm. In some places they are more frequent than others, but usually one does not have to travel far to find one."

"And the closest one of these is in Minnesota?" asked Jack.

"Of that I cannot be certain, for I do not have the ability to know where they are all hidden. This is because Eden Scars are a creation of Eden, not Euxinus. And at any given time, I know where only one is located," said Buck, trying to reroute the conversation. "As I said before, we must go to the Land of Ten Thousand Lakes; from there the map of where we need to go will become clearer. Do you know how close we are?"

"Well, it's about a day's ride by train to the Twin Cities," said Jack, stopping on the sidewalk before the alley to allow a fleet of Mack dump trucks to enter the junkyard. He swung his arm out to prevent Buck from advancing as the last truck driver honked his horn in appreciation. Jack nodded and pressed on past the alley, only to stop on the other side, puzzled Buck was not with him. He turned around to the sight of terror on the Breedling's face.

"Buck?" Jack closed the gap between them and looked about the street, but found no sign of anyone, not even a passing automobile. They were alone. He placed a hand on Buck's shoulder.

Buck's eyes moved slowly to meet Jack's gaze as a chilling sense of guilt curled in his gut. Had he imagined it? Buck absentmindedly moved away from the Trickster and stood in the center of the alley, his eyes staring at nothing.

"Jack, did you hear that?" he asked, needing validation that what he had heard was not simply in his head. "Did you hear a woman scream?"

Jack clapped his shoulder. "Ey, what of it? Women scream all the time."

"AHHHHHHHH!"

Buck did not dilly-dally and darted through the alley.

"Bloody hell," cursed Jack under his breath, following the Breedling.

Buck slowed his pace and peered around the corner of a hosiery factory. Down the perpendicular alley were two men, one standing guard and the other on the ground with a woman pinned beneath him. The woman let out another scream, her legs flaring underneath the man and her body thrashing to get free. The man raised a hand and slapped her across the face. Buck's body tensed as his fingers gripped the wall, attempting to dig his fingers into the hard brick. The sudden desire to take action consumed him as the woman cried out for help, but over the grind of the junkyard, no one else was likely to hear. Buck rolled back his shoulders, prepared to charge down the alley, but Jack pulled him back by the scruff of his jacket.

"Are ye plum crazy?" whispered Jack, spinning him around.

"Jack, let me go. That woman is in trouble."

"Buck, there is always some dame in trouble," said Jack coldly, the trickster within clawing out from behind the emotions he managed to unshackle from his talk about Iona.

"But we can help her," said Buck, wishing he had not allowed Jack to distract him with talk of Eden Scars. He would now have to choose his words carefully, for he could only set the stage, not force action.

"And what do ye propose we do? Waltz down there and ask 'em to stop?" said Jack.

"You have a better suggestion?" challenged Buck. He wanted to press the importance that Iona would never let such a misfortune occur, but to do so would influence the Trickster too much and in doing so would cheapen the act. He watched the Trickster's face tighten, a conflict raging inside him, his fingers tightening and relaxing until, finally, he relinquished his hold.

Jack inched to the edge of the building and peered around the corner at the two men. He watched the man on the ground wave a pocketknife above the woman's face, subduing her cries to submissive whimpers. The sight was enough to appeal to his innate sensibilities.

"All right, Buck," Jack said, turning back to the Breedling. "Give me a minute; then follow. Ye take the lookout; I'll take the other fella."

"The what?"

"The big fella standing guard," snapped Jack.

Buck nodded and stepped in line right behind the Trickster.

Jack peered around the corner and waited for the lookout to turn away before stealthily tiptoeing along the brick wall toward the trash heap. He crouched low, readying himself to make his move and within a few seconds, he leapt out from his hiding spot and tackled the man who was on top of the woman. Jack left no room for the knifeman to counter and he punched him, connecting with his large nose and the corner of his thin mouth.

In response, the knifeman pointed his small blade at Jack's neck.

At the same time, Buck charged down the alley armed with a metal rod and struck the other man in the back of the thigh. The big fella groaned, nearly taking a knee. Buck sprang back to reposition his stance, but he received swift retaliation, unprepared to defend himself. The man quickly nabbed him by the scruff and tossed him like a ragdoll. Buck landed on the trash heap, knocking wooden pallets and debris across the ground.

The big fella then reached for Jack and placed him in a chokehold, pulling the Trickster off the knifeman.

Jack thrust his right elbow backward in an attempt to connect with the man's chest, but his assailant attacked first with a jab to his side. He tried to double over from the instant pain, but was restricted.

The knifeman regained his feet and wiped a trickle of blood from his slanted jaw line. He estimated Jack with unadulterated contempt.

Jack spat in the knifeman's bloodied face.

The knifeman smeared the saliva across his sleeve and smiled crookedly as he balled his fists and jabbed at Jack's abdomen with a few rapid punches.

Buck mustered himself off the ground to get back into the fight. His body ached, but he managed to wield his weapon and took another swing, this time connecting with the guard's knee. The man roared as his leg crumpled beneath his weight, releasing Jack, and simultaneously they both fell to the ground.

"Jack, get up," said Buck, preparing his stance to combat the knifeman, but without warning, a force knocked him on his ass, his weapon dislodged from his hand.

"I'm gonna skewer your flesh, boy," threatened the knifeman.

Buck shuffled sideways like a crab and rammed against a steel can. He looked around for his weapon and saw it within the pile of wood. He tried to reach for the metal rod, but a firm grip creased his throat, restraining him from his purpose. The knifeman pulled him close to his face, his yellow teeth crooked in his decaying mouth, his breath reeking of death.

"I think I'll start with that pretty face of yours." The knifeman pressed the blade into Buck's cheek.

The pain was unlike anything Buck had ever experienced, and from deep within, a horrified scream projected from his chest as the blade sliced through the curve of his cheek and a cool sensation trickled underneath his jawbone.

"Buck," wheezed Jack, propping himself on his hands and knees, ready to rejoin the fray, but when he lifted his head, the knifeman was standing at arm's length away from the Breedling. The man's eyes were bulbous, and in a fit of panic, he released Buck, dropping his knife. The Breedling made a quick retrieval of the weapon to defend himself, but his attacker turned and ran before he could even use it. Jack wrapped his arm around his abdomen as he got to his feet and watched the guard hobble after his companion. Still winded, he managed to breathe well enough. He glanced over at Buck, the Breedling holding the knife out in front of him.

"Buck?" Jack moved toward the Breedling slowly, as though coming upon a wounded animal. He gave Buck a quick once-over for any injuries other than the cut on his cheek. He met the Breedling's gaze and offered a pleasant expression. "There ye are. Ye all right."

"I . . ." started Buck, his eyes falling to the knife in his hands.

"May I?" asked Jack. He moved in closer, disarmed the Breedling, and observed the substance on the blade, the color shimmering. "No wonder the coward ran off," he said. "Probably thought ye were some kind of demon, maybe even the Devil." Jack chuckled uncomfortably at the irony of it, considering it had only been a few hours since he had thought the same, and with less proof.

Buck's face flushed with anger. "I am no demon," he muttered. "Demons are volatile, careless creatures, full of Hades' sense of villainy and hatred. How dare you compare me to them?"

"Don't get yer knickers in a twist. I mean no harm," said Jack. "It's just, if I was to come across someone who bleeds gold, well, I might think the same." He rotated his wrist for Buck to see the shimmering residue on the blade.

"What is that?"

"Yer blood. Yer cut looks like it might leave a shiner, but it appears to be clotting quickly—uck, it looks god awful."

Buck lifted a hand to his face and touched the tender wound, capturing some of the cool residue on his fingers. "I do not understand," he said aloud.

"What, ye didn't know the color of yer blood?"

"Why would I?" said Buck, as a thunderous pounding from the junkyard stole the volume of his voice. "This has never happened before."

Jack lifted his eyebrows. "Ye've never been cut?"

"No, the protection of the Fates always stopped such things from occurring."

"Well that seems to have rubbed off, mate."

"Indeed," agreed Buck as he cradled his cheek.

Jack examined the blade. "Ye know, if I didn't know any better," he said, "I'd say this was real gold dust encased in sticky sap." Jack smeared the blood on his trousers, closed the pocketknife, and put it in his coat. Out of the corner of his eye, he saw the woman lying on the ground and turned to her. He followed the tear in her brown skirt, her bloomers exposed but still intact. His gaze moved to her abdomen and caught the sight of a dark red staining her salmon-colored blouse, her chest rising weakly.

"Jack, she is alive!" shouted Buck, recognizing the woman's

face from the train. He crouched down next to Mara, the action all too familiar to him and in a flash the woman vanished and in her place he saw Iona lying on the ground, her hair slick with rain and mud, and her tears mixing with the droplets hitting her face. Buck shook his head to push the image from his mind.

"Oh, rotten hell," Jack swore. He squared his stance, but was somehow incapable of moving to her aid. "Buck, we should really . . ." Jack looked at the Breedling, whose concern for the woman was a haunting image, and for a moment, he saw the scene of a mother and son. It was then his feet found their sense of urgency, and without command, they moved forward. He bent down, put one arm under her shoulders and the other under her knees. He lifted the woman, cradling her in his arms, pressing her against him tightly to put pressure on the wound, despite the fact the movement added discomfort to his ribs.

"Jack," said Buck.

"Come on, Buck," said Jack, turning toward the sidewalk. "Johnson Emergency Hospital is not far from here. We can take her there; then ye and me are on the next train heading north on the Milwaukee Road."

"Sure, Jack," said Buck, getting to his feet. He followed the Trickster out of the alley, staying a step behind to conceal the grin breaking across his face. He had not thought the opportunity would come so easily, and with the first act almost complete, he was certain retaliation lurked close by. He kept a sharp eye out for Hades and his demons, but despite his intention, vigilance would not be enough.

SHANTYTOWN

Posted on either side of the street, two Model T cars with a pair of horses hitched to each Ford stood like chariot sentinels at the entrance of the Shantytown, which consumed and surrounded what was once Union Square. The ersatz village sat in the shadow of the Everett Street Depot; its crimson brick gleamed in the midmorning sun, and the clock tower at its center remained silent despite the top of the hour, its three-thousand-pound bronze bell unable to ring. Jack and Buck passed through the makeshift archway comprised of packing crates and plastic sheets. Most of the small dwellings were misshapen structures, built from cardboard boxes, spare wood, and scrap metal with a small mixture of broken tents and ragged sheets. Black barrels marked the path through the temporary village, burning hot with fires in their bellies, providing light and warmth despite the sun and late spring heat. Standing around one of the first barrels, a crowd of mortals was roasting some kind of meat over a crude grill, their pants pockets inside out, signifying the Hoover flag. Their bodies were unkempt and as grungy as the ramshackle structures they now called home. Their faces were full of hopelessness, their voices low, whispering about a chance of rain even though there was not a cloud in sight.

Jack curled Mara closer to him in order to hide the spread of the bloodstain on her blouse. The readjustment created stress against his rib cage, forcing him to catch a breath, but he dared not loosen his grip for several pairs of curious eyes watched them as they passed. To the right, two long-bearded men standing in the doorway of a metal shack smoked their pipes and passed judgment on the newcomers, though they chose to do so privately. The men around the rusty grill did the same and went back to their business. He avoided colliding with a crotchety old crone, carrying a basket of rotten fruit and flies, by sidestepping a few paces, and he swung to the left to avoid a troop of children kicking a ball back and forth. The crone shrieked as they used her as an obstacle, and she shook her wooden cane at them in outrage, only making the children laugh at their own shenanigans.

Buck slowed his pace, falling further behind Jack, his senses overstimulated by the active surroundings. He found himself drawn to every sound and movement, judging every pair of eyes he came across. He, too, avoided the kids at play, although he was partially intrigued by their game and had an odd desire to join them. When he found nothing out of the ordinary about them, he lost interest and scouted a young woman hanging stained sheets on a wire while two young boys chased each other around her, both of them brandishing wooden sticks like swords. Next, he came upon a little girl dressed in a polka-dotted dress, sitting across from a small boy who was wearing an oversized black fedora. Two miniature cups sat on the tiny table in front of them and a broken ceramic teapot between them. The boy handed the girl a bouquet of wilting weeds as she giggled. The little girl took the gift and plunged her nose into a yellow flower as if to smell something pleasant. She placed the bouquet on the table and leaned in close to the boy. She closed her eyes and kissed the corner of his mouth. The boy's face flushed instantly, and the little girl giggled again. Buck considered the scene, drawn in by their innocence. For a moment, he forgot the reason he had been watching them in the first place. Their mortal ways were stealing him away from his mission and opening his eyes to a notion he had not yet witnessed.

"Soap, get your soap here!"

The call of a man's voice pulled Buck back from the normalcy of mortal life and he refocused his attention on a man standing on top of a large wooden box and holding a bar of soap in his bony fingers. The clothes on his back looked like nothing more than a potato sack. Buck rounded a cluster of onlookers to get a better view. The man's long black hair and pallid skin were undeniable—*Hades*.

"Soap, soap for sale, all trades be honored!" The alluring tone in Hades' voice drew a crowd, but he ignored them and leapt from his soapbox. In a few strides, he towered over Buck. His red eyes flickered, and with a snap of his fingers time slowed, everything around them fading into paused silence.

Hades bent over and put his cheek next to Buck's face. He inspected his wound, now an angry, crusty scab resembling dried pus. Hades breathed deeply, smelling the air in mockery, before moving in close and whispering in Buck's ear.

"Ah, the smell of sulfuric blood," said Hades. "How incredibly unexpected. It has been ages since I inhaled the scent of my ancestral home in Eden. Mmm, so fresh. Oh, Bartholomew, how you continue to amaze me."

"What do you want, Hades?" asked Buck, though he already knew the answer to his question. He felt the warmth of Hades' touch sear his cheek, the Devil's pale fingers brushing against his skin. He winced, but refused to give into the Master of Hell's taunt.

"Come now, Bartholomew." Hades pulled away and began to circle him like a buzzard. "Let me relish the scent of your defiance and betrayal."

"I betray nothing," Buck countered, rooting his feet.

"And yet you obey the command of another," said Hades, stopping in his tracks. "Enlighten me, Bartholomew. How did you, a mere soulcatcher, a slave, manage to exercise free will?" Hades paused for an answer, but Buck did not offer one. He snarled. "I don't know how you did it, but mark my words: I shall discover your secret."

Buck watched Hades closely, the Devil's stare lingering on the cut occupying his face as though he were trying to find the answer.

"What do you want, Hades?"

"Very well, young squire," spat Hades, his voice hardening. "Before this day is done, Stingy Jack shall be worthless to the one he loves."

"Is that what you came here to say?" asked Buck, letting out a chuckle. "To warn me of your plan?" He laughed a bit more, feeling a sort of perverse satisfaction.

"Silence," hissed Hades.

Buck choked on his laughter as Hades brought his face mere inches away from his nose. He swallowed hard.

"Tell me the whereabouts of my siblings and I shall let your charge continue his quest unscathed, for I will have no need of the Shepherdess," offered Hades.

"As I told you before . . ." began Buck.

"Do not play me for a fool, Breedling," said Hades.

"Fool or no, Creator Hades, both of them are far from your reach," said Buck, standing his ground, but only just.

Hades' eyes blazed with fury and flames burst in his hand, casting a scarlet glow on his face. "What makes you think you have the right?" said Hades, his voice uncharacteristically pinched. Then he changed his demeanor, twisting his mouth into a crooked smile, somewhat amused by the Breedling's gallantry. "Poor Bartholomew," he taunted. "Must be so perplexing to not be as you should, such a pity." He drew away, standing tall once more, and cast the fire from his hand. "You may have escaped your wretched masters, but you have weakened yourself by losing their grace. And as for your young master, he is not here to protect you."

Buck recalled Hades' orders to Tezcat to find Charlie. Had the Demon General already captured him? Buck tried not to fidget, but he could not prevent the flash of panic.

Hades' grin widened.

"You leave Charlie out of this," said Buck, unable to keep the words locked inside.

Hades snickered. "As I once told your new companion, Stingy Jack, when he said those same words to me about a certain Shepherdess—this is your doing. Charles Reese is a part of this odyssey now, and despite your grandstanding, he has no choice. You took that from him the moment he rescued you from that pitiful inferno. I shall send him your regards when he is brought before me." Hades bowed and turned his back.

"You are bluffing," choked Buck, with a single step forward. "Charlie is far away from here."

"Ah, but not far enough," said Hades.

"Hades, I swear by the Golden Faun, if you . . ." Buck took another step forward in threatening fashion, but Hades swooped down in a crouch, meeting him at eye level once more. Buck fought to keep his wits, but his fear was too strong. His eyes did their best not to betray him, but they did. If Hades truly wanted to cause him pain, there would be no stopping him. Buck curled his fist, prepared for Hades to strike, but the ancient Master of Hell simply stared at him until he felt like a speck of ash.

"The next time you speak my dear sister's name, Bartholomew, it will be to tell me where she and my brother are hiding," warned Hades. He let his threat linger between them for a moment. He then pulled away and returned to his soapbox, thrusting a hand in the air with a bar of soap.

"Soap, soap for sale, all barters welcome!" the rasp of his voice boomed, returning time to the Shantytown.

Buck watched the crowd come to life again as they rushed to Hades. He stood numb with his thoughts of Charlie, the nightmares he had seen. His mind began to theorize the worst, able to imagine the horrific pains that Hades' demon generals, each with its own special skill of torture, could inflict upon the fragile mortal. He began to feel the strength of his charge bend to the breaking point. No, the Apothecary was sending help. Charlie would be safe. Buck forced his concerns for his friend aside and collected his thoughts. He turned away from Hades and found Jack only a few feet away. He went after the Trickster, leaving Hades to make his latest deals with the destitute mortals of the Shanty. He needed focus to make certain Jack completed his trials before leaving Eden. And the faster the Trickster completed them, the quicker he could get him to Euxinus where Hades could neither track nor tempt Stingy Jack. Buck caught Jack's stride and moved in as close to him as possible, maintaining a sharp eye.

"Buck, do ye mind, mate, or do ye wish the woman be thrown to the ground?" said Jack as Buck bumped into him.

"Of course not," said Buck, evening his pace and looking up at Jack, mostly to see if Mara had regained consciousness. Her condition, however, was the same. "Jack, are we close?"

"The hospital is just beyond the Shanty," said Jack, exiting

Union Square, only to stop short. "I don't understand," he said. "It should be right here."

Across the street, a vacant lot stood sandwiched between two clay stone buildings, the sign of the Boston Store mounted by the door of the building on the corner. Jack turned back into the Shanty and approached an old spinster who reeked of mothballs, sitting on a broken rocking chair with a blanket of newspapers in her lap.

"Excuse me, Mama," said Jack, forcing a civil tone.

The spinster lifted her shaky head, jiggling wrinkled flaps of skin. "Morning, young man," she greeted in a low alto voice. "What can I do for you?"

"Can ye tell me what happened to the hospital across the street?"

"What was that, sonny?" asked the spinster.

"The hospital," said Buck. "Do you know what happened to it?"

The spinster eyed Buck and smiled, delight filling her whole face. "Torn down in '31, it was."

Buck thanked the spinster for her assistance and followed Jack as he stepped out of the Shanty.

"Jack . . ."

"Just give me a second, Buck," grumbled Jack.

"I don't think we have that kind of luxury," said Buck, as occupants within the horseless carriages eyed them judgmentally. It would only take one of them to inquire about the woman for an uncontrolled scene to occur.

Jack sighed. There was only one other place close enough to take her, where no one would ask questions. "Dixie Diamonds," he said, with a touch of defeat.

"What?" asked Buck, hurrying across West Michigan Avenue.

"Dixie Diamonds," repeated Jack. "It used to be the Oddy Palm Garden before Prohibition, but when liquor was outlawed, Tomas Oddy, the owner, transformed it into a burlesque speakeasy. Now, from what I've heard, it's a hush-hush brothel."

"Why there?" asked Buck. From his experience in Ziemba's Speakeasy, he was unsure how such a place would be much help.

"The Madam, Dixie Diamond, was the Canary during the Garden's illegal heyday, a top-notch one to boot. She takes care of the girls. She'll be able to assist us with our—problem." Jack repositioned his hand over the woman's stab wound, his fingers sticky with her blood.

"What makes you think she will help us?" asked Buck, weaving around an obese man who did not move himself from his path.

"Dixie and I go back a ways," said Jack, and he left it at that.

Buck sensed the Trickster was hiding something, but he was too alert to push for more information, his eyes busy scanning the avenue for Hades' spies. They crossed Third Street without delay, although a blue Lincoln nearly clipped them in front of the Hotel Atlas as it pulled away from the curb.

"Buck, stop drawing attention," said Jack from the corner of his mouth, catching the Breedling gawking.

Buck ignored Jack and caught sight of a woman in a bathrobe peering out through the corner window of her hotel room on the second floor. He drew his eyes away and tried to make his observations less obvious after that. His gaze turned toward the Public Service Building and he watched several mortals walk through a variety of entrances, the center one distinguished by a Roman numeral clock. None of the mortals bothered to give him or Jack so much as a glance, but that did not stop Jack from repeating his admonishment, warning him to look away. Buck complied as they stopped in front of an iron gate wedged between brick and the white-glazed terra-cotta of the six-story Enterprise Building.

"Well, don't just stand there. Open the gate," said Jack, the bundle in his arms almost dead weight.

Buck pushed on the metal bars, but the gate did not budge. He pulled them toward him and the iron moved slightly, only to catch with a heavy jerk. It clanged loudly.

"Buck, uncouple the chain," said Jack.

Buck uncoiled the lifeless snake, taking care not to make any more noise. Once unwrapped, the weight of the gate caused it to swing open. Buck forced the entrance a bit further so Jack could fit through. With care, Jack made sure not to bang the woman's head as he entered the shadows of the alley.

Buck performed one last scout of the avenue as he secured the chain, unable to identify a single otherworldly creature, unaware that two winged spies sat perched overhead on the roof of the Enterprise Building. Satisfied with his scan, Buck caught up with Jack, the gate squeaking as it settled back into place.

The Roarin' Twenties

*J*ack rolled into Milwaukee on the 8:15 out of Chicago with the appearance of a vagabond. His filthy clothes reeked of manure and he knew his attire was not suitable for his intended destination. He braved the wintery streets, wandering for hours before he managed to secure a suit, which he stole out of the back seat of a Lincoln. A few blocks away from the scene of his crime, he sweet-talked a cigarette girl into letting him use one of the rooms in the gentlemen-only Hotel Antlers to freshen up. The bath was divine considering he had gone without one for months. He lathered his body clean and picked the grime out of his nails. When he was finished, Jack assembled the three-piece suit and put it on. The fit was snug, but he was willing to sacrifice comfort for one night. He would just have to remember to keep his movements small. He studied himself in the mirror as he groomed his hair and continually muttered the password to get into Dixie Diamonds.

"Yer momma ain't got no socks," he whispered as he straightened his black tie. "Lookin' sharp, Jacky boy."

Jack left the Antlers and arrived at Dixie Diamonds just as the evening festivities were underway. The whole speakeasy resembled a chapel, decorated in gold and ivory with carved wood and copper features arranged harmoniously. The grand room was alive with an extraordinary wealth of chatter, music, and the occasional outburst of laughter. The polished marble floor was full of people, everyone standing or sitting at glistening black oak tables. Each person had a glass in hand—some with moonshine, others wine, and a few with near-beer. Some of the ladies held feathery fans, while most of the gentlemen brandished cigars. Everyone was dressed in the latest New York or Parisian fashions and all of the Who's Who of Milwaukee were there, most notably the Diamond's proprietor and brewery tycoon, Tomas Oddy.

Jack kept to the shadows along the back wall near the windows of what was once the main entrance. Elegant sheets of midnight velvet hung from the ceiling, covering the windows around him, confining the secrets of the Diamond inside the building. He surveyed the room as the trickster within him itched to put his inherent skills to use. Near him, a round table of gents with good luck charms sitting in their laps played poker. Jack watched their game for an hour, committing to memory every man's tell and pertinent details. None of them was at a loss for words, so he learned a great deal. When he could not learn any more useful information, Jack wandered over to the edge of the bar, passing through swirls of smoke, swanky jazz notes, and the twinkle of studded incandescent electric lights mounted on the graceful arches of the ceiling.

"What'll ya have, sir?" asked the cheerful bartender. He placed his palms on the counter at the ready to serve.

"Got any whiskey back there?" Jack nudged his head toward the bottles on the mosaic mantel that surrounded the grand mirror.

"Fresh out, but we got some moonshine and a few bottles of red left," offered the bartender.

"A glass of yer cheapest red will do," requested Jack.

"Comin' right up, sir."

Jack leaned up against the bar as the bartender poured him his drink. He paid the man and continued his observations. On the opposite end of the bar, a voluptuous woman sat propped on top of the counter like the statue of some African goddess. On her head, she wore a four-tiered bronze headpiece with gold ocher rhinestones and a black feather.

"Oi, barkeep, who is that woman?" he asked.

"Ya kidding me, sir, right?" asked the bartender.

Jack gave the bartender a nasty glare.

The bartender swallowed and pulled at his collar. "Not from around these parts? Well, sir, that there is Dixie Diamond herself, Queen Bee of the Speakeasy scene, the buzz of hush-hush Milwaukee."

Jack stared at her, enchanted by her form. Her bronze dress and chocolate complexion shimmered as if they had the power of the sun. A black-feathered boa draped around her neck and down her bulky arms. She sat cross-legged with a lime-green garter playing peek-a-boo through the slit in her dress. Jack surveyed the gentlemen swarming her and noticed they all, one by one, offered the goddess a trinket.

"Barkeep, tell me about the men," he added with a hint of jealousy.

"Who, them? Hounds, the lot of them," said the bartender with disdain in his voice. "Come from miles around to ask for her hand. Damn fools. The Diamond is a lot harder to crack. Money, jewelry, mansions in upstate New York—now you tell me, mister, what respectable Midwest Canary would want to live in upstate New York? She's got all that and more here."

Dixie Diamond giggled raucously at the men and blew several kisses.

"And what about the short, stumpy fella?" inquired Jack. He eyed the man circling in on the commotion.

"Mister Oddy?"

"Ye mean Tomas Oddy?" Jack turned to the bartender. "Owner of the Oddy Brewing Company?"

"One and the same," said the barkeep. He puffed his chest proudly.

"Hey, bartender, ya gonna make me wait all night?" shouted one of Dixie's many suitors from the other side of the bar.

"Enjoy your evening, sir," said the bartender. He tipped his hat and took his leave.

Jack sipped his wine and nearly spit it out. He swore under his breath, damning Woodrow Wilson and his bloody Prohibition. He set the glass down, disgusted, and watched as Tomas Oddy placed a cherry-sized diamond ring on Dixie Diamond's finger. Her face lit up, yet he found a hint of disapproval in her eyes. Maybe she did want to fly away to upstate New York. Nonetheless, she giggled heartily, which caused the gents around her to glower.

"There's always tomorrow, boys," her voice chimed over the clamor.

Tomas Oddy extended his arm to Dixie and escorted her to the stage. The Diamond Band struck up her signature tune and the crowd whistled, cheered, and then grew silent. Dixie took center stage, braced the microphone with one hand and belted out the start of the song.

"Your ladies are too good for you . . ."

The music vibrated through the floor as the blues of the tenor sax, the snap of the snare drum, and the foundation of the piano energized the room. Dixie sang with a rich, husky voice, her presence on stage raw and infectious.

"So, what ya think, mister? Ain't our Dixie a jewel?" asked the bartender, his hands busy drying a glass.

"Ye mean she always sings like this?" Jack turned his head in disbelief. He had heard a great many singers over the course of his wanderings, but none came close to the commanding pipes of Dixie Diamond.

"Yep, there ain't a song our Dixie can't slay," bragged the bartender as he set the glass under the counter.

"Remarkable," said Jack. He looked back at the stage, bewitched by the African goddess. He had his mark. "A fine jewel indeed," he added. Jack attempted another sip of his warm wine, but could not stand the bitter taste and set it back on the counter. "Well, me good man, I bid ye well," he said.

"And to you, sir, enjoy your evenin'." The bartender began to wipe the counter as Jack left a sawbuck next to his half-empty glass.

Jack ventured out into the sea of people to find his in, the right crowd to introduce him to Dixie. He started out with a flock of young gals who turned out to be the Diamond Girls. They wore an array of colorful flapper dresses and matching sequined headbands with fluffy white feathers projecting out of their foreheads. They cooled their flushed faces with black-handled fans.

"Evenin' ladies," greeted Jack, putting one hell of a charming smile on his face.

"Well, hello yourself, handsome," giggled the Diamond Girl in the pale pink dress.

It did not take Jack long to convince them he was the heir to some wealthy fortune out west, but the Diamond Girl in the scarlet flapper dress named Lydia saw right through his ruse. She simply rolled her eyes at the mindlessness of her burlesque sisters.

Jack paid Lydia no heed and let her storm off with some of the ladies, which left him alone to cozy up with a set of identical twins. Their names were Winifred and Merryweather, though they preferred Winnie and Merri. Dixie's number ended and the audience cheered with ample applause. A confident smile radiated from the Canary's face as she bowed and Jack followed her with his eyes as she moved off the stage to the arm of Tomas Oddy. The band went back to playing and the joint filled again with the clamor of voices.

"Ladies, why not introduce me to yer Madam?" said Jack.

"But Jack," said the twin named Merri with a pout. She puckered her lips, revealing a hidden dimple in her left cheek.

"We thought you liked us," said the twin named Winnie with a similar pout, though her puckered lips did not reveal a dimple.

"I do, pigeons," said Jack. He gave them both a pat underneath their pointy chins. "Forget I even mentioned it." Jack kept his expression cool.

Winnie and Merri looked at one another, each knowing the others' thoughts. It was never good business to upset a trick, least of all not one from wealth such as Jack Rutledge. Dixie would not be pleased to know they had lost such a find.

"Oh, no," squeaked Merri. She shook her head and disturbed the frills of her royal blue dress. "We can introduce you, surely." She nudged her sister.

"Oh, yes, it would be no trouble," agreed Winnie, tempted to hit her sister back.

"Then shall we, ladies?" Jack smiled as he escorted them closer to the stage.

In an alcove in the far side corner, the three entered the ranks of an elite circle. Judging by the jewelry each woman wore around her neck and the brand of cigars the men smoked, Jack knew *he had come to the right place. He gave a hearty chuckle as the group burst into laughter at one of Tomas Oddy's jokes. It was hardly worth a hiccup, but it was more a matter of sucking up— an art form Jack knew well.*

"So, Dixie, any good offers tonight?" asked a handsome man with a long face.

"Why, Boris, when are you gonna leave that sweet wife of yours and give me some sugar?" teased Dixie.

The men in the circle whistled at her response while the women giggled bashfully, unsure if they should condemn the Diamond for her adulterous choice of words or not. Jack saw their uneasiness, but when he looked at the prize wrapped around Boris's arm, it was clear that his wife had enough confidence to match both Dixie and her husband.

"Who is that striking creature?" Jack whispered to Winnie, admiring the woman's radiant beauty: her soft complexion, her thin pink lips, her clothes, even the orange hibiscus flower decorating her dark hair.

"Her?" Winnie nodded toward the woman next to Boris. "That's Mrs. Petrovich." She paused to take in her glow, her stomach already showing off the soon-to-be new arrival. Winnie swooned over the image of motherhood, lost in a fit of fancy.

"Winnie," whispered Merri. She nudged her sister from behind Jack's back.

Winnie fluttered her eyes. "Yes, well, she and her husband Boris moved here not so long ago from Russia. They are by far, next to Madam and Mr. Oddy, of course, the most well-connected pair in this joint."

"Do tell," said Jack. If he played his cards right, he could bait two for the price of one.

"Well, you see . . ." Winnie started.

"Well, you see," interrupted Merri. "Converting the Oddy Palm Garden into a burlesque speakeasy was Mister Petrovich's idea . . ."

"Hey, I'm telling the story," snapped Winnie.

"But I always get to tell this part," said Merri.

"Well, it's my turn to have a go at it," said Winnie.

"Not likely," said Merri as she reached in front of Jack and gave Winnie a shove.

Winnie huffed and pushed Merri back, accidentally ripping off one of the baby-blue tassels on her dress.

"Ladies, ladies . . ." Jack tried to keep his voice down so as not to draw attention, but the twins did not stop. "Ladies, please!"

Conversation in the circle ceased and all eyes fell on the three of them.

"You selfish brat."

"Toad . . ."

"Cow . . ."

"Jezebel!"

"Ladies!"

Winnie and Merri stopped pawing each other and looked over at their Madam. Their faces blushed in utter embarrassment as they realized the childishness of their actions. And in front of Tomas Oddy! They wanted to die. The girls let go of Jack, curtsied, and silently excused themselves.

"It seems you had your hands full with those two, mate," teased the gentleman next to Jack. His curlicue mustache shimmied as his nose wiggled.

The circle broke into light laughter as Jack readjusted his suit jacket and tie. He put his best foot forward and gave a half smile, masking his true intentions with a hint of embarrassment. He caught Dixie's eye, but did not linger there long. Under the circumstances, it would be best for her to come to him. Dixie whispered to Tomas Oddy and then took a step into the circle. Her presence quieted the amusement.

"My friends, it seems we have a schnorrer in our midst," announced Dixie.

"Oh, come now Dixie, leave the poor boy alone," said a woman with bobbed hair. "Can't you see he's embarrassed enough as it is?" She snickered under her breath, having found Jack's humiliation a bit of sporting fun.

"Nonsense, Flora," said Dixie. "A strapping young man, of what would you say, twenty? He looks right as rain to me."

"More like Clark Gable," said the only woman smoking in the bunch. The rest of the women giggled at the absurdity of the comparison.

Dixie put her hand to her chin and inspected Jack. "I can see it, Bertha. Yes, he has a certain charm about him. What's your name?"

"Jack."

The circle burst with laughter again. Even Dixie Diamond could not resist the temptation. "Jack? I was hopin' for a little something more than—Jack. Is that all?"

"Jack Rutledge," he replied. "And I be twenty-one, if me age be in question."

"Well, Jack Rutledge," mocked Dixie playfully, "since you went through all the effort, I'll let you have a go."

"A go?" Jack kept his voice at a level fraught with embarrassment. He did not want to seem too eager. If she wanted to play him, he would be sure to do her one better.

"Suiting, boy—are you daft?" asked a rotund man, blowing a puff of smoke above his evenly parted hair.

"No," said Jack in defense.

"Well, then, propose to the lady," said Flora.

Jack looked around the circle and then at Dixie. He bowed low and held down his head. "What be that which the lady requires?" he asked in a chivalrous tone.

The women gasped as the men cleared their throats. None of them expected old pleasantries.

Jack kept his eyes on the ground, but could not keep the smile from his face and waited patiently for Dixie to answer him.

Dixie blushed, stunned by such flattery. She began to fan her face. "You may rise, young sir," she gasped with heavy breaths.

Jack lifted his head and straightened his posture.

Dixie took a step or two forward and leaned in close to him, her lips kissing his ear. He smelt the aroma of gardenia on her dark skin. "Meet me at the alley door, midnight, after the show." She pulled away from Jack, just as Tomas Oddy swooped in and took her by the arm.

"Come, my dear, you're due back on stage." Tomas Oddy glared at Jack.

Jack gave a gentleman's nod to name him the victor, at least for now.

Tomas Oddy was not at all satisfied, but he kept his head. It was best not to make a scene in front of such distinguished guests. "Well, ladies and gentlemen, I believe it is time for Dixie to prepare for the evening's show." Tomas Oddy turned away from Jack.

Dixie winked at him before following.

"Oh, and Boris," said Tomas Oddy as he passed, "we will talk more about our business later, tomorrow, perhaps?"

"Certainly, Tomas, business can wait."

Tomas Oddy nodded and escorted Dixie to the stage.

Mr. Petrovich kissed his wife's hand and then placed it with his on her belly. "Let's go, my-ah sladkaya."

As the Diamond Band began to play what would be the overture to the night's performance, Jack made his way back to the far corner of the bar. He kept his eyes wandering the rest of the night, biding his time until he would be alone with his latest trick—the Diamond of Milwaukee.

Dixie Diamonds

A s they walked through the shaded alley, Jack became nostalgic for the Roarin' Twenties—the music, the illegal booze, the gambling. He remembered sneaking in this way to the back door of Dixie Diamonds the first night he had come to Milwaukee. He knew the path well, having used it countless times after that, and smiled up at the white stone and black windows of the Hotel Charlotte as though greeting an old friend. To his right, he expected to see another familiar structure, but instead of the dazzling architecture of the Bijou Theatre, a giant building, empty of any real character, stood in its place. Looking further down the alley, Jack's eyes registered the brick wall blocking the street view of Wisconsin Avenue. The bricks appeared relatively new and it dawned on him that if the situation arose, there was only one way out of the alley. He then lifted his gaze toward the towering skyscraper of the Majestic Building.

Jack stopped in front of the back door of Dixie Diamonds and stared at the scratched wood, predicting an unpleasant reunion. With little effort, he envisioned her breaking out the old pistol she kept under her pillow and shooting him first chance she got, before giving him a chance to explain himself. The scenario would be unreasonable, considering the last time he had seen the

Diamond of Milwaukee he'd been robbing Tomas Oddy. It had not been the first time he had pulled off such a lucrative heist, but it had been for this reason that he had made a rule long ago never to return to any establishment or have contact with any individuals he conned. He had enacted the rule after a series of altercations that came from cheating nearly every man in the Five Points neighborhood of New York City.

"Fool me once, shame on you. Fool me twice, shame on me," he mumbled and knew he would have to handle this arrangement with the utmost finesse, for no matter which way the chips fell, Dixie was not going to take seeing him well.

"Jack, what are you doing?" asked Buck.

He took a few steps past the door and laid Mara on the ground. "Buck, I need ye to stay over here with her."

"What? Why?"

"I need ye out of the way," said Jack. "For now."

Buck cocked his head.

"Buck, Madam Dixie is not entirely fond of surprises, least of all from me."

"You mean tricks?" Buck crossed his arms.

Jack shrugged. "Call it what ye like."

"Are you going to ask her to help?" Buck lowered his eyes to the bloodstain on Mara's blouse.

Jack followed the Breedling's gaze and tried his best to appear convincing. "Dixie is a good woman," he said, although it was hard to know if she had changed over the years. For once, he was betting on optimism. He placed a hand on Buck's shoulder. "I have no doubt she'll help. Just let me butter her up first." He grinned.

"All right, I will stay here, but make haste, for I do not know how much longer we can keep this up," said Buck. He knelt next to Mara and, as instructed, pressed his hand against her wound.

"Are ye referring to Iona's trial?" asked Jack, wondering if the events ahead would detain them further from getting back to the train yard and on their way.

"No Jack, it is Mara I speak of," said Buck, avoiding his gaze. "I fear she will expire before she is given aid."

Jack left it at that, although he had a nagging suspicion the Breedling was hiding something from him. He stood in front of the door and knocked. The sound of his hand on the weathered wood sobered his thoughts, and his only concern was how he was going to broach conversation with Dixie. He gave the door a few more earnest knocks.

No answer.

Jack knocked a third time with four good taps, but still no answer. He tried once more, this time knocking out *shave and a haircut*. The door opened, and in the empty space a woman appeared. He recognized her at once.

Dressed in nothing but her white undergarments and a crimson corset, the vixen propped her right arm against the doorframe. Her forearm draped across her brow slightly, shadowing the glow of her porcelain face. Her full cherry lips and platinum blonde hair accentuated her Jean Harlow–esque beauty. Her long, slender legs and diminutive chest gave her a unique innocent look, but Jack knew better than to trust the appearance. He watched as she lifted her amber eyes from the ground, a habit of hers when sizing up gents that came to call.

"Business or pleasure?" she quipped before seeing the grin on his face. Her demeanor drastically changed, and her voice grew icy. "Well, as I live and breathe, look what the wind blew our way—if it ain't the Stench of Chicago himself."

"Fine to see ye too, Lydia." Jack found her more enchanting

when she turned on her vixen charm.

"You've got some nerve comin' back here after what you done." Lydia dropped her arm to her side.

"After the night we had, Lydia, doll," teased Jack. They had had no such night, but he liked to get a rise out of her.

Lydia flicked up her chin. "Don't cajole me, Jack Rutledge. I ain't ever been your doll. 'Sides, Dixie's plum over your wretched ass."

"So she did miss me." Jack kept his voice sly and playful.

"No, Jack, she misses her money. And if you had any gumption . . ." Lydia stopped short as a commanding female voice sounded from somewhere behind the cracked door.

"Lydia, why haven't yaw let that johnny in?"

Half of Lydia's face disappeared behind the door. "Just a stray from the Shanty, he ain't got any lettuce."

"We can strike a deal," remarked the rich female voice, its owner still a distance away.

"Madam, I don't think his like is worth . . ." objected Lydia.

"Lydia, don't gainsay me, now let him in!"

Lydia pulled her head back around the door. "Pig-headed cow," she mumbled, and she cracked a cheesy smile. "The Madam welcomes you," she sang through clenched teeth and gestured for Jack to enter, swinging the door wide.

Jack vanished from the doorway to retrieve Mara as Lydia huffed. He knew she was anticipating some grand entrance, although it would not be what she expected. He heard her nails tapping on the door when he reappeared in the doorway, Mara in his arms and Buck behind him. He caught her pupils dilating and felt the sting of her glare on the back of his neck, the uneasy yet familiar sensation lifting the tiny hairs on his neck. He was certain it meant something, but he did not give it another thought.

Lydia closed the door behind them and locked it.

The vestibule was as Jack remembered, warm and inviting, comfortable. The sparkling chandelier cast pixie-like rainbows on the silver-hammered trefoil ceiling. The scent of flowers attacked his nose, which was meant to trick any johnny into thinking he had just wandered into some forbidden garden, a tactic Dixie crafted well to tantalize her guests. Slightly to the right, the dark mahogany rail of the staircase led to the second floor, where the ladies' quarters were, and climbing the ascent on the plaster veneer were photos of the Diamond Girls. On the other side of the bannister, a short hallway stretched to the back door of the stage, where two benches dressed in royal purple satin sat just a few feet away. Jack walked over to one and placed the woman with the swollen eye on her back, crossing her hands on her chest.

Jack twisted his body but did not move from his spot on the floor. He looked down at Buck's worried face and bit the inside of his cheek. He placed his hand on the Breedling's shoulder and lowered his head to whisper into his ear so that Lydia could not eavesdrop.

"Just let me do the talkin'," he whispered. "We'll be out of here in two shakes of a lamb's tail."

Buck tilted his head in agreement.

"Just keep yer hand pressed on the wound," Jack continued. "I'm not sure if she's still bleeding." Jack ran his unbloodied hand through Buck's hair and messed it around. It was an awkward moment for the both of them, but he figured it best to make the scene for Lydia.

Lydia simply rolled her eyes and crossed her arms as the floorboards at the top of the stairs groaned.

Jack moved to the banister as Buck knelt over Mara and pressed gently on her side; her face distorted a moment, but she did not open her good eye. Jack leaned against the large knob of the rail and watched the busty woman descend the stairs. Her chocolate-colored skin radiated with tiny sparkles and, above her head, a set of chopsticks peeked out of the sloppy bun of her brunette hair. Her black and royal purple corset with lime-green lacing did not restrain her large figure but instead accentuated her curves. The black sleeves of her dress covered her thick arms and its skirt hid her strong legs.

"Welcome," she purred, her voice alluring. "What be your poison, johnny?" Midway down the stairs, the woman must have recognized him, for she finished her descent with great speed, her heels clacking beneath her.

Jack half expected her to embrace him, despite how they had left things, but instead of the typical forgive-and-forget personality Dixie was known for, she gave him a ripe slap with a vigorous hand. His head rotated from the force of it, and he opened his mouth wide in order to realign his jaw.

"Ye still can give a good wallop," he said, turning his head forward and met her hand for another slap. "Fair enough, I deserve that." He turned his head. She gave him a third slap.

"Lydia, run along upstairs," ordered Madam Dixie with a sharp snap of her fingers.

Lydia's arms immediately stiffened at her sides and she scuttled up the stairs, mumbling under her breath. "Good-for-nothing mark of the Devil."

"Jack, you black hearted scoundrel," said Madam Dixie as she smacked him in the shoulder. "I ought to throw your no-account skint ass out for what you done!"

Jack slid his hands in his jacket pockets and admired Dixie's attempt at ruthlessness. She was not hardly good at it, for as much as she might be angry, she was harmless. A trait of hers he had found most alluring, after a cat-and-mouse start to their relationship. It had been an unforeseen affair, and he had let it go on far too long. Jack watched her as her rant became more animated, negating to listen to anything she said. He stepped forward to catch her attention and when he did, she took another swing at him. This time he was more prepared, counted on it even, and grabbed her wrist, blocking her attempt. She pulled back once, but he did not let go and instead kissed the back of her hand, turning on his manipulative charm.

The action temporarily subdued her anger, her demeanor taken by his chivalrous gesture, as he portrayed the character of the Jack Rutledge she first met.

Jack let go of her hand; it floated as though it wished he would take it again, but he refrained. It was best to leave her wanting more.

"Jack," whispered Buck, his voice cautiously entering the shared moment.

Madam Dixie dropped her arm and glanced over Jack's shoulder before brushing him aside to obtain a better view of her unexpected guests.

"Jack, you've got some gall," said Madam Dixie, anger boiling in her tone. She moved towards Buck, but Jack intercepted her.

"Dixie, now, wait. Let me explain." Jack held up his hands to halt her.

"Damn right, you'll explain."

"I came across them on the train."

"Who are they, Jack?" demanded Madam Dixie.

Jack thought for a moment. What could he say that would sound remotely true? He was a great liar, the best, but Madam Dixie was no twit. She was sharp as a tack and bamboozling her was not easy. In fact, she had an uncanny knack of seeing right through his white lies, one of several reasons he had been taken by her.

"Speak, Jack. I don't have time for any of your tomfoolery. I need to see my girls are ready for the night. You have five seconds."

Jack panicked. Madam Dixie's impatience was not giving him enough time to respond with a plausible answer.

"My name is Buck," he heard the Breedling say. Buck got to his feet and bowed, hiding his hands behind his back. "Pleased to make your acquaintance, Madam."

"That don't right explain who you are, boy," said Madam Dixie, miffed by the boy's politeness. "Who's the woman?"

"She . . ."

"She's the boy's mother," interrupted Jack as Buck went back to his task.

Madam Dixie raised an eyebrow, unconvinced.

"She and the young whippersnapper got separated when our train was stopped by Bulls north of Wadsworth. It just so happened I came across him hiding in some hay."

"Where were you headed, boy?" asked Madam Dixie.

"The Land of Ten Thousand Lakes."

Jack shot Buck a scowl then laughed. "Ye know me, Dixie, a lone wolf to the bitter end, but the kid was adamant about finding his mum. 'Sides, I needed a good lookout to get back on the train. I mean, I couldn't have him screaming his sorry little head off to alert the hounds."

Madam Dixie judged Buck, his round, ivory face too adorable to portray a lie. Her eyes did not linger on him long, though, as she considered the woman's plight. She walked over to them, ignoring Jack, and loomed over Buck's shoulder.

"What's wrong with her?"

"She was attacked in an alley not far from here by two men

we were traveling with. One of them stabbed her." Buck lifted his hands from the wound, revealing the stain on her blouse. His palms were stamped with her blood. "We tried to take her to the hospital, but it was no longer there. Please, we need your help."

Madam Dixie stared at the woman and expressed her sympathy toward the state of her broken body. She placed her chubby hand on the woman's head and stroked her ratty, brown hair. There was a familiarity in how she traced the curve of Mara's face, as though she knew her, and Jack wondered who, amongst all of Dixie's friends and acquaintances, she could be. Madam Dixie looked at Buck again, her expression skeptical about their introduction as mother and son; however, as Jack suspected, she did not verbally question the connections, careful not to deny the battered cyclops what was claimed to be hers.

"This does not come without its price," she decided finally.

"Dixie," said Jack, somewhat surprised she did not display her usual good grace, but it only proved that time had indeed reshaped her.

"You know the rules, Jack. Nothing in my cat house is free of charge." She removed her hand from the woman's face. "Bring her upstairs and I'll have my girl Maddie see to her."

Jack walked to the bench and bent over to retrieve Mara. He picked up the woman and they joined Madam Dixie near the banister.

"Well, put your mind at ease, sugar," said Madam Dixie, taking Buck by the chin. "Your lady is safe here." She made a face at the grotesque sight of the cut on his cheek. "What an unpleasant souvenir," she added.

Buck tried to pull his head away and expressed his discontent when she did not let him go.

"There, there, young Buck, I meant nothing by it," said

Madam Dixie, releasing Buck. "Now come, we don't want the poor woman to bleed to death in my vestibule." She presented a soft smile as large dimples creased the corners of her mouth.

Jack nudged Buck and he came around, his demeanor expressing reassurance, at least to Mara's safety, but Jack could tell he was still wary of her intentions. Buck offered a smile and followed him as they ascended the stairs. On the top landing, Dixie called for Maddie as he noted the familiar doors lining the plaster veneer walls. He named each room in his head and wondered if all the same Diamond Girls occupied them.

"Maddie," Madam Dixie called again.

Jack looked down the hall, and at the far end, a figure appeared from the last door—the room that had once been the residence of Winnie and Merri.

"Maddie, girl, come here," said Madam Dixie with a maternal tone.

The short figure shuffled briskly down the hall and within the last few feet Jack was stunned to realize the girl's youth. He suspected she was no more than fourteen at best.

Maddie stood poised, only an inch or two taller than Buck. An oversized off-white dress with stitched pockets fell from her broad shoulders and did nothing to accentuate her figure. Her peach-colored complexion gave her face a radiant glow. Her thick, wavy hair tried to cover the misfortunate affliction on her face, but it was unable to do so. On her upper lip, a slit broke the flesh that extended to her nose. It was no wonder, then, that her doe eyes were so somber. Jack frowned at the sight of her wasted beauty.

"Maddie, please escort these two gents to your room. I would like you to tend to—my word, I never did catch her name."

"Her name?" mumbled Buck.

"Yes, silly boy, her name," said Madam Dixie.

"Mara. Her name is Mara," said Buck in a daze.

"How quaint," said Madam Dixie, with a hint of sarcasm. "Are you sure?"

"As far as I know," said Buck. "It is what she has called herself for quite some time. She no longer goes by her given name. And, truthfully, she never told me what it is."

"That's quite all right, sugar," said Madam Dixie. "Maddie, please tend to Mara's wound, and see that she is given a suitable dress."

"Yes, ma'am," replied Maddie with a curtsy, her voice rich and full with a throaty sound.

"Jack, would you be so kind to carry Mara down the hall and then join me in my quarters? We shall discuss the terms of our arrangement."

Jack nodded and followed Maddie as she escorted them to her room.

Maddie's room was aglow with candlelight, as the black-painted windows did not allow any daylight in from outside. Jack laid Mara on the daybed nestled up against the brick wall. Maddie placed the back of her hand on the woman's brow and then her cheek. She studied her shallow breathing, satisfied it was steady. She pulled a pair of scissors out of her pocket and cut away the woman's blouse, only to pause. She looked over her shoulder.

"Jack, I believe ma'am asked you to meet in her 'uaters."

Jack found it hard to understand Maddie's words, her lisp strong and heavy, but he was able to venture a guess at what she was saying.

"Be sure to send in the boy," she added.

"You mean Buck?"

Maddie nodded and went back to her preparations without giving Jack any further acknowledgment.

Jack made his way back to the door with his bloodstained hands stuffed in his pockets.

Buck stood with his arms crossed.

"Don't worry, Buck," Jack whispered. "Dixie's word is ironclad."

"That is not what has me concerned, Jack," said Buck. "She has asked for something in return."

"Eh, nothing is given without getting something in return," said Jack.

"And would you ask Mara for something in return for saving her?" challenged Buck.

"Of course not," barked Jack. The Breedling's accusation hurt him somewhat in his current state.

"Good," said Buck, his body relaxing as a shadow of a smile broke on his face, his eyes watching Maddie. "Tell me, who is Dixie Diamond?"

"What does it matter?"

"Does it have to matter?" asked Buck.

Jack fidgeted and felt his face express how uncomfortable he was. "I came here nearly fourteen years ago, fancying to make Dixie my latest mark. I had fashioned me way into her good graces by being someone I wasn't and over the course of a few weeks, I managed to squirrel away hundreds of dollars from high-end types at the poker tables. Tomas Oddy didn't take too kindly to me winnings and when I was accused of cheating, it gave him an excuse to throw me out. But Dixie got me back in, said she liked having me around. It was then that she became less than a mark and, well, I had a moment of weakness is all. I let me guard down and one night, after too many drinks, said some things I shouldn't have, mostly about Iona. She listened and I found meself taken by her. I know I shouldn't have, after what had happened to Iona. I swore never to get close to anyone like that again, but at times Dixie reminded me of her. I should've known better, but the heart wants what the heart wants and mine grew tired of being alone. So maybe it was fear of Hades, or maybe me own ill-suited nature, but like so many who got too close to me, I drove her away the only way I knew how. I betrayed her."

"So when she called you a scoundrel, she was right," said Buck.

"Yes," said Jack. "And now I have me chance to wipe the slate clean. Besides, no one leaves without paying the house. I'll haggle our payment, whether by coin or favor. And we'll be on our way."

Buck did not answer and simply stepped aside.

Jack patted Buck on the head as he passed. "Oh, by the way, the girl, Maddie, needs yer help. Don't do anything I wouldn't do," he said with a mischievous wink and headed down the hall.

SPELLBOUND

B uck sat on a wooden rocking chair next to the bed in Maddie's room. He fiddled with his hands, his fingers still sticky with blood. He occupied his mind with thoughts of Jack, and he hoped the Trickster was sincere about wiping the slate clean with Dixie. If so, it was possible Jack could complete two of his three acts before they left Milwaukee. The prospect was enough to cloud his initial uneasiness about Dixie, and instead of dwelling on it, he lifted his gaze from his lap and observed Maddie, whose hands were diligently at work. He watched her for a moment before darting his eyes around the room, because he did not want her to accuse him of staring, even though her beauty was a sight he wished never to turn from. For, unlike Jack, he did not see the deformity on her face.

The room was quaint, with candles burning like watchtowers all around the room. On the ceiling, woven circles dangled like vines as they spun slightly with feathers and beads interlaced in the web of the sphere. Buck remembered seeing them once before, long ago—dream catchers, if memory served. The walls were not dressed with wallpapering or paint, just exposed brick. He kept himself occupied until Mara let out a distressed gasp and then he returned his gaze to the bed.

Maddie's hands were floating over Mara's pale face, the girl's expression growing troubled. Her thin lips grew rosier, her cheeks warmed with blush. She waved her hands across Mara's chest and then the wound. With every breath, blood seeped through the broken flesh. The skin around it was a swirled pinwheel of black, purple, blue, and red.

Buck diverted his attention again, the sight making him squeamish and for some reason he felt it improper to look at her naked flesh. His gaze traveled to the other side of the room where a grand vanity and dresser stood against the wall, set aglow. Above the long, narrow dresser hung a crooked rectangular mirror, most of the glass having been shattered and pieces missing. On the smallest of the three dressers sat a large white ceramic bowl and on the other side of it, in the far corner, a three-fold screen cut the corner at a diagonal. Several pairs of silk stockings and white gowns were draped over the top. Buck's eyes passed along the blackened windows and finally came back to Maddie as she finished her preliminary examination.

She appeared focused, but he caught her checking on him from the corner of her eye. He could not guess at what she was thinking, but there appeared to be a hint of displeasure that flickered across her face and her body suddenly became unsure of itself. Then she snapped back to attention and returned to her task. At one point, she closed her eyes and released a low whistle. She did this several times before placing her hands in her lap, allowing the room to fall into a meditative state.

Buck dared not move, but a slight shift in his weight caused the rocking chair to creak.

Maddie opened her eyes with a scowl.

He offered an apologetic look, but she, having been disturbed, rose from her stool and went to the other side of the room to retrieve the ceramic bowl from the dresser. Her feet glided across the wooden floor as she returned to the bed, placing the bowl on the nightstand. She pressed the cloth into the water, disturbing the orange hibiscus flowers floating on the surface. She twisted the cloth and cleaned the wound. Her face grew grim as she worked, quickening her pace.

Buck had no idea the show of discomfort was because of his staring, not realizing any other girl might welcome the attention, but not Maddie.

"Could you hand me that bottle of whiskey?" she said, pointing beyond Buck's shoulder.

Buck collected the green bottle perched on a trunk behind him and passed it over to her, catching sight of the blood still on his hands.

Maddie took the bottle from his unsteady hand, and he retracted his arm, resuming his fidgeting. Maddie ripped out the cork with her teeth and spit it onto the floor. She threw back a swig and then took another before offering it back to him.

"Oh, no thanks," said Buck. He was through with the destructive vice and never wanted to touch another drop.

"It'll take the edge off." Maddie tipped the bottom of the bottle toward him, the liquor sloshing against its glass cage.

"The edge off what?" Buck was not familiar with the expression, nor was he sure why she was being insistent. He figured she had a reason, much like Charlie had had a reason, but he was not sure why her voice was telling him one thing and her face something different. She spoke with cordial tones, but her face bore a mark of judgment.

"Can you understand me?" asked Maddie. "I mean, it's just that in my experience, it usually takes several tries to convey my meaning."

"Understand you? Certainly, I can understand you just fine," said Buck with an insecure smile. Was she testing him?

Maddie hesitated and tried her best not to sound cross. "That is very sweet of you and all, but you don't have to be like that."

"Like what?"

"I know my voice is not the most pleasing on the ears," said Maddie as she burned the tip of a sewing needle.

"Maddie, I could listen to your voice for eternity," admitted Buck. He bit his lip as his cheeks warmed.

"You are an odd goose," she said in response, not at all taking him seriously.

"So I am told," Buck mumbled, feeling foolish.

"Your loss," she shrugged and guzzled down another pull, making a face to combat the sting of the alcohol. She poured the whiskey over the woman's wound, but Mara did not flinch.

Buck smelled the dizzying scent of whiskey mixing with the iron in her blood. He felt faint, and he swallowed back the saliva in his throat.

Maddie threaded her needle with some catgut string. She then poked it through one side of the stab wound to the other. She continued in a crisscross pattern. Her hands were steady, much more than Mara's increasingly sporadic breaths. Wrinkles formed across Maddie's brow as trickles of sweat rolled down her cheeks. A strange and yet wonderful tingle spread from Buck's toes to his brain and he found himself afloat, even though his feet were on the floor. He became smitten by her beauty, though he had not the word for it. Maddie tightened the catgut and the two sides of torn skin melded back together. Deep red blood seeped through the stitching, staining the white sheets shades of red and pink. She made four more strokes and tied off the thread, biting away the excess. She set the needle back on the nightstand and reached for a tiny wooden bowl.

"What is that?" Buck asked.

"This is gentian and astra. It will help stem infection and heal the wound faster," said Maddie, and she smeared the strange substance onto Mara's skin.

"She will be well, then," said Buck, not posing the words as a question but rather as a statement.

Maddie looked up, astonished. "She's dying," she said, unable to take his naive disposition any longer. "Do you not have any concern, any sense of despair, any feeling at all, or must you stare at me some more?"

Buck did not know how to respond. With the exception of Iona, his dealings with death had always come in the form of souls, the lifeless by-product of mortality. He watched Maddie's frustration melt, changing into something like sympathy—or maybe it was still anger. He could not tell for sure. He looked at Mara, her breaths shallow, her face as white as Hades' pallid skin. He examined her patched wound and then his hands. The red stain of her blood still graced them. It triggered the memory of a conversation he and his mentor, the Apothecary, had had about mortals and how they died. The Apothecary had explained the four fundamental things mortals needed to live: air, water, nourishment, and warmth. *Take one of these away, Bartholomew, and the life of a mortal will diminish.* He had asked then about their fragility and why some were easier to break. The Apothecary had not been so forthcoming with his answer, and instead he had responded with, *Mortals are incomplete . . . for any creature that can bleed is vulnerable to death.*

Buck rubbed his fingers together. It was then, for the first time, he realized the importance of blood, registering a thin sheet of

Mara laid upon him, a piece of her life in his hands. Buck smelt the iron and his throat pinched. He felt sick. His face numbed and his mouth salivated. He frantically began to rip at his skin, but the blood would not come off. Aware of his struggle, Maddie grabbed the ceramic bowl and knelt down in front of him, setting the bowl at his feet. She picked up the rag and wrung out the water, which was already pink. She reached for his trembling hands and took hold of them, one at a time.

"Does it come off?" Buck whispered.

"Of course it does," said Maddie, gently wiping the blood away.

Buck flinched.

"It's all right," she reassured him, keeping her voice calm.

"Buck," he offered.

"It's all right, Buck," she said. "And I'm sorry for yelling. It wasn't my intention to upset you."

Buck smiled. The sound of his name coming from her lips was sweet and pleasing. His hands felt weightless in her care and the motions of her strokes were hypnotic, the cloth caressing his skin. His anxiety dwindled as the red disappeared from sight. Maddie removed the cloth, dipped it back into the water, and wrung it out. Buck leaned forward to smell the remnants of Lilies of the Valley in her hair, taken in by her spell.

"There, all gone." Maddie removed the cloth and examined his hands one more time.

Buck inspected his hands with her. His palms, fingertips, wrists, they were all clean. Nothing but ivory skin remained. Her soft fingers massaged his hands, and as she rotated his wrists, she pinched him. Buck felt a sharp pain pierce his flesh as though he had been stung. He looked at Maddie's face and, to his horror, it distorted, revealing the slit in her lip and the abnormally large flare of her nostril. The heat in his hands crept to his elbows and rose into his shoulders. Buck tore away from her grasp and sprang from the rocking chair.

"Buck?" Maddie tried to reach out for him.

Buck moved around her with such alarm that he lost all sense of direction and cornered himself against the dresser. He saw her eyes watching him with curiosity as the heat entered his chest, causing him to breathe heavily. The burning sensation made him want to jump out of his skin.

"What . . . have you done . . . to me?"

Maddie sat perplexed, as though confused by his reaction. She studied him closely as he pressed his hand against his side.

"You're him," she gasped, looking from Buck to the woman in bed. Maddie rose from the floor and glanced down at the pink water at her feet.

"What . . . have . . . you . . . done?" repeated Buck. The sickness inside him magnified, and his brain was unable to control his faculties. His eyes watered from the pain as the stitch in his side threatened to split him from hip to shoulder.

"Buck, it's all . . ." Maddie attempted, reaching out, but he retreated, bumping against the dresser.

Buck's skull filled with a thick fog, and everything swirled as he fell to the floor.

Maddie rushed to his aid and placed her hands under his chin to cradle his head. "Buck," she whispered, her voice worried.

Buck blinked, unable to see her. His thoughts were a whirlwind, and when he squeezed his eyes shut, he lost all ability to hold himself up. The pain spread through his lower abdomen to his legs, until it consumed his whole body, searing his insides with white-hot fury. It was then he knew what was happening, despite not having experienced it himself. Buck tried desperately to remember the creature that could inflict such pain, but the boiling sensation in his brain prevented him from accessing any knowledge of the creature.

Beware, Master Breedling, came the Chameleon's warning, *beware of the Wickers.*

As a young Breedling, Buck had spent a great deal of time in the Tales Teller's library learning about the creatures of Eden. He would later discuss his findings with the Apothecary, who divulged stories about mortals and tested his knowledge on the differences between amid souls and spirits. His mentor would go on to talk about the Animawalkers—the children of the Black Tortoise— and their offspring, the Animalia, the animals of Eden. It was on rare occasions the Apothecary would speak about Wickers, the cursed descendants of Eden's first family. Of what he knew, such mortals were born with an additional amount of Hades' flame in their bodies, cursing them with great deformities and a venomous touch. The Wicker's Curse was a detrimental infliction with the ability to infect any creature made of flesh, known to drive victims into madness or force the victim to act indiscriminately ruthless. In all his travels, Buck had never encountered one of the damned, but shortly after his imprisonment, rumors had reached him that the Fates had given charge to one of his kin to hunt down the remaining creatures as punishment. Apparently, one remained free.

"Buck?"

Buck's head drooped to the side, but Maddie used her hands to lift it back up.

"Buck, blink if you can hear me," she insisted.

Buck heard her voice clear as day, and yet he felt so far away. He began to slip out of consciousness, but Maddie gave him a little shake.

"Buck, stay with me." She took hold of his hands.

Buck sensed the heaviness vanish and his eyes became more alert. His breath slowed, and the searing pain dwindled under the protection of her touch.

"Maddie," he whispered.

"There you are," she said with a smile, and caressed his hands with her thumbs.

"Water . . ."

Maddie shook her head. "Not now, brave one. First you must heal this woman if you are to survive my spell."

"I—I do not understand," Buck muttered. "What spell?"

"My healing spell," said Maddie. "I'm like you, Buck—well, not exactly like you, I mean I'm not immortal, but I'm a healer, like you."

"Me?" said Buck. "I am no healer. I . . ." He trailed off.

"You are now," said Maddie. "And who better than the champion of Earth and Sea."

Buck's eyes widened.

"Just listen, Buck," insisted Maddie. "I'll explain everything to you, but first we must see to the healing of this woman. I was able to patch her body, but her soul is in turmoil, and if not mended, I fear she will die. I assure you, it was not my intention to place this burden upon you, but it was the only way to wake your ability, as promised, and because of that my spell lives in you now. I'm sorry you're in pain—if I could draw it out of you, I would—but all I can to do is keep her pain from destroying you."

"Her pain?" Buck glanced back to the bed, Mara's body still a picture of death. "You mean . . . ? But how—No, I cannot be responsible for her. Not like this."

"Regardless of what you want, Buck," said Maddie. "This responsibility is now yours and you must act. Like I said, I mended

her body, but her soul is beyond my power now—but not yours."
She wrinkled her nose, lifting her harelip into a snarl.

"How?" asked Buck. "I do not know what to do."

"I was told you knew," said Maddie.

"Who told you?" asked Buck. "What manner of magic is this?"

"Later," said Maddie. "Now, please, I know you carry within
the words that will mend this woman and return her life. Will you
accept this responsibility set before you?"

Buck's heart sank with the realization Mara would die if he
did not do something. He closed his eyes, trying to bring himself
to accept what Maddie was saying. It was hard, but the thought
of Charlie ignited a sense of understanding he could accept,
wondering if this was what unwanted responsibility felt like.
Buck lowered his gaze to his hands nestled in Maddie's soft
embrace then elevated his chin, and to his surprise, he could no
longer see the deformity on her face. He twisted his hands in hers
and she let go of him. Almost instantly, the heaviness settled in,
his head tingling with dizziness. Buck waited a moment to collect
himself before moving.

"So does this mean you'll help?" Maddie stared up at Buck.

Buck did not answer right away, as the white-hot sear
pushed to his shoulders again and his mind searched for
Charlie's voice. *Because, Buck,* he recalled, *you do things you
don't want to do to survive, pure and simple. So you ain't got
a choice in the matter.* Buck let out a gasping sigh. If he had
any hopes of continuing his charge, he needed to rid himself
of this pain or suffer losing more than his chance to fulfill his
promise to Iona.

"I believe in you, Buck," said Maddie as she rose.

Buck's ears twitched, having never heard such an utterance
addressed to him. He struggled to walk over to the bed, and

when he reached the footboard, he crawled his hands along the mattress for stability. He then hovered them over Mara, his ivory face now red as if burned by a summer sun. Buck sensed the pain moving through his chest and settled his palms back on the bed. His lungs seized, laboring his breath, and the fog returned to his skull. He felt his body crumbling under the weight of Maddie's spell. He glimpsed Mara's face and was unable to find the words.

"Buck . . . "

"I have not the words." Buck closed his eyes, desperate to find some. The whirlwind in his brain was making rational thought difficult.

The priest closed his gray eyes and began to speak. Some of it was in my own tongue, some in Latin, I think, and then he spoke a phrase to which I can neither repeat nor provide any translation for.

"Damek," said Buck. He knew the prayer well. The one the Apothecary had used to heal the priest's dying mother. Could such words save Mara now? If there was a chance such power could pass through him, he had to try. Buck set a hand on Mara's clammy forehead and one over her broken side. He bowed his head and with steady breath whispered his words.

"May the earth rise up to meet you . . . may the wind be at your back . . . may the waters calm your spirit . . . may fire vanish from your sight."

Buck repeated them as Maddie approached the foot of the bed, expecting to see a change in the woman's condition, the healing of her wounds, but nothing had changed. Her body still lay broken and unconscious. Maddie glanced at Buck. His veins were large, threatening to burst from his skin. He was going too far. Maddie rushed to him and grabbed his wrists to break him from his trance. She yanked him backward into her chest and wrapped him in an embrace. Buck's body went limp in her arms.

"You did what you could, Buck," she whispered, kissing the back of his head. "Hopefully, it will be enough."

A Cat's Price

"It's open," called Madam Dixie's voice on the other side of the closed door.

Jack cracked the door ajar. "Ye decent?" he asked as a few of the Diamond Girls peeked out into the hallway.

"Heavens, Jack, am I ever?" she said.

Jack heard the subtle tease in her voice, which was quite different from her sharp temper in the vestibule. It gave him pause, weighing what it meant. He entered anyway, conscious to remain guarded. The scent of gardenias, which since meeting Dixie had become a nauseating fragrance, welcomed him into the room. It vexed him in a way, for once he had carried a fondness for the floral scent.

"Well, don't just stand there, Jack, have a seat," said Madam Dixie as she wrapped a lime-green shawl around the straps of her lacy black gown. She gestured to the lounge chair in the middle of the room. She busied herself at the small vanity, which doubled as a bar, lining up several shot glasses and filling them with top-shelf whiskey. She then unscrewed two mason jars of moonshine.

Jack sat on the upholstered chair and leaned against the single arm. He glanced around the room, finding it in the same condition as the last time he had seen it. Two electric lamps, posted in opposite corners of the room, provided enough light to set the mood. Burgundy satin sheets still covered the mattress of the four-poster bed and thick burgundy decorated the bedposts, pulled back like stage curtains with golden tassels dangling at the end. They had faded a little, but then again it may simply have been dust. Strips of wallpaper were peeling more profusely from the wall, leaving yellow flecks of adhesive on the black carpeted floor. Dixie had told him once that the carpet was to cover up any unwanted stains. The thought of her words made Jack look at his own stains, Mara's blood dried on his ghostly skin. It was an unusual sight, for rarely were his hands dirtied red.

Jack fiddled with his hands, a tad unsettled by the sight, and distracted himself once again by looking about the room. His instincts gnawed at him, and he had a sinking feeling Hades would appear at any moment to taunt him, like before in McGregor's Tavern, and tempt him to do some wicked deed against Dixie. For the moment, they were alone, but that fact did not deter his paranoia. What did, however, was the thought of Mara. Jack looked down at his bloodied hands again. It had not been the first time he had rescued someone during his many years of wandering, but to be an instrument in saving a life was another thing entirely. It was an intoxicating feeling, one which Jack had not felt since Iona's death, and he wanted to sustain the high for as long as he could, prompting him to break even with Dixie.

Dixie's hand came into view, offering him one of the shot glasses. He took it greedily, in an attempt to dull any lingering disastrous thoughts that would keep him from his task, and when she offered a second, he drank it for good measure. He was not concerned about getting drunk, for it took a great deal for him to feel the slightest buzz. Little did he know Dixie had concocted a practical potion and mixed it in his liquor.

Madam Dixie handed Jack a third shot glass, distracting him enough to wipe the blood off his hand with a damp handkerchief. Jack hawed back the shot and made a noticeable face, finding an odd, bitter aftertaste. He glared at the bottom of the glass with a suspicious eyeball as though peering through a scope. He felt strange for a brief moment, forgetting what he had been thinking about, his sense of awareness plummeting.

"There," said Madam Dixie, taking the shot glass and replacing it with one of the mason jars. "No need to fret over the sight of blood."

Jack took a drink of the clear liquid as she made herself comfortable on the lounge chair, wearing her confidence like a coat of armor.

"Drink up, Jack," she said, taking a swig herself. "You'll need the liquid courage for the task I have for you."

"Say yer piece, Dixie," said Jack, feeling the onset of a premature buzz clouding his comprehension. "I'm . . ." He paused to reach for the right words that would tell her he did not have time for games, but somehow he lost his train of thought. "What is it ye want?"

Dixie's lips curled, pleased her remedy was already taking effect. She lifted her free hand and pulled the chopstick from her bun, allowing her hair to fall. She sat up straighter with a commanding posture rather than a seductive one and took another swig of moonshine.

"I want revenge, Jack," she said. "Revenge that won't come back on me and my girls. So I want you to be my henchman."

"Henchman? Revenge? Revenge fer what?" asked Jack.

"Do you remember my head girl, Bianca?"

"Ye mean Birdie, that cute dish? The sweet Southern Belle? Sure, I remember her. What about her?" he said, eyeing his reflection in the mirror, alarmed by his dazed expression. He blinked, and instead of himself, he saw Iona. He blinked again to remove the hallucination from his sight, but when he looked back at the mirror, her face was full of terror and her fists were pounding on the inside of the glass. She was yelling at him, mouthing words he could not decipher, and he suddenly wondered if this was what Alice felt like as she gazed upon the looking glass.

"Jack," he heard Madam Dixie's voice.

"Hmm," he said, turning away from the mirror. "Right, what were we talking about?"

"Birdie," said Madam Dixie.

"Yes, her," said Jack. His hand fed his mouth a hefty gulp of moonshine.

"A few nights ago, a no-account by the name of Jeb came into my house plum drunk, demanding to see Birdie. Naturally, I told him the girl was indisposed, but he wouldn't listen. He got a little rough and a few of the girls tried to help, but you can imagine what a poor excuse of a sight that turned out to be. It was like kittens trying to fight off a gorilla. Why, one blow from that man's fist could kill a man dead. At least that's the rumor I heard. You know the type, thinking they're better than the likes of James Jeffries or Jack Dempsey. Now, those men were real boxers. Anyhow, Jeb managed to fend us all off and made a path for himself fumbling up the stairs. He kicked in Birdie's door and from the vestibule, I heard the commotion of his bullish tantrum."

"What about yer muscle?" asked Jack, referring to the Diamonds' enforcers.

"Well, ever since you hightailed out on me with my money I haven't been able to afford decent protection."

"What, cats on the house weren't good enough?" he teased, though his words came across crueler than intended.

Madam Dixie crinkled her nose. She leaned forward as though to slap him, but she abandoned the physical attack for a verbal one. "You know as well as I that my girls weren't always whores. And if you had any lick of sense, Jack Rutledge, you'd keep such lewd comments to yourself." She got to her feet and went back to her dresser for another shot.

"Then what happened?" asked Jack, cashing what was left of his liquor.

"Well," said Madam Dixie as she turned around, placing her hands on the dresser behind her. "After he made a royal mess of things in her room, I tried offering him a replacement girl for the night, but he wouldn't hear of it. One of my girls eventually let it slip where she was, to keep him from hurting me some more, and while I was touched by her loyalty, she should never have told him where to find Birdie. I had Lydia follow him because, unlike the rest of the girls, she has a strong constitution.

"After it all happened, Lydia came back and told me the whole story. She had followed Jeb to the Eatery, where he discovered Birdie having drinks with some johnny. She watched him barrel towards the table and make a horrific scene of it all. He grabbed Birdie by the arm and dragged her down the stairs and into the street. Lydia followed them for several blocks from a safe distance, Birdie's voice calling for help every step of the way. Her screams eventually caught the attention of a group of working men, so Jeb cut down an alley. Lydia lost sight of them for a few minutes and when she caught up, Jeb was nowhere to be found and Birdie was lying dead on the ground."

"He killed her?" said Jack, attempting to get to his feet, but he got no further than raising his butt off the chair before the room spun. He fell back against the arm of the chair, his head too heavy to bear. He stared at the ceiling, the crown molding a solid sheet of chrome. His body relaxed, and he dropped the empty jar onto the floor. He felt tired, but an anxious sort of tired. He knew there was something that he had been doing, something important, but now he had no ambition to continue his forgotten mission. His eyes drooped as Dixie's blurred face came into view.

"Poor Jack," he heard her say as though he were under water. "Seems you have a problem holding your liquor."

Jack felt her fingers press against his temples and begin massaging them counterclockwise. The pulse was hypnotic, and he struggled to hold onto a conscious thought or remain aware of himself. As she continued, the smooth rhythm grew sharper. He tried to shake her penetrating trick, but she had pushed too deep, ensnaring him in her spider web. He felt himself slipping away as his eyes closed.

"Can you hear me, Jack?" asked Madam Dixie.

Jack moaned in response.

"Good," said Madam Dixie. "Now what is it I want from you?"

"To be the instrument of yer revenge," said Jack in a monotone voice.

"And, as my instrument, you will find Jeb and pay him back tenfold for killing Birdie," said Madam Dixie.

"Yes," said Jack. "I will kill him." The words sat heavily on his tongue, and deep inside himself, he knew they were wrong, that killing was wrong, but he also knew on the surface that he could not refuse his madam's wish.

"You will go to the Eatery and find this Jeb," said Madam Dixie. "You will hunt him down, and you will kill him. And, when the deed is done, you will leave this city and never return."

"Yes, Madam," said Jack, fully compliant.

"Good," she said, removing her hands from his scalp. "Now, get out," she added with a crisp snap of her fingers.

Jack's eyes popped open. He needed only a few blinks before the details of the ceiling came into view, his vision clear again. He rose from the back of the chair, his head lighter than before, unaware he had just pledged to commit murder. He met his reflection again, though this time a rather ruthless face mounted his determined expression. He tried to manipulate his face, but there was nothing he could do to change it, his faculties no longer in his control. His puppeteer was pulling his strings.

He got up from the chair and headed for the door. He twisted the knob, but paused, his free will trying to break through Dixie's charm. He turned back toward her, the woman he had made his mark all those years ago. She was not as he remembered, her free spirit now darkened, and he wondered if it had been because of him or time itself. He wanted to ask her, but he could not formulate the words.

"Stop your gawking, Jack," shouted Madam Dixie, her tone cross. "I said get out!"

The command in her voice pushed his feet out the door, leaving the Madam of the house to her gardenia perfume and aged whiskey.

Jack walked down the hall, giving no thought to retrieving Buck from Maddie's room. He flew down the stairs, his need for vengeance driving his pace onward. And without so much as a backward glance, he exited Dixie Diamonds.

BLEST

The beautiful vibrato lured Buck back to consciousness as he opened his eyes. At first, his surroundings looked unfamiliar, but soon the details of Maddie's room became familiar again. He rolled his head along the back of the rocker, causing it to teeter. A wool blanket scratched his chin, and its mothball smell tickled his nose. His body was cozy, a sensation reminiscent of lying in one of the Apothecary's healing beds. He batted his eyes again, finally catching sight of Maddie putting Mara in a lacy nightgown. It was black with gold stitching, which made him wonder if it was a symbolic gesture. The colors of the Black Tortoise and the Golden Faun stirred a sense of pride in him and for a brief moment, he smiled at the thought of being called their champion.

Buck watched Maddie place Mara's head onto the pillow and lift the covers to her chin. She folded the blanket back and tucked it in, locking the woman into a cocoon. Then she tilted her head to meet his gaze.

"Ah, you're awake," she said, smiling. "I thought I lost you for a moment there."

"How is she?" Buck's voice came out low and hoarse. He tried to swallow, but his mouth was too dry.

"She's well," said Maddie, returning her gaze to the woman.

"You've done what you can." Her expression was thoughtful, as though trying to decide if she knew the woman lying in her bed. Maddie brushed her hand across Mara's forehead and tucked a strand of hair behind her ear. When she was finished, she retreated behind the three-fold screen, her shadow cast on the wall. There was a moment of stillness before she lifted her dress over her head, revealing a much tinier figure.

Buck watched the shadows as she let the dress fall, the arch of her back dipping low to the curve of her hips, following a set of slender legs. Somehow, he knew it was inappropriate to watch, but he found it hard to turn away. Her form was truly mesmerizing.

Maddie's hand reached for one of the gowns draped over the screen and slipped it over her head, the shadow of her curves disappearing. She came out from behind her hiding place dressed in a gown made of white silk that hung from her broad shoulders and was more flattering than the oversized dress.

Buck's heart unexpectedly fluttered as she glided over to her dresser.

She took hold of her hair and twisted it together in a bun behind her head. With the one hand, she tied an orange ribbon around her head. Then, she picked up two tin containers on her dresser and brought them back to her healing station beside the bed.

"If there is something you wish to say, I wish you would say it," she said, setting the two containers on the nightstand.

"What are you?" asked Buck.

Maddie's nose wrinkled into a displeased snarl, making the deformity on her face more pronounced, but Buck could no longer see it.

"I'm not a what, Master Breedling," she said. "I'm a who."

Buck sprang from the rocking chair, disturbing its rest and

causing it to pound against the floor. The wool blanket fell away from him, and he felt a sudden chill from the absence of his cozy nest.

"Your outburst is not necessary," she said, tinkering at her nightstand. "I told you I would explain. Now, sit back down before you keel over."

Buck wanted to protest, but he knew she was right, for he could already feel his legs giving out from underneath him. He begrudgingly returned to the rocking chair, but he was thankful he did not have to hold himself up. He was tempted to reach for the blanket, but he left it on the floor. Maddie looked at him again, once he settled, turning squarely in her chair to address him.

"As you have undoubtedly noticed," she said, placing her hands in her lap, "there is a deformity on my face. Of course, there are many plagued with the same condition, but the severity of my abnormalities runs much deeper than a cleft palate. I am what you call a Wicker, a cursed descendent from the line of Cain. At least that is what I was told."

"Who told you of such things?" asked Buck.

Maddie simply smiled. "He said you would be impatient," she said with a bright laugh.

"Do not protest to know me," said Buck sharply, unsure whether to fear Maddie or trust her. "You know nothing about me."

Maddie's merriment faltered, and her face became solemn. "You're right, I don't know you, but I do know about you." She rolled back her shoulders and fixed her eyes on Buck. "Who I am stems back before my birth. I don't know much about my parents, only that my father was a mysterious yet prominent businessman and my mother was a well-educated woman, both of whom had made nightly appearances here to appease the gossip circles or entertain politicians and upper management in all walks of business.

"Madam Dixie told me that shortly after Prohibition began, many of Milwaukie's elite lost a great deal of money, particularly in liquor investments. This was also true of the Diamond's proprietor, Tomas Oddy, who—thanks to my father's keen sense—convinced Oddy to turn the Palm Garden into a burlesque speakeasy and set up drop-off points and hideouts for bootleggers between the Wisconsin and Illinois borders to Canada. At the helm, my father made a great deal of money, and not long after, many joined his lucrative enterprise. It wasn't to last, however, and in the summer of '24, one of my father's closest associates ran into trouble with Al Capone."

Maddie shifted in her seat and did her best not to show how uncomfortable she was, but Buck watched her intently enough to notice the sorrow mounting on her face.

"I have tried so desperately to remember my parents' faces, but all I see are ghostly shadows. I was four at the time it happened, when men with tommy guns came bursting into the house, killing the servants. My mother had hidden me under the floorboards in my closet and told me not to come out. I remember her tears, but I don't remember my own. The house was full of too much noise, and as I lay in the dark, I curled up and pressed my hands against my ears, praying it would stop."

"Did your mother return for you?" asked Buck, his voice softer and concerned. Maddie's tale strengthened his virgin sense of empathy.

"No," said Maddie. "She never did come back for me." She lowered her eyes and sighed before describing what happened next, noting it was only hearsay from what Madam Dixie had told her. She talked at great length about what had transpired on the front lawn of her home. How her parents were both beaten. How her father had been thrown into the back of the gangsters' vehicle and how they had left her mother half dead in the street, until some neighbors helped her to the hospital, where she convalesced for two days before disappearing.

"Then how did you get here?" asked Buck. "I mean, did no one come looking for you?"

"Of course not," said Maddie. "Aside from my parents, only our servants knew about me. And even if that weren't the case, why would anyone look for a monster?"

Buck leaned forward in the rocking chair, trying once again to see the deformed flaw on her face, but was unable to find it. "But you are not a monster," he said.

Maddie lifted her gaze. "It is sweet for you to say," she started.

"But you are not," protested Buck, rising from his seat. He felt dizzy for a moment, but managed to remain on his feet. "I know monsters, and you are not one of them."

"Buck, please do not patronize me," said Maddie, turning away from him. "You don't know. You couldn't know." She paused, long enough to feel his hand on her shoulder. She tilted her chin to see him standing over her.

"Then tell me, Maddie," he said, lowering himself to his knees. Buck took her by the wrists, placing his palms on the back of her hands to prevent any further unpleasantness from her touch. "Who would take pity on a cursed creature?"

Maddie choked back a surge of tears and cleared her throat. She told him about her rescuer, the tall man with bronze skin and a long black robe. He had opened the trapdoor and coaxed her out of her hiding place with a powerful command in his voice. She had not been terrified by him, rather more curious about why he was not scared by her shocking form. She described the familiar features of the Apothecary and went on to say how, before any officials arrived, he had carried her from the house and brought her to Dixie Diamonds. Listening to her story, it sounded similar to Father Van Lewen's tale, and it became less difficult for him to accept that his mentor had again intervened in the affairs of Eden—which begged the question, were there others, and how many?

"Maddie," said Buck. "The tall man, did you strike a deal with him?"

Maddie's face sharpened. "Of course not," she said, pulling her hands out of his relaxed grip. "I didn't ask him to save me or bless me with this gift." She curled her fingers into fists.

"But he must have asked something of you," said Buck, more anxious than he would have preferred.

"Sure, but not in any way that constituted making a deal," she said. "Besides, I never thought it would happen. I mean, I was only four at the time and I had just lost my parents, and a complete stranger presented me with magic, telling me things no one else would believe."

"And what did he tell you about Earth and Sea? About me?" asked Buck.

Maddie got to her feet so fast that Buck only had time to reach for her hand. It prevented her from getting away, and she tripped over her feet, crashing into his arms. Buck embraced her, getting a true sense of her worth, for she radiated pure starlight.

"Please, Maddie, what did the man tell you?" he asked again.

"A fairy tale," she said, her voice the remnants of a timid child. "Of four siblings betrayed by an evil trinity and what became of them. He spoke at great length of Earth and Sea, the lost queen and king. He said that one day a champion would return them to their seats of power. He called you a Breedling, though he said nothing more, only that you had emeralds in your eyes. I had envisioned you in many different forms over the years, but I never expected you to be a teenage boy." Maddie squirmed and waited for Buck to release her. She repositioned her hips and twisted at her waist so that her left eye could look at him. "He then told me about myself, what I was. He scared me with such nightmarish stories about Wickers, telling me that, one day, I too would lose all notion of self and become a detestable creature. It was then that he asked me if I would be willing to assist him."

Maddie reached a hand down the inside of her gown and pulled out a small vial attached to a leather strap around her neck. She held it out in her hand for him to examine, the visible black shard surrounded by clear water sealed inside.

Buck's eyes widened in astonishment. "How? He gave this to you?" he said, reaching for the vial, but Maddie quickly placed it back under her gown.

"He said it would conceal my most shocking deformities from others, but not all of them."

"And did he tell you what it is?" asked Buck.

"Only that it is a blessed relic of Sea, one of three left in the world, and that with it, I would have the ability to heal others. He asked me then if I would be his seventh, and of course I agreed. How was I to say no? It was then he professed my reciprocation for his generosity. He said, '*The champion of Earth and Sea will not know of his gift, for it was given unbeknownst to him. He will know the words to heal the mortal soul and by combining the power of the vial and the strength of the Wicker's curse, you will awake this magic within him.*' And after my healing spell awoke your power," she said, reaching for her cloth on the nightstand, "it appears you also have the ability to heal yourself as well."

With care, she pressed the cloth over his cheek and wiped away the yellow scab, revealing his ivory pigment with no mark in its place.

Buck winced, his cheek still tender, but the feeling was only temporary.

"There," she said with a smile. "All better."

A silence fell between them as they stared at one another. Maddie leaned in closer, their noses nearly touching.

"Aww," came a sarcastic voice from the doorway. "How quaint, little Madelina has found herself a johnny."

"Lydia," shrieked Maddie as she pulled away from Buck. "I didn't hear you come in."

Buck turned and peered over the bed to see Lydia propped against the doorframe, still dressed in her undergarments.

"Is there something I can do for you?" asked Maddie, her hands behind her back, keeping the cloth hidden.

"No," said Lydia in a sighing tone as though bored. "Madam sent me to see if you needed a hand."

"I have everything well in order," replied Maddie.

Lydia lowered her gaze to Buck. "I bet you do," she teased with a knowing smirk.

Buck used the bed to get to his feet. "Tell me, Miss," he said. "Have Madam Dixie and Jack settled an accord?"

"Well, I just saw him a moment ago, heading for the stairs. If you hurry, you can catch him," said Lydia. "And with the task Dixie has asked of him, you might want to stop him."

"Why?" asked Buck. "What has she asked him to do?"

Lydia shrugged. "Don't know really, but I suspect she's looking to exact revenge on the two men that wronged her by having one do away with the other. You know, an eye for an eye and all that."

"Wait, Dixie has asked Jack to kill someone?" Buck's gut

tightened, and though he could hardly believe it, he knew Hades was somehow involved. But how? How could the Master of Hell have possibly known this was where they would be? He was already having a hard time with the Apothecary's foresight. He was not ready for Hades to have the same ability.

Buck kept his eyes on Lydia, anticipating she would shift into something else, but if she were a demon, she never changed nor gave him any inkling she was one.

"Where is he?" he asked finally.

"At the rate you're going, probably already done the deed," said Lydia sarcastically.

Her laughter prompted Buck to act, and without another word, he rounded the bed and charged toward the door. He wished he did not have to pass the vixen upon his exit, but there was no other way out of Maddie's room. He grabbed his jacket and brushed against her folded arms as he left the room. He felt warm stinging nettles creep along his limb, and rather than give himself away from the concern mounting beneath his face, Buck ran down the hall.

The Tall Man's Promise

"Buck, wait," said Maddie as she raced down the hall after him. He was already down the stairs by the time she reached them. Her light feet swiftly carried her downstairs as he opened the door, her bare feet landing on the rug where tiny drops of blood stained its threads. The vestibule filled with the sound of rain as they stood quietly, his back to her. There were so many things she wanted to say to him, but all she wished was for him to say something instead. She had failed to tell him the most crucial part of her story, that she had not only met the tall man once, but twice. A year ago, in fact, on the eve of her thirteenth birthday. The tall man had appeared in her room without warning, her alarmed scream stifled by the bundle of sheets she had been carrying.

"Pleasant evening, Madelina," said the tall man.

She stood, too flabbergasted to respond.

The tall man crossed the distance of her room, his brown cloak sweeping the floorboards, and offered himself a seat at the foot of the bed. She set the sheets in her basket but kept her distance from the man who had rescued her, who until now she had thought a mere figment of her imagination. In her heart, however, she always knew him to be real, for his gift to her was proof he existed. She clenched the vial around her neck, fearful he might reclaim his offering.

"Fear not, young one," he said. "I have only come to reaffirm our agreement."

"It was the least I could do," Maddie said, cutting him off. She bit her lip, apologetically.

The tall man smiled as he considered her. "Rightly so, but it was unfair of me to ask one so young to pledge such an oath. You had just lost your whole world."

"And you gave me a new one," said Maddie, cursing her tongue for once again speaking out of turn.

The tall man laughed. "I see the years have sharpened your mind, Madelina."

"Please don't call me that," said Maddie. "That is not my name."

The tall man's merriment faded, his tone turning somber. "One day that name shall find you again, young one. On this I give you my word."

"You promise?" said Maddie.

The tall man nodded.

Maddie smiled at his reply, and it rekindled in her a sense of hope that there was still a chance to reunite with her parents. She approached the bed and sat next to him, placing her hands in her lap. She studied his bronze skin for a moment, wishing she had the courage to ask how old he was, where he came from, but she knew better than to ask questions that would meet silence. Besides, it did not matter. She was alive because of him.

"Do you remember the story I told you?" he asked after a moment.

"Of the four siblings and the Champion of Earth and Sea," she said. "Of course I do."

"And will you assist me Madelina? Will you be my seventh?"

"Your seventh what?" she asked. *Her question was met by silence. She took a deep breath.* "Yes," *she said, and held out her hand.* "If I am to meet the Breedling you spoke of, I will unlock the healing power within him as you have asked."

The tall man looked at her hand with an uncertainty she was not prepared to consider, and she suddenly felt a tad foolish.

"It is how agreements are sealed," she offered. *"Take my hand."*

The tall man indulged her, his massive hands swallowing her tiny one.

She acted the motion of shaking hands and said, "There, now we have an accord."

"Be well, Madelina," the tall man said. *"May what has been lost to you return, and may that which has been denied to you make you whole."* And with that he was gone.

Maddie watched the rain droplets twinkling against the inside light, unaware it had been the last thing Buck had seen before his imprisonment. The earthy smell conquered the floral perfume inside, and she saw his body shake as if he were having some waking nightmare. She positioned herself in front of him, barring his escape, and was shocked to see twisted despair on his face. She looked into his eyes, but he was worlds away, lost in some memory. She lifted her hand to his once-wounded cheek and brushed it. Buck closed his eyes, acknowledging her comforting presence, and in that moment, a surge of longing struck her heart. She could not imagine he felt the same way, uncertain if a Breedling could love at all.

"You can stay," she said.

Buck opened his eyes. "And I would like that," he said, taking her hand. "But I cannot."

"I know," she said somberly. "It's . . ." She sighed. "I had to try. But will you entertain one question before you go? Why him? Why Jack Rutledge?"

Buck smiled at her. "The tall man may have called me the Champion of Earth and Sea, but I am not the only one."

"You mean that callous blight-heart?" said Maddie. "Jack Rutledge, a champion?"

"Yes," said Buck. "And it is imperative I find him. Do you know where Dixie might have sent him?"

Maddie stumbled on her words before managing, "If Lydia is right about his deadly errand, then he will be at the Eatery. There you'll be looking for a man named Jeb. He's a man of burly stature. Has a head the size of a melon, a crooked nose, a lazy eye, and scratch marks across his left cheek. From what I heard, his face became deformed because of all the abuse he took in the boxing ring, which is where he was known to be a gorilla of a man, but never here, and especially not to Birdie. He was always so gentle with her, like a beauty and her beast. Still don't believe he killed her." She paused and bit her lip. "You'll stop him—Jack, I mean."

"It's not my place to choose Jack's course of action," said Buck.

"Not even if it is to save him from the influence of someone else?" asked Maddie.

"What do you mean?" asked Buck.

Maddie gnawed on her lip. "Well, what if Jack weren't in his right mind? I mean, what if he had no choice? Would you stop him then?"

"Of course," said Buck, "but I can hardly see Jack being manipulated by anyone."

"Well, you don't know Lydia like I do," Maddie began. "And if Jack Rutledge is as strong-willed as you say, I'm certain Dixie asked the vixen for a tonic to coax Jack into completing her task."

"Tonic?" said Buck.

"She drugged him."

Buck's eyes enlarged and though she had no idea what he was thinking, it was clear he had to find Jack and stop him as quickly as possible. She watched him reach into his pocket, and he placed two coins in her hand.

"For services rendered," he said.

Maddie looked at the coins and felt their unusual weight. Pressure mounted under her skin and with intense speed. It traveled the length of her arm and into her chest, stealing her away as the vision of water entered her mind and the taste of peanuts filled her mouth. She heard singing, an old folk tune she did not know. The water shimmered, and she was suddenly standing alone in the center of a dark street, with no stars overhead, just a sweep of blue. She felt weary and smelled the scent of rotten eggs. She watched the sky ripple as flashes of scarlet burst inside a series of lampposts. It made her jump, and the animalistic scream of a woman terrified her. Maddie brought forth a heavy breath as Buck came into view, the smell of fresh rain replacing sulfur. He had a concerned look about him, his lips slightly parted, weighed with a question he did not ask. She sighed, resigned to keeping her vision to herself, for she could keep him no longer. She placed the coins back into his palm, and closed his fingers around them.

"No payment is required," she said with a tired smile. "Besides, I can see you will need these more than me."

Again, Buck's lips parted with a question, and again he did not speak. He merely put the coins back into his pocket.

"Here," she added, untying the ribbon in her hair. She coiled it like the rind of an orange and placed it in his now empty hand. "Something to remember me by." She then stepped aside to let him pass.

Buck breezed out the door into the rain, but stopped in the alley, the cool droplets hitting his bare skin. She watched him stare at the ribbon, his thoughts again somewhere else. He gripped the keepsake in his hand and turned back to her. She never gave him a chance to do anything more, as she went out into the rain and kissed him.

Maddie pressed against Buck's lips with an uncharacteristic ferocity, but considering the Diamond Girls had been her only teachers in such a matter. She held her position, but started to feel uneasy, for Buck was not kissing her back. She wondered then if he even knew what kissing was. She pulled herself away to ask, but in response to her retreat, his lips pressed against hers.

It lasted long enough for her to have to catch her breath, and when she finally pulled away, she saw the innocent astonishment on his face. She watched his eyes as they inspected her flattening hair. A chill ran down her back, realizing how close her gown was to her skin. Patches of peach flesh were becoming more visible through the transparency of the fabric. Maddie shivered, and instinctively she pulled him into her, to keep his eyes from her apparent nakedness. She buried her face in the crook of his neck and felt safe in his arms as they embraced her. She wished to stay wrapped in them forever.

Buck relaxed his hold and forced her to withdraw. He cupped her face with his hand as she closed her eyes, nuzzling against his gentle touch. He lingered long enough to memorize her face and without a word, he ran down the alley in search of Jack.

Maddie opened her eyes and stared at the brick wall in front of her. She had the urge to turn, but she could not bear to watch him leave. The droplets of rain mixed with her tears as she began to sob. She screamed, pressing her hands into her abdomen, and leaned forward. She cursed the tall man and his promises. How cruel it was to have put her in his path, only to be torn from it. Never in her whole life had anyone given her so much and in one stroke taken so much away. She held herself firm, taking control of emotions. Maddie lifted her head, her eyes meeting her shadow on the wall. The raindrops hit her head, rolled from her brow to her nose, then onto her closed lips, only to roll to her chin and fall to the ground. Maddie's chest ceased moving. It was not possible. The drop should have entered her mouth. She lifted an unsteady hand to her lip and met the touch of flesh. She turned her head, but it was too late, Buck was gone.

Was it true? She had to be sure.

Maddie rushed indoors, her drenched body dripping water on the floor. She raced down the hall to her room, trying her best not to slip, her footsteps making more noise than ever before. She half-expected to run into Lydia upon her return, but the vixen had done her task and called Buck away toward whatever dangers awaited him, like some siren beckoning a sailor to dash his ship against the rocks. Maddie burst through her bedroom door and went straight to her dresser.

Maddie stared at her fragmented reflection, allowing the pieces to come together, the image of her face revealing the miracle. She gasped. Her deformity was gone. She moved closer to the mirror and rubbed a hand along her lips. They were whole. She reached for her necklace and slipped it over her head. She set it on the dresser and waited for her body to wither, to morph into the hideous monster underneath her glamour, but she remained unaltered.

It was more than she could have hoped for, more than she thought the Breedling's powers could achieve. Giddiness built inside her, ready to burst, but out the corner of her eye, she caught sight of an image shifting in the mirror. Maddie turned around and glanced across the room at the bed. Her hands shot over her mouth to conceal her scream, her eyes swelling in disbelief. Sitting upright, Mara stared back at her with both eyes open.

"Sweet Madelina," whispered Mara. "My-ah sladkaya."

Maddie rushed to the bed and threw her arms around her mother's neck. The tall man had kept his promise.

EYE FOR AN EYE

The fluorescent lights reflected off every watery surface, giving the illusion that a bloody massacre had taken place in the intersecting streets. Buck stood underneath an overhang a block away from the Eatery, catching his breath. He could sense Jack's presence, his tether to the Trickster still strong, despite the shroud of an unnatural haze. At least, unnatural to him. Aside from that, it was the only darkness he felt between them, which meant there was still time. He puffed a few ragged breaths, which made his ears pound, temporarily muting all sounds of the rain and the commotion spilling out of the establishment. It was no wonder then why he did not hear the strut of high heels heading toward him.

"You'd better hurry," came the faint sound of Lydia's voice.

Buck glanced over his shoulder and saw the vixen standing underneath the lamppost, an umbrella in her hand, which matched both her shoes and the shimmering scarlet of her flapper-style dress. Curls decorated her hair and a sequined headband, adorned with a brooch made of feathers and other shiny materials, crowned her head. Her skin was pasty against the color of her outfit and her face was overly painted, her lips the color of ruby.

"What do you want, Lydia?" asked Buck, not nearly as challenging as he could have presented himself.

"Nothing from you," she said, with a mixture of baleful delight. "I just couldn't pass up the opportunity to miss all the fun. I mean, this chase will be a gay ol' time. Don't you agree?"

"What did you do to him?" demanded Buck, finding his backbone.

"Hmph," snorted Lydia, her expression overtly disappointed. "I didn't do anything to him and I'm insulted you think I would degrade myself by using something so primitive." She stepped up onto the sidewalk, increasing her height. "I merely gave Madam Dixie a few options on how to tame the thief. Because frankly, Bartholomew, I'd have used much more than practical magic," she added, as a flash of red flickered in her eyes and she curled her lips at his instant recognition.

"Oh, yes, Bartholomew," she said with jubilant triumph. "You see me now, don't you?" Lydia snapped her fingers and a spark of flame appeared between her fingers.

Buck stared, the trick hardly changing his bewildered expression. How could he have missed it?

"Ah," Lydia squealed with exaggerated fanfare. "Can it be true? Have I deceived the Great Bartholomew, Breedling of the First Grade, the Fates' Most Beloved? Creator Hades will be most impressed."

"That may be," growled Buck, trying to figure out which one of Hades' demon generals was standing before him, for even though revealed to him, he was still struggling to sense her demonic aura. "But you will also have to explain to him how you failed."

"Care to wager on that?" said Lydia with a snarl. "My remedies are foolproof. Stingy Jack will have no choice but to heed the siren's order and usher in his own doom."

"I'll stop him," said Buck, his tone more cocky than confident.

Lydia cackled. "Then this shall be an event worth spectating," she said.

Buck balled his fists, unsure if it was wise to confront the demon in a physical fight, but before he could make up his mind, he heard shouting behind him. He turned away from Lydia and saw a bulky man burst through the crowd gathered at the entrance of the Eatery. Shouting commenced, followed by the appearance of Jack hollering at the man to stop as they both took off down Clybourn Street. Buck sprang off the balls of his feet and dashed after them, leaving Lydia to watch the action, although from her vantage point they would soon pass out of sight.

Buck splashed through puddles as the rain pelted his face. It was difficult to see several feet in front of him, but he let his tether to Jack be his compass. On either side of the street, the buildings turned into a shadowy wall, locking their chase into a proverbial maze until he passed St. Paul Avenue. Then the dark walls gave way to the obstacle course of the train yard.

Buck paused at the fence and scanned the yard for Jack. There were long chains of stationary railcars scattered across various tracks. Off to the right, he caught sight of the bulky man disappearing underneath a boxcar and saw Jack's shadow closing in behind him. Buck followed the fence until he found an opening, and he headed into the yard. It became difficult to see again as he ran, but he watched Jack dive into the mud and slide toward the boxcar with ease. The outline of the Trickster's body lurched back, heaving what he could only assume to be a piece of Jeb's clothing or part of the man himself. Jack tugged again as he got closer.

"Jack!" he shouted, his voice interrupted by a single crash of thunder. "Jack!" he tried again.

Buck could not tell if the Trickster had heard him or if Jeb had managed to give him the slip, because as he leapt over the fourth track in front of him, he saw Jack fly backward into the mud. The Trickster recovered quickly, scrambling forward on hands and knees before disappearing underneath the boxcar.

"Jack!"

Buck sprinted and reached the boxcar with purposeful speed. He crawled underneath it, his small size an advantage. A conductor's horn blared, vibrating the metal above him, but he did not bother pausing to cover his ears, letting the overpowering ring deafen his hearing. On the other side, Buck scrambled to his feet, spotting the approach of a locomotive. Ahead of him, it became clear both Jeb and Jack were trying to get in front of it—Jeb to put a barrier between him and his pursuer, and Jack to prevent the latter. Buck darted after them, his muddy clothes weighing him down.

The light from the engine beamed, casting their shadows long against the ground as the train drew nearer at a slowed pace. Buck picked up his stride, straining every muscle in his legs, and reached for Jack, managing to grip the tail of his coat. He pulled back with all his strength as though he were reining in a horse. He felt his grip jerk and collided with Jack in what would have been a comical stunt had anyone been watching.

Jack screamed as his prey threw its body in the air and cleared the track just before the train restricted his path. He wrenched his head, his eyes dilated and empty of reason. With a chop of his arm, he cut away Buck's grasp and glared at him with a glazed expression, bursting with fury.

"Argh, what have ye done!" shouted Jack, his voice barely audible over the rattling of the passing train. "The bastard is getting away!"

"Jack, you need to stop!" shouted Buck. "This is not you. Whatever Dixie did to you, she is manipulating your indecent nature."

"So, what of it? Don't like what ye see?" said Jack crossly. "Well, get used to it, because this is what the Trickster looks like!"

"Even so, the trickster within you is not a crazed animal," said Buck, being mindful to keep his distance.

"Bloody hell, I didn't ask fer this!" Jack yelled in a recognizable fit of frustration. He began to pace, slopping through the mud. "I was just fine without ye. I could've wandered with what little peace I have left!"

"Jack, the only peace you know died two centuries ago," said Buck.

"Hold yer tongue, ye worthless little wretch!"

"No, you need to snap out of it," said Buck. "Dixie drugged you to make you compliant. You need to see that, feel that. Think about it. Is this truly what you want, to commit murder for her? You are not a cutthroat."

"Argh, shut up," growled Jack, tugging at his hair.

"Listen, Jack," challenged Buck. All he needed to do was keep pushing. "What would Iona say?"

"Iona's dead!" shouted Jack, his defeatist words putting a crack in his masked expression.

"But she does not have to be. You can still save her, but not like this, not at the cost of your own soul. She needs you. I know she still speaks to you in some way, trying to reach you. Listen to her. Hades is trying to force your hand."

"What are ye jawing about? Hades has nothing to do with this!"

"Of course he does," said Buck. It was then Buck recalled what Maddie had said to him. *He was always so gentle with her, like a beauty and her beast.* The phrase resonated with him so strongly that an epiphany stuck him. "Jeb never killed his beauty. He loved her."

"Poppycock!"

"I tell you, that vixen Lydia is one of Hades' demon generals, and whatever story she had told Dixie was a lie. Jeb would never have harmed Birdie, just as you would never harm Iona. Lydia killed Birdie, and she used Dixie's grief and need for revenge against her in order to turn you into the weapon she needed. But you cannot be that weapon!"

Jack pounded his feet in the ground and roared, his struggle evident.

"Please Jack, turn away from this; let me help you," said Buck, and he offered his hand. If he could just connect with Jack long enough to cast a healing spell, maybe he could rouse him from the hypnotic fog.

Jack planted his feet and stared at the Breedling, even as the barricading train removed itself from his path. He absentmindedly lifted his arm, but stopped short, distracted by yet another engine horn blasting through the yard.

"Jack, wait," said Buck, panic evident in his voice. He could already see he was losing the Trickster's attention. "Please, just take my hand."

Jack rotated away in search of his prey and watched as Jeb headed toward the switch track near one of the elevators, the red lights illuminating his brawny physique.

"Jack, listen," said Buck, gripping the Trickster's hand. He squeezed it tightly and muttered the Apothecary's healing prayer under his breath. He had no idea if it was going to work, but he had to try something. Jack did not pull away, but his gaze remained on his target. "Do not let Hades do this to you," he continued.

"You are too strong-willed to fall victim to his scheming. You are Stingy Jack, the Trickster of Tricksters, the unclaimed soul, the Eden Wanderer. Fight it! Do not give into Dixie's revenge; do not forsake Iona's soul."

The Trickster let out a heavy breath.

Buck relinquished his grip, noticing the shift in their tether—the haze was lifting. Whatever influence Jack had been under released him.

Jack stood silent, his attention fixed on the switch track.

Buck followed his arrowed gaze and saw Jeb struggling to break himself free. The man's cries for help broke through the brief stillness as the approaching train blasted a warning call, its speed barreling through the yard. It was then that Buck realized Jeb was in its path, the engine spotlighting the terror on the man's face as he fought to dislodge his foot clamped between irons. The situation was grim and all Buck or Jack could do was stand at a distance and watch as the train made its murderous pass while the rain rinsed their clothes.

"Jack," said Buck, in a soft voice.

"Leave it be, Buck," said Jack, and he sloshed through the mud to the nearest open boxcar and sought refuge inside.

Buck lingered for a moment alone, numb by the ordeal. He had been so close to losing Jack, too close. If he had not grabbed his coat when he did . . .

"Well played, Master Breedling," applauded Lydia.

"Go away, Rachel," said Buck, finally able to sense the demon general's true identity.

Lydia walked into his line of sight, her scarlet heels in one hand, her umbrella in the other.

"So, you finally figured me out," she said.

"Yes," said Buck. "Now get out of my sight, demon."

"But aren't you curious about how I did it? How I orchestrated this little play?" she teased.

"I want nothing from you," said Buck. "I am not concerned with the secret of your trickery," he lied.

Lydia giggled. "Did you actually just say a lie?" she said. "So the rumors are true. There is something wrong with you. How extraordinary."

"That may be," said Buck, losing his ground in this battle of wits. "But there is nothing more you can do here."

"Of course there is, soul stealer," said Lydia, issuing a derogatory name demons used to address Breedlings in order to get under Buck's skin. "I can make you doubt yourself."

Buck did not want to give it away in his expression, but the demon general was right. He did doubt himself.

Lydia laughed at his uncomfortable posture.

"Go away, Rachel," he growled.

"I shall, Bartholomew. Believe me, I shall, but don't think your victory here means you have won. Sure, you saved Stingy Jack for the time being, but there is still plenty of time before you reach the Ferryman," she said. "And besides, despite the setback, I still get to claim Jeb's soul for Hades."

"Mark of the Devil," said Buck under his breath.

Lydia giggled. "Sticks and stones, soul stealer," she teased and turned to depart. "Oh, and before I go," she added. "A little parting gift from me." She bent over and kissed him on the cheek, her warm lips searing his skin.

Buck tossed his head to the side.

"As always, Master Breedling, it has truly been a pleasure, and most entertaining. I look forward to doing it again," said Lydia. She gave Buck a polite bow.

Buck returned the formal gesture, although reluctantly, and

watched Lydia as she danced toward the switch track, taking her laughter with her. The flashing red lights ahead engulfed her shadow, and in the blink of an eye she disappeared, leaving a trace of red fabric in the mud. A large raccoon continued to wander up the tracks in her place, and he could not help but wonder how long Rachel had been posing as Lydia or if she had always been the Diamond Girl. If so, he had to give Hades credit for his foresight.

Buck waited until he could no longer see any sign of the raccoon's bushy tail before joining Jack in the dry confines of the boxcar, which, unlike their previous car, did not have a comfortable surface. He huddled against the wall just inside and kept his eyes attentive on the yard. He pulled in his knees and hugged them against his chest. He needed to be more cautious going forward, but more importantly, he needed to anticipate Hades' next plan of attack.

From the Library of the Tales Teller
Fool Me Twice

O n the anniversary of his first meeting with the Devil, Stingy
Jack came upon the outskirts of the Village of Lentil. He
traipsed through McGough's Orchard, searching for food to
tame his hunger. Most of the trees were bare, the apples already
harvested for the season, but the blackthorn trees were plentiful
with ripened sloe fruits. Their trunks were thin, covered with dark
bark, most of them small, almost shrub-like, but some reached
unnatural heights, where the best fruit lingered at the top.

Stingy Jack heard a rustling of leaves and crouched down to the
ground to avoid detection. The crunching of leaves drew closer,
and from around the edge of the row stepped a familiar man with
black clothes and long, thick black hair.

"Top of the mornin' to yaw, Jacky," hissed the familiar raspy
voice.

"Ah, Hades, I was wonderin' when ye were goin' to show,"
said Stingy Jack as he rose from the ground and brushed off his
tattered clothes.

"Our deal was a year, was it not?" said Hades, taking a bite
of an apple.

Stingy Jack practically licked his lips at the sight. "It was," he said, giving a fake forlorn sigh. "It's just I was lookin' forward to the festivities of Samhain. Lentil is known to have one of the best throughout the countryside. It had always been me mother's favorite celebration, having brought me here once when I was a wee tyke. Will ye perchance grant me the day?"

"Of that I will not," said Hades, tossing the half-eaten apple over his shoulder. "I will not make an exception for ye, Jack. Yer melancholy trick will not work on me."

"Then it appears I have forgotten who I be speakin' to."

"It appears so," said Hades.

Stingy Jack lifted his arm overhead and pulled a berry from the tree. He rolled it through his fingers, the berry's waxy texture and pale purplish skin a tantalizing treat. With all his powers of deceit, he lifted his gaze, his longing stare coveting the prized fruit above.

Hades lifted his gaze as well, ensnared by the mortal's desire. "Be that yer time is now mine," he said, "will ye join me in a small snack?"

"Ye mean, eat of the vine?" asked Stingy Jack, lowering his gaze to meet Hades' stare.

Hades' fiery eyes danced. "Something like that," he replied, without giving away his motive to deny his rival this final mortal pleasure.

"Then by all means," said Stingy Jack, preventing humor from saturating his words. He stepped away from the tree.

Hades scaled the tallest blackthorn, its thick trunk jutting out of the earth five feet, before breaking off into a vast weave of branches.

Stingy Jack roared with laughter as Hades pulled berries from the tree. "I didn't think it would be this easy."

Hades placed the gathered berries in his pocket and looked down at Stingy Jack. In the grass, he spotted shavings of bark lying at the mortal's feet, which somehow he had missed before. He lowered his eyes directly beneath him and saw embedded in the trunk of the tree the source of his nemesis's merriment. In the bark of the blackthorn was a gleam of silver—the Trickster's cross. Outraged, Hades blasted a bolt of fire from his hand, setting the tree closest to him aflame. He could not believe he had forgotten the Trickster was in possession of the blessed relic.

Stingy Jack momentarily choked on his celebratory cheer, but he resumed his laughter as the flames jumped to several trees until the whole orchard was on fire. He collapsed on the ground and began to cry from the pain in his sides, his hysteria all consuming.

By the time the heat became too unbearable to stand against his mortal flesh, Stingy Jack picked himself up from the ground and walked over to the tree Hades was trapped in.

With fury in his throat, Hades shouted at Stingy Jack. "Let me down from this tree!"

"As I said, not clever," snickered Stingy Jack. "And ye call yerself the Devil."

"I call myself no such name," roared Hades. "I am Flame; the Scarlet Phoenix; Hades, the Master of Hell. And ye will . . ."

"What, fear ye?" mocked Stingy Jack, snorting a whiff of smoke from his nostrils. "I fear ye not, Devil. I merely find distaste in the notion of ye laying claim to me soul."

"I shall do more than lay claim to it, mortal," threatened Hades.

Stingy Jack sighed. "And so, we find ourselves at yet another impasse."

"Let me down!"

"I will, Devil, if ye promise to leave me be fer ten more years. I should be thirty by then, and if I should die befer our next encounter, ye are not to take me soul."

Hades swore, hating Stingy Jack for his cunning. "So be it!" he shouted over the crackle of the blaze. "I shall not be back fer ye 'til the ten years are done. Trick me once, shame on ye; trick me twice, shame on me. Attempt a third, Stingy Jack, and I shall unleash a wrath upon ye unlike any has ever seen!"

"Deal," said Stingy Jack as he removed the silver cross from the trunk of the tree.

Hades jumped down as the blackthorn caught fire and vanished before his feet ever hit the ground.

Stingy Jack ran through the burning row of trees, now choking on the thickened smolder, and managed to make it to the safety of the road. He stood, coughing the smoke out of his lungs, and watched as the flames spread over the dry autumn prairie towards the Village of Lentil. The church bells rang frantically, their warning rousing the entire village from their evening slumbers.

Stingy Jack stared at the horrific sight as the fire threatened to consume the village as well. It was then, perhaps for the first time, under his self-inflicted armor and beneath the festering trickster within, he felt a flicker of remorse, that in years to come, would become the inextinguishable torch of hope Iona Covington would see in him.

Irish Fists

Buck wove Maddie's ribbon between his fingers, thinking about the touch of her lips, and the reassurance of her embrace. It brought about a strange sensation he could not name, but it did not last long, for he became overwhelmed by stirring questions, and there was one in particular that kept badgering him. If Maddie had been the Apothecary's seventh, then what did that make Father Damek Van Lewen? How many breadcrumbs had the Apothecary made? And had they been made simply for him or did they serve a higher purpose? The questions kept coming after that and he knew the only way to get any answers was if he and Jack made it to Euxinus.

Buck rested his head against the corner of the door, staring at the swiftly moving countryside as the freight train sped them into the Land of Ten Thousand Lakes and closer to their destination. Even though the train was not heading in the precise direction they needed to be going, Buck could sense they were close, a couple hundred miles as the crow flies. He closed his eyes for a moment and sifted through the map the Tales Teller had placed in his head, allowing it to fill him with longing to go home.

"Home," he mumbled under his breath, the word like the lash of a whip on his tongue. It was bad enough he had to return to the sulfuric nightmare, but worse, he had no idea what lay between him and the Eden Scar that would take him there.

Buck opened his eyes and began to flex his powers of perception. He could not sense the presence of any demonic aura, which did not give him any ounce of reassurance. It would have been easy for General Rachel to double back after retrieving Jeb's soul and hop the train. He tried his hardest to discern her presence, but either she had managed to conceal herself again or she was not on the train. Never, in all his years, had a demon of the Octet fooled him with a mortal disguise. It unnerved him because he had always been able to detect the difference, for like Euxians, demons and angels did not possess souls of their own and so lacked the ordained spark, given only to mortals by the blessings of Flame, Wind, and Sea. Even when the Octet were in the form of their respective animals: raccoon, weasel, fox, blue jay, raven, hare, cellar spider, or jaguar, he could always tell them apart from the true Animalia—the animals of Eden. Just the mere thought that Rachel had used every ounce of trickery and camouflage at her disposal stirred his worry and doubt—*So the rumors are true. There is something wrong with you.*

Buck sighed. How could he protect Jack if he was broken?

The opportunities he had created for Jack in Milwaukee had both succeeded and backfired. He had been prepared for Hades or one of his generals to intervene, but nothing as elaborate as a long con orchestrated by a demon. It hardly mattered now, because without the second act of compassion complete, he needed to start from scratch, and he prayed wherever the train stopped there was someone who knew Jack.

Sure, you saved Stingy Jack for the time being, but there is still plenty of time before you reach the Ferryman. Rachel's threat stewed in his head and his cheek twitched, marked with the warmth of her warm lips.

Buck glanced over at Jack; the Trickster's head slumped with his chin tucked to his chest, his eyes closed. They had not spoken since leaving the Milwaukee rail yard, but frankly, there was nothing to say. He wanted to prepare Jack with knowledge of what Euxinus was like, the order of its trial proceedings, or even the truth about his involvement in Iona's death, but none of that mattered, nor was it the right time. In Jack's current state of mind, it was doubtful he would even retain it, let alone listen. So instead, he let him rest. Buck looked down at the ribbon in his hands again. He lifted it to his nose and breathed in the faint smell of lilies, using it to calm his defeatist nerves while it forced his heart to flutter—the emotion still unknown to him. He returned the keepsake to his pocket and felt the chill of another object, and his breath caught. He dared not pull out the silver harmonica, even though it was already too late, for he could not help but think about Charlie.

* * *

The freight train jolted to a halt, resting in the yard of the Milwaukee Road Depot in Minneapolis. The clamor of voices carried from the platforms near the passenger train into the bustle of the yard. Buck was able to rouse Jack from his rest, before rail workers inspected the car. The Trickster's movements were lethargic, but he managed to follow Buck onto the platform. The depot rose magnificently above them as they drew under its shadow, the superb Renaissance Revival architecture boasting prominent cornices and a decorative pinnacle above the clock tower. Jack and Buck walked through the arched doorway, the concrete giving way to a waxed marble floor. The risen sun pierced the glass of the paneled windows and the light hit the chandeliers dangling from the wood carved ceiling. The detailed plaster walls and various arches gave the room a sense of grandeur, which Buck lingered to admire before joining Jack outside. The clock rang its hourly duty, alerting all those who could hear that the time was seven o'clock. Shortly after, the whistle of a conductor's horn announced the passenger train's departure from the depot.

"Buck," said Jack as two men in suits rushed around them to get inside. "About last night."

"No need, Jack. You were not yourself," said Buck.

"Yes, but about what ye said, about Lydia," said Jack. "Ye really think she's a demon?"

"Yes," said Buck. "And not just any demon. She happens to be one of Hades' generals who goes by the name of Rachel."

"And she killed Birdie," said Jack.

"It appears so," said Buck. He studied the Trickster's expression. "Are you square?"

"Not yet," said Jack, with a deep breath. "But I will be. Still in a bit of a fog, but I'm starting to understand what happened. What's real and what isn't."

Jack stepped off the sidewalk, walked diagonally across the street toward the corner, and proceeded to the steps of the Federal Office Building. He did not bother to look both ways, though oddly enough it made little difference. For aside from the fleet of parked vehicles lining the curbs, the city street was empty.

"Jack?" shouted a jubilant voice.

Jack and Buck turned at the same time, each on his guard for an enemy, but approaching them was a man dressed in respectable denim trousers, a T-shirt, and a navy-blue vest. His carroty hair, both wild and thick, brought out the fairness of his complexion, and in turn, his fair skin brought out the scatter of freckles on his face, which still held its youthfulness. His string-bean stature gave him a gangly appearance, despite the meat on his bones.

"Do I know ye, mate?" Jack asked, finding something vaguely familiar about the Irishman, but his mind had not fully recovered from Dixie's concoction to retrieve his memories so quickly.

"Oh, how silly of me," said the Irishman. "It's been, what, twenty some years since ye last saw me. Can't expect ye'd remember me. I mean, I was only knee high to a pig's eye back then, but blimey, Jack, ye haven't changed a lick. Why, ye don't look a day over twenty-one. It's me, Danny, Danny O'Toole."

Jack tilted his head in recognition, but the memory still escaped him.

"Bloody hell, Jack, don't tell me ye already forgot the Yards. They used to call ye Irish Fists, especially me kin Patrick."

"Patrick," mused Jack aloud. He scrunched his face, working though his hazy thoughts. "Yer Trusty Pat's kid brother from Chicago?" he paused, giving the Irishman another looksee. "Well, ye were Trusty Pat's kid brother."

The Irishman laughed. "Ey, not anymore. I even got me some runts of me own now," he said and extended his hand to Jack. "Say, this yer kid brother?" he asked, noticing Buck.

"What?" said Jack. "No, this is Buck, Buck O'Reilly, he tagged along with me on the ride up from Milwaukee."

"O'Reilly, huh?" said Danny. "Well, any friend of Irish Fists Jack is all right by me." He extended his hand to Buck.

Buck stared, baffled by the carrot-top Irishman. He had hoped for them to meet someone Jack knew, but this seemed all too convenient. He studied the Irishman's face, judging his eyes, but he doubted the accuracy of his observational skills. So he took the man's hand, and the instant they touched he sensed the purity in Danny O'Toole's soul. The strength of it caught him off guard, but he knew the Irishman was a mortal like Father Van Lewen and Charlie, someone he could trust without question.

"Pleasure to make your acquaintance, Danny O'Toole," said Buck.

"Pleasure to meet ye as well, young Buck," cheered Danny, his face lit up with a grin. He threw an arm around Buck unsuspectingly and ushered him toward the stairs. "Ye know, Buck, yer friend Jack and me older brother, Patrick, go way back," he continued with a twinkle in his eyes, reminiscing about his boyhood hero as though the memory were fresh in his mind.

Buck glanced over his shoulder at Jack, but the Trickster merely shrugged.

"Take a seat, Buck," said Danny, sitting on the third step.

Buck took a seat on the second step while Jack perched himself on the low stone railing, keeping himself removed from the conversation in order to remain lookout, but also to give himself more time to feel alert.

"Tell me, Danny, how do your brother and Jack know each other?" asked Buck.

"Well, now that's a story, isn't it?" said Danny. "Ye see, me brother, Patrick was the best damn bookie the Yards has ever seen. Sure, the fights were fixed and most of them illegal, but it was a job, and Pat was good at it. He became the guy everyone trusted, and I mean everyone. Now, I wasn't allowed to go with him when he was working the boxing racket. Me mum wouldn't let me. But one day I wore him down and he let me tag along. I stayed out of the way and watched the matches from a ringside seat. Everything was great until the seventh match, when a boxer by the name of Jeb Zabodowski entered the ring."

"What did ye say?" asked Jack, getting to his feet, looking down at Danny.

"Jeb Zabodowski," said Danny. "Ye know, the King of Dives."

"Jeb Zabodowski!" squealed an approaching woman.

Buck, Jack, and Danny all looked at the platinum blonde standing in scarlet heels, which matched her railene-style dress.

"Lydia?" said Danny, getting to his feet. "As I live and breathe, what a surprise." He embraced the seemingly coy woman.

Jack and Buck stared gobsmacked, both of them frozen in utter horror by the vixen's appearance and her friendly exchange with Danny.

"Oh, where are my manners?" said Danny. "Lydia, may I introduce Buck O'Reilly and Jack 'Irish Fists' Conway."

"No," gasped Lydia, placing a gloved hand on Danny's arm. "You don't mean the Irish Fists Jack who stopped the hooligans from beating you to death."

Danny chuckled. "Ye remember."

"Remember?" said Lydia with a flirtatious cackle. "How could I forget? You only told me the story about a hundred times. I swear I could tell the whole thing myself."

"All right then," said Danny. "I just started talking about the seventh match."

Lydia smiled at the challenge. "Piece of cake," she said, and turned her attention to Jack and Buck, who both glared back at her. She curled her lips into a sly grin.

Jack grabbed Buck by the forearm to prevent him from doing something foolish. Danny was safe as long as they maintained the charade the demon vixen had in play.

Lydia went on about how Patrick had given Danny the cash box when the brawl broke out and told him to hide under the ring. Then, how one of the cheated spectators found him and chased him into the boxing ring. Neither Buck nor Jack were listening at this point, each of them missing the part about how Jack had climbed into the ring and rescued young Danny.

"And that's when the fuzz showed up," said Lydia. "Irish Fists had not only saved you that day but saved your brother, Patrick, as well."

Danny clapped and gave Lydia a bravo. "Oh, and speakin' of Irish Fists," said Danny, engaging Jack. "What do ye say, Jack—we could use a hard-hittin' mate like yerself today." Danny looked at Buck. "Ye don't mind if I borrow him fer a few hours, do ye?"

Before Buck could answer, Jack stepped forward. "Of course ye can," he said. "The kid and I were fixing to part ways when we got to Minneapolis anyway."

"Huzzah, one more fer the cause!" cheered Danny and turned to Lydia. "Well, Lydia, darlin', it was swell to see ye."

"And you as well, Danny," said Lydia.

Jack turned to Buck and held out his silver cross.

"Jack, where did you get this?" asked Buck in an intense whisper.

"Never mind that," said Jack. "I need ye to stall Lydia while I get Danny away from her. And if she's a demon like ye say, then use it to slow her down or send her back to Hell. It's worked on Hades, so chances are it will work on her. Ye just have to make sure it touches her skin."

"All right," said Buck, stuffing the cross in his jacket pocket.

"Ready to go, Irish Fists," said Danny, smacking a hand on Jack's shoulder.

"Lead the way," said Jack, and he followed Danny toward Second Ave before disappearing from sight.

"Aww," moaned Lydia as she procured her signature weapon with a snap of her fingers, a morning star mace with red-hot spikes. "And here I thought I was going to have all of you to play with at once."

"You will have to settle for me, Rachel, because whatever you might have planned for Jack by using Danny, you will have to go through me first."

"With pleasure, soul stealer," said Lydia. "I'll dispose of you; then I'll corrupt Stingy Jack, and for good measure I will present Danny O'Toole's soul to Hades." She twirled the mace in a circle and took a formidable stance.

Buck wasted no time and ran across the street. He ducked behind one of the vehicles as a ball of flames broke through the window and set it on fire. Buck kept low as he inched forward to the hood. He looked beyond it, expecting Lydia to be standing by the steps, but all he saw were her heels. Buck made a dash for the cover of the next vehicle and the next, each one bursting into flames on the inside. When he reached the corner, Lydia was waiting and grabbed him by the collar of his shirt, forcing him to his feet.

"I'd forgotten how boring it is to spar with Breedlings," she said. "There is no fight in any of you."

Buck reached into his pocket as Lydia dragged him out into the middle of the intersection. He struggled, but put forth the effort only as a formality. He did not want her thinking he was scared, when truthfully he was, but he needed to move past it. She tossed him on the ground and he rolled along the street. He attempted to get up, but Lydia pressed one of the morning star's spikes against the exposed skin on his lower back and drew a line from hip to hip. He screamed and sank immediately back to the ground, pressing his cheek against the concrete.

From his limited view, he watched Lydia's bare feet circle past. When she was gone, he saw three children peering out from behind one of the parked trucks a few yards away. He could not quite make out their faces, but their eyes stared at him, undecided whether to run for help or remain hidden. Buck did not begrudge them the latter, for there was nothing any mortal could do to help. What did give him pause, however, was that he was mere seconds away from dispatching a demon, and to have witnesses—he could not dwell on that now.

"Bartholomew," cried Lydia. "You poor, pathetic excuse of creation." She crouched in front of him.

Buck acted on pure instinct and thrust himself forward. With his left hand, he stopped the morning star from hitting his face, the metal spikes piercing clean through his skin. He screamed from the pain, but more so to give himself motivation as he slammed the silver cross against her exposed chest. Lydia met his roaring scream with a siren wail. After a few seconds, she leaned forward and forced strength into her weapon arm, twisting the spikes. Buck screamed, but he did not release her. Steam began to rise between the cross and Lydia's skin, as iron-hot fire inched through his arm. Buck gritted his teeth and shouted with all the voice he could muster.

"May flame vanish from sight!"

In the blink of an eye, Lydia disappeared and Buck fell hard against the concrete. His body ached and it suddenly hurt to breathe, but he could not lie in the street. He needed to get to Jack. Even if he had managed to send Lydia back to Hell, chances were she was not alone. Buck slowly got to his feet and stuffed the cross back into his pocket. He glanced down at his left hand, his skin drenched with golden streaks of blood. He took Maddie's ribbon and wrapped it around his tender flesh. He glanced down the street to address the children, but they were no longer in their hiding place. He hoped they were somewhere far away and safe.

Buck took a deep breath and focused on Jack, despite the grueling pain. He was close, maybe five blocks away. Buck took a step forward, ready to run after him, when the coursing flame in his arm crackled and he felt the unmistakable presence of Hades.

TEAMSTERS

"Jack, are ye well?" asked Danny, as he and Jack turned the corner onto Fifth Street. "Ye look a little peaky."

"Where is everyone?" asked Jack, his eyes searching every inch of the quiet downtown street. They had only seen a few vehicles since leaving the station.

Jack felt uneasy, though he could not tell if it was because he had a compelling urge to be amongst more commotion in order to keep Danny camouflaged or if it was because Lydia had appeared. Her stalking prowess, although impressive, put him on high alert for Hades to make an appearance. It could be because he had given his silver cross to Buck. All of them had him vexed, but he felt naked without the protection his heirloom gave him, almost as though he were missing a part of himself. When Buck caught up, he would ask for it back. That is, if he caught up. In the back of his mind, he was skeptical of the Breedling's ability to fight.

"Jack," said Danny.

Jack felt the Irishman's hand pressing against his chest, his arm fully extended. He noticed Danny standing in front of him as his mind shifted attention, realizing the street was busier with both vehicles and pedestrians. He looked overhead at the sign and read *Marquette Avenue.*

"It's the boy, isn't it?" said Danny.

"What?" said Jack, trying to reengage.

"Buck," said Danny. "Yer worried about him. That's what's got ye all distracted. I mean, ye haven't heard a single word I've said this whole time, have ya?"

"Buck's a capable fifteen-year-old. He can take care of himself," said Jack, although unconvincingly.

Danny scrunched his face, his eyes serious—a trademark he no doubt had learned from Trusty Pat. "I know ye don't believe that, Jack," said Danny. "If ye need to go back . . ."

"No," said Jack, casting his eyes about the street and out the corner of his eyes catching sight of a bushy tail that resembled the backside of a raccoon. Without even blinking to make sure he was not imagining it, Jack grabbed Danny's outstretched hand and hurried them across Marquette.

"Jack, slow down," said Danny as he pulled his arm away and forced Jack to double back to him like a dog to its master.

"Danny, let's just go," said Jack with an uncharacteristic eagerness. "Ye said we were going to meet up with yer mates, so let's do that. I'm ready for a fight."

"A fight?" said Danny, cocking his head. "So ye weren't listening to me."

"What's the big deal? Ye asked for a hard hitter. I'm ready to go," said Jack, his sensibilities in question. He was beside himself. A wadded-up bundle of nerves and hypersensitive to everything around him. It was the worst sort of feeling imaginable, and it stirred a forgotten fear he had not felt in nearly two centuries. Jack looked at Danny, the thirtysomething man he had met as a child, a coincidental fate similar to his encounter with Liam McGregor, the bartender. Was it some cosmic joke, or was fate trying to teach him a lesson? Never before had he reencountered so many old acquaintances in such a short amount of time, and so far none of them had ended well. It needed to stop, he wanted it to stop, and he was going to do whatever it took to keep Danny away from the influence of Hades and his demons.

"Jack, I didn't bring ye along to fight," he heard Danny say.

"Fine," said Jack. "Then let's meet up with yer mates."

Danny sighed as three trucks buzzed past them and turned around up the block, forming a barricade at the intersection. "Ye know, it's funny what one does and doesn't see when they're young. But I see ye now, Jack, and I understand what I missed when I first met ye."

"What are ye talking about?" asked Jack, his attention stolen away by the beeping of horns as he watched several men exit the lobby of the nine-story Andrus Building up ahead and gather around the trunks. Several more horns beeped, rallying the men as a Lincoln rolled up the street and stopped at the blockade. The car honked. In response, a husky bloke with a mean face and greased hair stalked toward the antagonistic car and broke off the driver's side mirror with a baseball bat. The driver of the car made an impromptu U-turn and headed back to Marquette. Jack watched the vehicle as it merged with traffic, and he caught sight of Danny's patient expression.

"We have a saying in me family, Jack," said Danny. "Whether by kith or kin." He paused and stuffed his hands in his pockets, a glint of his youthful self appearing. "As a boy, Jack, it was no secret that ye were beholden to no one. Ye had no kin, held no confidence with anyone, and ye were always in the thick of trouble. On that day our paths crossed, I worshipped ye fer being a hero, but now I see the error of me boyish wonderment. Ye weren't me hero, Jack; ye gave me something much greater than that. Ye made me yer kith. Even if we never saw each other again, ye chose me as someone ye could confide in, someone ye could trust, because, ye built our connection upon an unspoken accord. Now, I don't know what happened between ye and Buck, but I do know that Irish Fists Jack only goes it alone if he wants to, and clearly ye don't. I can see it plain on yer face. Yer worried about him. And there's also something more to it than that, ye . . ."

"Stop," said Jack, suddenly feeling exposed. He could not explain it, but it was as though all his secrets were visible on his face, and he had a nagging urge for Danny to see him for what he truly was—a monster who was unworthy of friends or love. But the Irishman's reassuring expression softened nerves. "All right," he said. "I'll admit it. I'm worried about the kid. Now, will ye get off me about it?"

Danny's expression gave no sign of agreement.

"Shoot, Danny," said Jack with a heavy sigh, trying to think up a plausible lie to throw the Irishman off his proverbial high horse. "Will it help if I told ye we have a rendezvous lined up at the Hotel Ritz?"

"Then what's all the melancholy about?" asked Danny, his voice brimming with elation. "A man only has that look when a woman is involved."

"Let's just say . . ." said Jack, holding somewhat to the truth. He ran a hand through his hair, coming off embarrassed. "Last night, a dame drank me under the table."

Jack waited for a reaction and was grateful when Danny started to laugh.

"Oh, Jack, ye are as painfully honest as I remember," said Danny, throwing his arm around him. "Also, ye seriously have to tell me yer secret fer aging. Now come on, everyone's waiting at Curly's Café."

Jack let Danny lead him on up the street, past the Chevy truck blockade, and onto the next block. The smell of hot cooking oil filled the air as they finally gathered amongst the men standing outside the café. Jack studied each of the men in the cluster, checking for any hint of a glamour masking their true faces, but if any of them were not as they appeared, he could not tell. Some of the men held clubs with sleeves rolled up to their biceps, their expressions ready for a brawl.

"I thought ye said we weren't gonna fight," said Jack.

"We're not. They're just fer show," said Danny.

"Aye," said a wiry fellow in a plaid vest. "It's the numbers we be after. Rest of the teamsters are waiting fer us near the Cream of Wheat Building."

"Teamsters?" said Jack.

"Aye," said one of the men as he punched Danny in the shoulder. "Didn't ye tell him, mate?"

"Of course I did," said Danny, rubbing the tingle out of his arm. "But this knucklehead over here didn't hear a lick of what I said. Apparently, a dame drank him under the table last night. It may have damaged his attention span."

The men got a good laugh at Jack's expense, but he paid it no mind, nor did he give into their taunts, because the forming crowd had his attention.

"See what I mean," said Danny, as the men laughed again.

Jack remained attentive and less inclined to join the conversation near him as the men talked about the state of things while finishing their coffee and cigars. At one point, Danny handed him a cup, but the glass never touched his lips. Without paying close attention, he gathered what was going on, as none of the men were shy about speaking their minds. Apparently, Danny's older brother Sean's union had just announced its strike, and they were one of many posts to keep scabs out of The Market. Jack cringed when he heard the word strike. He hated strikes, hated them more than his forced sparing matches with Hades. Bad things happened far too often during strikes, men died, and right now that was something he was trying to prevent from happening to Danny. The only consolation was they were amongst others instead of alone. Plus, Jack had sworn never again to get involved in such dealings after participating in the infamous Pullman Strike. There was also talk about the Dunne brothers, a man named Tobin, and two other blokes, Skoglund and Dobbs, but again Jack only caught bits and pieces. He became so obsessed with his watchdog-like charge that he did not realize they had begun to walk or notice when the coffee cup left his hands.

The group of men stepped into the shadow of the Lumber Exchange Building as others began to gather around them. Jack quickly surveyed every new face, especially the small assembly standing outside the brick fortress of the West Hotel. He could not check them all, and he began to second-guess his "camouflage by crowd" strategy. He had anticipated a group, not a whole massing. His stomach somersaulted as he sensed eyes on him. He whirled, but was unable to find his stalker.

"Jack," said Danny, positioning himself on his right.

The call of his name broke Jack away from his search. He turned to Danny, the Irishman's expression a strange mixture of concern and enthusiasm.

"Danny, we should get off this street," he said, keeping his voice at a whisper.

"Nonsense, Jack. All is well. Yer among friends here," said Danny, but his eyes betrayed his doubt.

"Danny, ye don't understand." Jack paused as a group of men walked around them to join the mob in the middle of First Avenue. "I ain't safe," he added, leaning into Danny's ear so only he could hear it.

Danny's eyes widened, and all of his merriment melted from his face. The Irishman looked about the street, trying to see if he could spot anyone who did not belong, but there were too many unfamiliar faces.

"What sort of trouble are ye in, Jack?" asked Danny.

"Danny, I . . ." started Jack as the hairs on the nape of his neck prickled. He looked beyond Danny, and in the sea of drab colors and scruffy faces, he saw the flow of scarlet. His line of sight was only open for a few seconds, but it was enough to see her face. Lydia grinned at him, and for the first time he saw the shadow of a raccoon shroud her expression. He sensed the air stiffen and he felt his bones ache. The men began to move slower as time shifted. The churn in his gut returned, sensing what was coming.

"Jack," said Danny, peering off in the direction he was looking. "What's she doing here?"

Jack immediately grabbed Danny by the arm and rounded the corner, his expedient impulse igniting the other teamsters into a frenzy. In his haste, he had not taken stock of his surroundings, for if he had, he would have noticed the delivery truck approaching. Jack heard the battle cry of the teamsters behind him and the thunder of their collective pursuit. The men gained on him and Danny, several outmatching their stride. As more closed in around them, Jack lost his hold on Danny.

"Danny," shouted Jack as the charging men swept the Irishman up in their wake. He could only identify Danny's movement from the carrot top on his head. He managed to ride the current and, with precision, maneuvered himself along the curb to intercept. The men furthest in front halted all at once as though on command and the rest of the teamsters banked themselves together to form a wall. As the men closed in ranks, Danny sped through the cracks and found himself out in front and alone.

"Danny!" shouted Jack. "Get out of the way!"

But it was too late.

Time slowed to a grueling crawl as the approaching truck swerved. Jack slammed into the wall, unable to break through the mortar of men. He felt his bones settle, which discouraged any further outburst of struggle. He watched helplessly as Hades appeared in the street. Danny's face flushed a burning pink as beads of sweat became evident along his forehead. He saw Danny's body shudder as Hades drew his finger along his collarbone and circled the Irishman as though inspecting a rare specimen. The Devil flashed Jack a wicked grin that seemed to say, *This is on you, Stingy Jack.*

Jack tried to scream, but any plea refused to pass his Adam's apple. All he could do was watch in horror as Hades secured Danny by the arm and threw him toward the oncoming truck. The action moved at a snail's pace, and with the snap of his fingers, Hades vanished and time resumed its deadly course.

Brakes screeched as the truck crashed into the fire hydrant. Water shot up like a geyser, and in the instant chaos, Jack could not see any sign of Danny.

KITH & KIN

A loud burst of cheers exploded from the mob as the men celebrated their triumph. They began to disperse, talking amongst themselves, none of them at all concerned with checking on Danny's well-being. This was not surprising to Jack because it was possible Hades' glamour had masked his assault on the Irishman. He had witnessed such a spectacle once before during the Battle of Gettysburg. He had hid in one of the local taverns when the fighting broke out, not bothering to take part in the chaos outside. Jack had been content, which was why it did not come as a shock when Hades arrived. The Devil coaxed him into accompanying him on an errand and the two rivals ventured out onto the battlefield. Hades' presence naturally slowed time, and in that moment, he went out into the thickest section of the fighting and repositioned one soldier in the line of cannon fire. As Hades had put it, the man was overdue on his payment and he aimed to collect. With a snap of his fingers, the Devil reset time and no one gave another thought to the fallen soldier.

"*Let this be a lesson to ye, Jacky,*" Hades had said. "*For one day when I tire of our game, I will take what is owed me from ye too.*"

Jack had found the threat empty at the time, not realizing how serious the Devil had been. But now all he cared about was finding Danny alive. He let the men move around him like water flowing over a log stuck in the river. He did not want to seem too eager or draw attention to himself, for fear of making a scene. The teamsters paid him no heed as they regrouped at their post back up the street. Jack stared at the truck, its engine still running, water clogging the sewer drain, flooding the street. Once he had an open path, Jack approached the truck, expecting to see Danny's body in a pool of bloody water, but the Irishman was not sprawled on the sidewalk or on the pavement.

Jack shot a look at the driver, who sat hunched over the steering wheel, unconscious. He crouched down and peered under the truck, soaking his knees and palms. He did not find a corpse underneath, but on the other side, near the back tire, he saw a bundle lying on the ground. Jack moved eagerly around the hood of the truck, unconcerned about getting wet. He felt anxious again, hoping Danny was still alive. He took a deep breath when he saw the Irishman's unconscious body lying on the blacktop. There was a deep gash on his forehead, which was bleeding a red much deeper than the color of his hair. Over his torso lay another body, shielding him.

"Buck," said Jack, stepping off the curb into the forming puddle.

Buck immediately looked up at him. "Jack, behind you!"

There was no time for him to react as spikes slammed into his back. The force of the attack made him crumble, his body splashing face-first into the water. He blacked out for a second, the pain temporarily numbed, but when he regained his sense of awareness, fire burned between his shoulder blades. He spit out water as the hot spikes embedded in his back and dislodged from his flesh. He let out a groan, then lifted his head. He saw Lydia stalk her way toward Danny and Buck, a blazing morning star in her hand.

"I'm gonna revel in watching you bleed, Breedling," said Lydia. "I wonder how much blood you have to lose in order to die."

The threat of death compelled Jack to push himself off the ground and muster a shot of adrenaline through his body. He dashed toward the demon, locking her with his arms, and spun her away as though he were whipping her across a dance floor. She stumbled on her heels as she stepped to the edge of pooling water.

"Ye want Danny or the Breedling, bitch, ye gonna have to go through me first," said Jack, struggling to keep himself upright.

"With pleasure," sneered Lydia. She readied her weapon, twirling it twice. "I'm going to enjoy this, Stingy Jack."

"That's enough, Rachel," came Hades' voice, ordering his demon general to stand down.

"Creator Hades," said the demon, her expression stunned by the Devil's appearance. She stood straighter, though she held her readied position.

"As you can see, Rachel, Stingy Jack is in no state to be swayed. Your tonic has lost its hold on him and I'm afraid you are overplaying your hand," said Hades.

"But Master . . ." said Lydia, relaxing the morning star to her side.

Hades made a combative step toward Jack. "It's been awhile, Jack," he said. "I haven't seen this side of you since—when was it again? Oh yes, I remember—since you and I had our dance by the willow tree over a certain Shepherdess. Pity she had to up and die so soon after."

Jack responded by curling his fingers.

Hades smiled. "I'm sorry, Rachel, but you are battling the wrong Jack," he said. "Danny O'Toole is lost to you. Now his son, on the other hand . . ." Hades turned to look behind him.

Lydia followed her master's gaze and Jack shifted slightly in order to see three children standing in the street, their pale faces staring in shock. In the center of the trio was a girl, who stood a step ahead of the two boys flanking her and looked more like a boy herself the way her hair was short and how her clothes hung away from her frame. The smaller of the two boys was the spitting image of Danny with a carrot top head and fair skin full of freckles. He stepped forward, his face wet with tears, but the girl held out her arm to bar the small boy from taking another step. The other boy, whose eyes were the same bright blue as the girl and who stood a foot taller than the teary-eyed boy, readied his fists for a fight. It was clear the three of them were willing to charge at the monsters before them if it meant getting to the Irishman on the ground. That determination fueled the smaller boy. He tore past his weak blockade and ran.

"Danny, don't!" shouted the girl, as Lydia moved in to intercept the boy.

"Jack!" shouted Buck, throwing the Trickster his silver cross. "The water!"

Jack caught the heirloom and felt an immediate connection with the object. It whispered to him in a reedy voice, and he felt empowered. He listened to the instruction, the voice telling him the precise course of action. Jack looked at the expanding pool of water, noting that Lydia's toes were hidden underneath the flood. He watched Hades vanish, giving his general no space to retreat, and without a second's hesitation, Jack dropped to his feet and slammed the heirloom into the water.

The water crackled with streaks of lightning as though charged by electricity, and they attached themselves to Lydia, shocking her. The demon screamed in pain and vanished to escape the torture. It gave young Danny a free path to his father, his small feet splashing past Jack. The boy dropped to his knees and placed his hand on his father's shoulder.

"Is he . . ." the boy's voice was soft, his body trembling.

"He'll be well," offered Buck as he placed his unbandaged hand on the Irishman's forehead. He mumbled the healing prayer under his breath, but not so quiet that the young Danny could not make out the words. Instantly, the wound began to mend, leaving a crusty scab. "See?" Buck added, suddenly exhausted.

Young Danny nodded.

"Jack," said Buck, looking up at the Trickster. "We need to get Danny off the street."

In response to the suggestion, the sound of shattering glass mingled with the bubbling noise of the hydrant. The two older children came out from behind the geyser, picked up the unconscious Irishman under his armpits, and dragged him toward the corner building until they had to lift him over the broken shards to get him inside. Young Danny followed them.

Buck made his way over to Jack, the Trickster's posture hunched. "Jack," he said, noticing the puncture marks in his coat. There was no blood, but heat radiated from his wounds. Buck reached to touch him, but Jack's unexpected swiftness stopped him.

Jack grabbed Buck by the wrist. "Leave it," he groaned.

"But I can . . ."

"It'll pass," said Jack. "Just . . ." His breath caught as a soothing caress washed over his back, taming the fire in his skin. He sighed. "There," he said, and looked at the Breedling, noticing the golden blood staining the ribbon wrapped around his hand. "Yer hurt." Jack reached for the Breedling's hand, but the two older children returned. They helped Jack to his feet and with one arm over each of their shoulders. They led him through the door.

They entered a quaint barbershop, though from the look of things, no one had used it for some time. Layers of dust were collecting on the vacant chairs lined against the windows on either side of the double doors, and a sheet covered the barber chair in the center of the room. The countertop sink placed below the mirrored wall had an army of spiders laying claim to the abandoned scissors, jars of foam, and other instruments suited for a barber. The boy and the girl set Jack in one of the chairs nearest the door before separating. The girl went to tend to Danny Sr., while the boy went back into the street, no doubt to retrieve Buck.

The girl did not dilly-dally and headed for the counter. The faucet hissed as she filled two bowls with yellowed water. She draped a few cloths over her forearm and picked up the bowls, then carried them across the room, knelt down, and began wiping the blood away from the Irishman's head.

"Cousin Emma," said young Danny, his voice worried.

"Don't worry, Danny," said the girl. "Yer da's tough. He'll be all right." She gave her cousin a smile as the older boy returned with Buck. "Colin, bring him over here," she added to her brother.

The older boy brought Buck into the middle of the room and set him on the floor next to Danny Jr.

"All right, Danny," said the girl. "I need ye to use that bowl of water and soak that hand of his in it. Colin, keep an eye out."

The older boy nodded and went to his post at the door.

"Buck," said Jack weakly, his head leaning against the window. "What do we do now?"

"Ow," said Buck as Danny Jr. placed his injured hand in the bowl, the cold water taming the heat in his hand. "We have to go, Jack," he replied.

"Where?" asked Jack. He was in no condition to get far.

"The truck, Jack," said Buck, looking out the window, his

eyes rereading the side of the truck, *Minnesota Valley Canning Company - Le Sueur, Minnesota.* "The truck is our way out of here."

"But ye can't go," objected Danny Jr.

"Danny," scolded the girl. Then addressed Buck. "Ye'd be wise to leave. If the teamsters come back, they won't hesitate to harm ye or yer friend there. Without me uncle's testimony, they'll see ye as an enemy, one who hurt their own."

"Emma," said the older boy, stepping away from the door. "The men are lookin' this way. If the truck doesn't move, they'll come back."

"Jack," said Emma. "Can ye pick locks?"

Jack smirked. "Aye, lass. Oi, boy. Colin, is it? I need ye to stir the driver."

The older boy looked at his sister, who gave him a nod. "Sure thing, mate," he said.

"Right then," said Jack. "Help me up and let's get to it." The older boy helped him to his feet, and together they exited the barbershop.

Buck lifted his hand as droplets of gold fell into the bowl. He motioned to gain his feet, but young Danny grabbed his bandaged hand, and he flinched from the shot of pain.

"Wait," said the small boy, trying hard to sound more grown-up. "Ye saved me da's life."

"It was my pleasure," said Buck, hoping his response would appease the young mortal, but the acknowledgement of his action simply fueled the boy's courage.

"Please, sir, if there ever be the need to repay such debt, I, Daniel Patrick O'Toole Jr., shall be willing to do that which would be asked," offered the boy.

Buck held up his free hand. "That will not . . ."

"Please, sir," said Danny. He looked down at his father. "Me da would've done the same if it were me, he being an honest man, fer by kith or kin, someone always has to have our back in times of need. At least that's what he'd say." He looked back at Buck, his expression binding every word.

Buck felt an uncomfortable tingle of warmth in his hand, but it wasn't the same heat associated with Lydia's weapon. This was different, similar to the sensation he had felt when Father Van Lewen had reaffirmed his tether to Stingy Jack.

"I be in yer service 'til such time ye deem the debt repaid, on me honor as an Irishman and a son of an O'Toole." Danny Jr. kissed Buck's hand, partly because he saw it in a moving picture once, but in truth, it was out of respect—his first act at becoming a man. He released Buck, giving his hero one final look of remembrance, and then returned to his father's side.

Buck got to his feet, his legs unsure of themselves as Colin came rushing back in.

"Come on, Buck," said the older boy. "Time to go."

Colin escorted Buck out of the barbershop as his head reeled, captivated by the integrity, the honor, and the humility of Danny's son. It had always been an impossible notion to him, a mortal pledging any sort of fidelity to an immortal, but like the Tales Teller had said, *That word no longer carries its true meaning, Master Breedling, for now, all things are possible.* There was great magic at work here and Buck could not even begin to fathom who might be its master. Or if it had a master at all. He needed to speak to the Apothecary, he needed answers, but first, he needed to get Jack to Euxinus.

"In ye go," said Colin, as he lifted Buck onto the truck.

"Colin," said Buck, unwilling to leave without a warning.

There was no way of knowing if Hades would return once they were gone. "About what ye saw . . ."

"Let it go, mate," said the older boy. "We Irish are well-acquainted with the stories of Old Hob. Don't fret; if the Devil comes a-calling, we'll give him a fight."

Buck wanted to argue that there was no fighting the Master of Hell, but he was too exhausted and Colin was already closing the door. He leaned his head back and searched for Jack, who was resting on a higher perch of boxed sweet corn. The door latched, sealing them into a swell of darkness. A moment later, the engine revved and the truck jerked into reverse, before switching gears and moving forward.

Buck rested his eyes, letting the rickety clank of the truck sooth him. He tried to plot their next course of action, but his head was too full. A smile crested his face, relishing in the valiant act of Stingy Jack, having caught a true glimpse of Iona's Jack, the fierce loyalist who would protect those he cared about. He had come through for Danny despite Lydia's poison and his ruling nature. The transformation had been quite the spectacle. And now they were one step closer. All that remained was a deed for the unknown—a selfless act toward an immortal.

From the Library of the Tales Teller

The Eden Wanderer

*T*en *years did not pass for Stingy Jack before death found him along the outer ridge of Ireland. In fact, after his second deal with Hades, word of his character began to spread like the flames of Lentil and the world around him shrank. Bounties cropped up in every town to seize him by any means necessary and no place was secluded enough to hide the Trickster of Mortals. Near the Village of Fountainstown, a band of thieves captured Stingy Jack and turned him over to the local magistrate for a handsome prize. His trial was swift, for no one was willing to release the Penny-Pincher, the Arsonist of Lentil. The magistrate threw Stingy Jack into the stocks of the village square and sentenced him to remain there until his body was empty of breath. In the days that followed, the villagers made a spectacle out of him. They placed a jester hat upon his head and threw rotten fruits and vegetables at his face. It seemed far less than he deserved by the cries of those in the square, but aside from hanging or cutting off his head, both of which had been discussed, their laughter and ridicule was the best they could provide.*

Stingy Jack remained in the stocks for nearly a week, guarded day and night and given no food or water save for the rain that fell from the sky and the generosity of a little girl, who took pity on him and fed him a bowl of creamy oats, which helped him live another night. On the second anniversary of their first meeting, Hades came to visit the dying Trickster to pay his last respects. And in the witching hours of the night, the famed Stingy Jack gave his last mortal breath.

Hades wandered into the village square as the bells chimed twelve. Stingy Jack's corpse hung, rotting away in the night air. He looked at the guard next to the post, slumped over and incapacitated from the evening's drink. Hades approached the stage with little concern for wandering eyes and grabbed a patch of strawberry-blond hair. He lifted the Trickster's head, his eyes closed, his skin as pale as a full moon, and his lips the shade of concord grapes.

"Aww, Jacky boy," sighed Hades in a somewhat sorrowful tone. "I told ye I would get the last laugh." He let Stingy Jack's head flop and hit the wood of his binds. "Pity it had to end this way."

Hades stood in wait as the night drew colder, waiting impatiently for Stingy Jack's soul to leave his body in the hopes of tormenting him one final time before Everlyse's angel appeared to take it away. But his soul never left his body and no angel emerged. The church bells chimed the late hour of one, which stirred the drunken guard, but he did not wake. Hades folded his arms across his chest, in an attempt to keep the nipping wind at bay and cursed his sister under his breath for the chill in the air.

"I would appreciate it if you did not take the name of my mistress in vain," spoke a commanding feminine voice.

Hades turned around to face the new arrival. He half-expected it to be Lady Vala, his sister's Fallen angel, but instead it was

Everlyse's High Valkyrie General, Mist. The Valkyrie angel, who was known to only appear in Eden in the form of a mute swan, had abandoned the elegant visage for a rare mortal form. Her legs were as tall as a stork, but firm. She wore knee-high leather boots that added two inches onto her height, allowing her to meet Hades at eye level. Just above her knees, a short skirt, stitched with dancing white feathers, flattered her hips, with a train of various blues floating in the light breeze behind her. A stunning corset of silver and azure protected her chest as though it were a sheet of armor. Stitched to it in a crisscross fashion were loose sleeves with white lace, covering her arms to her wrists. On her head, a silver band gave her appearance a regal appeal, though her style was less than ladylike. Her attire was more appropriate for a battle setting. Her feather-white hair lay over her left shoulder in a single braid, and her exposed flesh blended with the bewitching night.

"Good evening, General Mist," greeted Hades with a hint of sarcasm.

Mist did not acknowledge the fiery deity and stood in front of the stockade, observing the deceased mortal. She extended her hand, closed her eyes, and concentrated on the soul's energy. After a moment, she withdrew her hand and turned to Hades.

"What have you done to this soul?" she asked.

"Whatever do ye mean?" asked Hades, smug.

Mist wrinkled her nose. "I have no time for your tricks, Creator Hades. Now why has this mortal's soul not left his body? What have you done to it?"

"As I said," replied Hades. "Nothing."

"Lies," proclaimed Mist. "This poor soul is scarred, tarnished by your wickedness and hatred. Such a soul is of no use to my mistress."

Hades grinned. He needed no invitation to con the Valkyrie angel, but she was making it rather easy. "Are ye certain?"

Mist changed her expression, second-guessing her initial assignment of the lingering soul, believing she had missed something of importance, for surely the Master of Hell was not trying to get her to claim this guttered soul. Mist glanced over her shoulder to steal another look at the corpse. The scars on his soul were undeniable, but there was something more hidden under Hades' handiwork. Mist took a step toward the stockade and reached out, ready to rip his soul from his body, but what happened next was unexpected.

Mist placed her fingers on Stingy Jack's head, and from his scalp, a surge of energy threw her backward and straight into Hades. The two immortals landed hard in the dirt, their breath knocked out of them. Once she regained any sense of self, Mist rolled away from the Devil and onto her feet. Hades sat up and shook his head. He could taste the lingering sensation of water in his mouth. He licked his lips, and sure enough, a mixture of salt and sulfur teased his taste buds. Hades began to laugh.

Mist scolded. "I see no humor in this, Creator Hades," she said. "I have not the time for your games." She walked in front of him, exiting the square, the bells striking the two o'clock hour.

Hades' laughter faded as the echo of the bell dissipated and silence returned once again to the night air. "Very clever, dear brother," he hissed as he stared at Stingy Jack. "No wonder I took a liking to this despicable creature. He kind of reminds me of you." Hades paused a moment, at the ready to greet the Black Tortoise, but as the minutes passed, the water deity never entered the square.

"Do ye hear me, Brother Sea?" shouted Hades, throwing his voice into the air. "What are ye waiting fer? Come and claim yer soul!"

Silence fell again, save for the little snores of the sleeping guard.

"Fine," shouted Hades. "If ye will not take Stingy Jack, then I will."

Frustrated, Hades approached the stockade. With a snap of his fingers, the lock burst with a puff of smoke. He then waved his arm and the heavy beam of wood lifted off the Trickster's shoulders. Stingy Jack's body slid from its prison and fell limply to the ground. Hades reached for the bundle, ready to draw out the Trickster's soul, but a warning shock rejected his attempt.

"Bloody Hell," cursed Hades as he quickly grabbed Stingy Jack by the collar of his tattered coat and threw his lifeless body across the square. He continued to swear obscenities until he heard the heavy sound of an exasperated gasp. Hades turned to the ragdoll lying on the ground and staring back at him was the Trickster.

"Who be there?" asked Stingy Jack, unable to see the figure towering over him at first. He blinked a few times, allowing his eyes to adjust, the familiar shape of his nemesis coming into focus. Stingy Jack scrambled to his feet concerned Hades was here to collect him. Was the Devil going back on his word? Stingy Jack patted himself down and felt for his silver cross. It was still safe in his inside pocket. He felt a moment of insecurity until his inner trickster resumed control of him.

"Surprised?" taunted Stingy Jack, aware of the disbelief on his enemy's face. He, too, was stunned by the turn of events, but he was not about to let his adversary see it. He wobbled unsteadily, doing his best to hold his weak structure upright in spite of his depleted strength.

"I be nothing of the sort, Jacky," said Hades ineffectively, his expression seething with disappointment. "As I said, I will get the last laugh at yer expense. Fer as ye can see, Heaven's representative did not wish to remain and retrieve yer guttered soul."

"Think what ye will, Devil, fer ye have lost," gloated Stingy Jack.

Hades roared with laughter, his fiery eyes filled with sinister delight.

"What be so amusing?" asked Stingy Jack.

"Ye think that because I have vowed not to take yer soul that Heaven will want it. Yer unsavory behaviors as well as yer dealings with me have banned ye from the lofty gates," lied Hades. "In me generosity I can see to it ye are taken care of, Jacky. Ye can move on from this miserable realm. Come with me and live on in me kingdom."

"Or else what?" asked Stingy Jack.

Hades shrugged. "Or else remain the soul of flesh ye are and wander the earth fer the rest of eternity."

"Then as ye say, give me a light and I will be on me way," said Stingy Jack.

"Ye be sure, Jacky?" asked the hiss of Hades' voice. For if the Trickster were freely willing to turn himself over, the blessing of his sibling would no longer protect him. "Eternity be an awful long time."

"That it may be, but ye would not begrudge me, Devil, if I chose to stay here. Our game can still go on, though clearly I have the upper hand, this being the third time I have bested ye," taunted Stingy Jack.

"Mind yerself, Jacky, even though ye be dead, I shall find other ways to make ye suffer," promised Hades as he reached for the guard's knife and small purse on his belt. From the leather pouch, he withdrew a turnip and began to carve the vegetable into a lantern. The shavings of flesh littered the ground until Hades was finished. From his own pocket, he withdrew a candle and lit the wick with a snap. The small light danced in the nightly wind as

Hades placed the ball of wax inside the turnip and closed the lantern. He then thrust the totem into Stingy Jack's hands. Hades traveled out of the square and, as he did so, his voice spoke his curse.

   "He was a lad who did it twice,
   shamed the Devil by a roll of the dice.
   His luck ran out the day he died
   and was left in Eden—no tears were cried.
   Who was this lad who cheated fiery torture and eternal bliss?
   Who was this lad who wanders now full of villainy and regret?
   He goes by the name of Stingy Jack,
   an unsavory character; an unsavory chap.
   With turnip in hand to light his way through the darkest black."

Scars

"Jack, do you mind?" grumbled Buck, tired of listening to the incessant clicking of the Trickster's lighter. He opened his eyes to the welcome of a soft glow, the turnip lantern alive with a belly full of flame. Buck sat up as the truck hit a bump, and he flew off his seat. He braced himself to keep from being tossed around like a rag doll and gave it a moment before settling back in.

"Tell me, what's our next move?" asked Jack. "Is this it? Is the Eden Scar in LeSueur?"

"No," replied Buck, shifting his weight. "But we are heading in the right direction. We will be some miles away from the town of Mankato when the truck stops. My hope is we will find the Ferryman before then, before . . ."

"Something else happens," said Jack, a touch of melancholy in his voice. He cleared his throat and continued, "And this Ferryman, he will tell us how to find the Scar?"

"Yes, the way will become clear to us once the Ferryman provides us with the words."

"Wait, magic words? Ye mean like 'open sesame'?" said Jack, letting out a forced chuckle.

"Jack, I have no idea what you are talking about," said Buck.

"There are no magic words, just words that, when said by the Ferryman, hold power. The tale of the Ferryman is the key to make the gateway visible and open to those who seek to pass through."

"Seriously, that's it? A story?" said Jack on the verge of mockery.

"Yes, Jack, and a tragic one," replied Buck. "Every Eden Scar is created by tragedy, the very worst injustices mortals can inflict upon each other, dating all the way back to the first."

"And the Ferryman?" said Jack. "He's like the Ferryman who takes souls across the River Styx?"

It was Buck's turn to let out a chuckle. "I guess you can make that analogy if it helps, but the Ferryman is merely a historian, a guardian. A single soul bound to eternal duty—well, unless the Scar is healed, of course."

Silence fell between them again as the truck's gears grinded and the tires swerved left. Buck leaned into the turn, but was keener to hold his balance this time. Slowly, the truck straightened again and continued over smoother surface.

"Have they . . ." started Jack.

"Have they what?"

"Have any of the Scars healed?"

"Some, over time," said Buck. "As a Breedling of the First Grade, I was given, on occasion, the charge to heal the wounds of Eden. Mind you, there were only a few dozen of us given such a task, and the Scars vastly outnumber my kin. Even in the infancy of our creation. The same can be said for those Breedlings who are charged with the prevention of Eden Scars, which is much easier than healing, but that is not to say both do not have an equal number of challenges involved."

"Is there one in particular ye haven't been able to heal?" asked

Jack.

"Well, the most notable Scar is the very first. I am sure you know about the death of Abel at the hands of his brother Cain."

"And what of the Scar in Mankato?" asked Jack. "How was it created?"

"Jack, I do not feel qualified to answer that," said Buck. "The Ferryman will tell us our story."

"As ye said before," said Jack. "But I want to know what sort of act would tear a rift in the fabric of space."

Buck laid his head on the box and looked at the roof of the truck. Talk of Scars only made him think about Charlie's cousin Jimmy and how he had no way of knowing if the boy's death had created a Scar. Even if that were not the case, he was certain it had established a rift between him and Charlie, an eternal reminder of the pain he had caused his friend. He felt his insides burn, bile rising in his throat. The scene of the boarding house played out in vivid detail as he and Charlie managed to escape the crawlspace, navigate the roof, and climb down the spout. At the time, it had not occurred to him how much he had taken advantage of Charlie's shock and kindness. He had had no right to place such a burden on his shoulders, nor to allow himself to be in his debt.

"Buck, snap out of it," said Jack, giving Buck a crisp slap across the face.

Buck blinked and shook his head.

"So ye were just about to tell me about the Scar of Mankato," said Jack, sitting back across from Buck.

Buck stared for a moment, letting his brain retrace its thoughts. He looked up at the lantern, its ghostly glow spotlighting a long-legged spider spinning a web. It did not occur to him, in that moment, whether the arachnid was anything other than what it seemed—another of Hades' demon generals, perhaps—but as he watched the spider weave with a delicate rhythm, it gave him an odd sense of clarity.

"The Scar of Mankato," he began, trying his best to remember what he had overhead while in his prison cell, "was created nearly seven decades ago on a frigid December morning, when thirty-eight Sioux men swung from the gallows. Now, I cannot tell you what transpired to bring about such tragedy, but I do know that on that day, a Breedling by the name of Annaliese tried to prevent it."

"How did she do that?" asked Jack. He leaned forward, placing his elbows on his knees.

"A miracle," said Buck, folding his hands in his lap. "It is a skill she and one other Breedling have the strength to orchestrate." He paused a moment to make sure he had retrieved the whole memory from the back of his mind before continuing. "As far as I am aware, she jinxed the executioner to ensure the ropes would not drop. In this way, it was her hope that she could change the minds of those in attendance and give them a chance to free the men before it was too late."

"Did it work?" asked Jack, resting his chin in the palm of his hand.

"Well, to some extent, I suppose," Buck continued. "The miraculous occurrence swayed some in the crowd, convincing them that *the Almighty* was telling them to spare the men. It was a good indication that Annaliese's plan was working, but as always, there was no way of factoring in the interference of Hades."

"I'm not surprised," said Jack through his teeth, the mention of his rival challenging his calm.

"As to be expected," said Buck. "Hades has had a hand in creating nearly every Eden Scar, ever since the first. And it is not a surprise he took a personal interest in the creation of this one. I think it was partly because he still held a grudge against Annaliese for keeping a very powerful soul from him. And as you know, Hades neither forgets nor concedes."

"What did he do?"

"From the whispers I heard, earlier that day Hades met with a man by the name of William Dudley, who had recently lost a family member at the hands of a Sioux warrior. Hades liquored him up well, though it did not take much to convince William to act vengefully. When the ropes did not drop, William made his way to the scaffold. Atop, he withdrew his knife and cut the main rope, carrying out the execution. All Annaliese's efforts had been in vain. And now, as you know, Mankato is marked as a place of great pain."

Buck sighed, feeling weighted by the account. "Tell me more about Iona," he asked.

Jack cracked a smile. "All right," he said as though he understood Buck's need to speak of other things. "She was never short on words. Or songs. She loved to sing, especially to the lambs. I'd teased her fer it on occasion, but she always had the right words to put me in me place."

"Like what?" asked Buck.

"Once she told me that it was only fair to give a creature made for slaughter as much beauty as was possible, fer how else could ye pay fer such sacrifice?"

"You are right. She certainly had a way with words," said Buck.

Buck's voice trailed off as the truck veered to the left again and came to a halt. The truck idled for a moment before the engine died and the driver exited the cab, slamming the door, his voice cursing out every damn teamster for his wasted trip. The sound of his voice dissipated, leaving Jack and Buck in a stationary silence.

"Jack," whispered Buck. "We should go."

"Give it another minute, mate," said Jack as he leaned against the box behind him.

"Jack, we do not have time for this," said Buck.

Jack locked his fingers and placed his hands behind his head. "What's a few more minutes when we wasted a whole day in Milwaukee because ye had to go poke yer nose where it didn't belong?"

"You cannot possibly mean that," said Buck, sitting up.

Jack chuckled. "Of course not, but still, it won't do us any good if we waltz out of here thinking there ain't nothin' on the other side of this door. So, while we're waitin', and since we're in a sharing mood, tell me something about Euxinus. I mean, all its creatures can't be ugly."

Buck smiled at the playful insult, appreciating this side of Jack's personality. "Well, I can assure you, Jack, there are many creatures that call Euxinus home. And yes, some are better looking than I, but there are others that are as hideous as they are dangerous." He paused and rubbed his thumb along Maddie's soiled ribbon.

"Buck," said Jack.

"What? Right, creatures . . ." said Buck. "Well, the creatures you will have to be most mindful of when we arrive are the Coymorphs, the watchdogs of Euxinus. Their mandate is to capture any unauthorized Euxian roaming the streets. If we are lucky, we will reach the Apothecary's residence before you have the chance to see one, although you will be sure to hear them."

"Who's the Apothecary?"

Buck considered his words. "He is the head of the Euxian council."

"And yer certain he will take us in after yer defection?" asked

Jack.

"I know he will," said Buck.

"What makes ye so sure?"

"I . . ." Buck stopped, cut off by the sound of the door unhitching.

╫ELLHOUNDS

Jack swiftly rose to his feet, pressing his body against the secondary door. He placed his pointer finger to his lips and signaled Buck to remain quiet, cocking his head just enough to keep him in sight.

The truck door swung open.

Buck lifted a hand to block the blinding stream of natural light, his maladjusted eyes missing sight of the man standing in front of him.

"What the devil are ya doing in here, boy?" exclaimed the truck driver as he grabbed Buck by the arm.

There was no time for Buck to react as Jack's leg barreled toward his face, hitting the truck driver square in the chin. The man loosened his grip and fell backward onto the concrete.

"Jack—what—why did you do that?" asked Buck, flustered. He moved to the door—the truck driver was unconscious as a stream of blood trickled from his mouth. "By the powers, Jack, you could have killed him."

"Come now, Buck, don't get yer dander up. He'll be fine," said Jack, reaching for his turnip and blowing out the candle. "Besides, the hearty Norwegian and German folk of this area have good, strong heads. He'll wake up with one hell of a headache, but he'll at least be alive." Jack hopped off the truck and studied the blood on the truck driver's face. He might have dislocated his jaw.

"Jack," said Buck, leaning out the door.

Jack held out his hand to stop Buck from getting off the truck. "Ye should wait right here. I'll have a look around."

"But . . ." Buck tried to object, but Jack disappeared from sight. He leaned back against the boxes, feeling uneasy. Jack was supposed to refrain from hurting anyone, and he hoped this little mishap would not set him back. Buck fidgeted with his fingernails.

"It would be wise to go after him," said a familiar voice.

Buck jumped in a fit of fright as he searched for the tabby cat. He saw the feline's glowing pink eyes coming out of the shadows. It jumped gracefully from a high shelf and landed nearly in Buck's lap.

"Master Chameleon," said Buck. "What . . ."

Before Buck could finish, a trumpet of howls sounded.

Buck jumped off the truck as Jack darted toward him, passing what looked to be a fleet of trucks.

"Time to go," said Jack as he breezed by him. He leapt over the unconscious truck driver.

"Best you follow, Master Breedling," said the Chameleon, jumping out of the truck and trailing Stingy Jack.

Buck heard scratching at the door on the far side of the garage, his instincts aware of the threat. "Hellhounds," he said aloud.

Their muffled howls chorused in response.

Buck turned on a dime and ran after Jack, toward the opposite end of the garage. "Jack, wait!" he shouted, getting the Trickster to delay. "We need to find the river," he added when he caught up.

"What good'll that do?" asked Jack. "I ain't fixin' to drown, nor be cornered by Hades' pets."

"We do not have to cross it. We just need the water's edge. If not, a good patch of trees will do; hellhounds cannot climb."

"Aye, there is a prairie surrounding the garage with thick trees on the outer rim. I caught a glimpse of it when I peeked outside. Oi, what's this?" said Jack, pointing at the feline standing next to the Breedling, but he did not get an explanation.

At the far end of the garage, what sounded like an explosion erupted as the door clattered to the ground.

Jack grabbed Buck and braced them against the rear of the last truck in the line. He gave the Breedling some hand signals to address their next move, but it became apparent that Buck had no clue what he was trying to convey. Jack sighed and mouthed for him to follow as they inched to the front end of the truck. He peered over the hood to gauge their path to the exit, the door several feet away. They would be out in the open, sitting ducks for the hellhounds to pick them off, but it was their only way out. Jack spotted one of the hellacious breasts prowling toward their hiding place, its mangy black fur gnarled into spikes. Its fiery eyes darted over every inch, and just as it glanced in his direction, Jack dropped into a crouch. He pressed his back against the rubber tire and looked at Buck, the Breedling's expression as hopeless as he felt. There was no way of getting around the beast.

"Master Chameleon," whispered Buck as the tabby cat brushed past Jack's leg and darted into the open.

There was a massive yelp from the hound, followed by a ferocious growl and the pounding of a chase. Jack peered around the tire at the exit, their route momentarily clear. He got to his feet, not even giving Buck warning of his intention, and made a break for it. He immediately jiggled the knob but it refused to turn.

"Bloody Hell," he cursed and rammed his shoulder into it, the force rattling the aluminum walls, but the door did not budge.

In response to the noise, the three hellhounds converged on their position, fanning themselves out in attack formation.

"Buck, catch" said Jack, tossing the silver cross at the Breedling. "Fend 'em off while I pick the lock."

Buck thrust the sacred relic out in front of him and took a step forward. The hellhounds cowered, but they backed down no further. They snarled, acidic drool dripping from their lips. Out the corner of his eye, he saw the tabby cat spring into action, placing itself between the hounds and him. The feline's back was arched high, its fur defensively fluffed. One of the hellhounds attempted to strike, but the cat defended, slashing the beast with sharp claws. It yowled and pulled away, keeping the cat's eyes distracted and opening it to attack. The second hound struck and batted the feline with a swipe of its bearlike paw.

"No," shouted Buck, and threw himself at the hellhound, pressing the cross against its muzzle.

The beast's fur sizzled and it threw its head back, enraged, knocking Buck on his rear. The impact dislodged the relic from his hand and the third beast stalked up to him so close that he could smell the burning sulfur on its breath. Buck braced himself, anticipating the hellhound's teeth sinking into his skin, but his dismal attempt at self-preservation was needless. Buck lowered his arms and watched Jack fend off the beast, grab the cat, and made a mad dash for the open door. Buck followed, not even pausing to slam the door behind him. They ran straight into the thickening mist, losing sight of what lay ahead, leaving the sound of howls behind. Buck edged Jack out for the lead and collided with the invisible obstacle first. His body ricocheted off the chain link fence, forcing him backward.

"Fates be damned!" swore Buck as the small egg on his forehead throbbed instantly. He rubbed his fingers over the swelling bump as the mist floated through the diamond-shaped holes in the twelve-foot-high fence.

"Here, let me hoist ye over," said Jack. He stuffed the heirloom into his pocket and set the bleeding cat on the ground. He cupped his hands and bent his knees.

"I can climb," snapped Buck, his aggravation stemming from the tenderness of his head and the throb of his backside.

"Don't be ridiculous," Jack insisted.

Buck allowed Jack to hoist him up as howls sliced through the mist. He grabbed a hold of the top and pulled himself up. He swung his leg over and straddled the fence.

"Here," said Jack, holding up the cat.

Buck took the unconscious feline, fearful the Chameleon was dead. He cradled it in one arm as he threw his other leg over and jumped. Jack landed next to him as the three hellhounds barreled into the fence, each one bouncing off it and disappearing back into the mist. In a flash, however, they returned, using their oversized paws to dig in an attempt to outmaneuver their prey. Jack turned his back to them and flapped up his coat to expose his rear. He wiggled it back and forth, taunting the beasts.

"Jack, must you infuriate them?" scolded Buck. He smacked the Trickster on the shoulder.

"Words from the wise, Master Breedling," said Lydia as she appeared from the fog, dressed in a delicate scarlet robe.

Jack stopped and straightened. "Witch," he spat.

"I must say, Bartholomew," said Lydia, lacing her fingers through the fence, "I have never had such an exhilarating chase. It makes me," she shivered. "Oh, so giddy inside."

"Call off the dogs, Rachel," said Buck.

"Oh, honey," said Lydia, holding onto her vixen persona. Her hand began to glow, the fence wire warming a dull orange.

The hellhounds stopped digging and waited in anticipation for their General to break through. "You, the Trickster, and the Fates' spy are mine," she continued. "Oh yes, I'm well aware of the Chameleon's movements. It's been tracking you ever since Milwaukee."

Buck curled the feline against his chest. It released a feeble meow of discomfort.

Lydia curled a smile as pieces of the fence began to melt away.

"Buck, let's go," said Jack, and together they ran into the gray cloud.

Jack kept out in front, not realizing Buck had fallen behind until he heard the Breedling call his name.

"Jack!"

Jack halted, alone in the fog. He tried to part the haze with his eyes, but nothing but dense mist surrounded him. The hellhounds blasted a set of trumpeting howls, their swiftness an uncanny stampede. Jack reached for his heirloom, preparing for the inevitable strike.

"Jack!" shouted Buck.

Jack spun around toward the Breedling's voice and took a few steps, but he was quickly deceived, the mist subduing his senses. The prairie grass rustled behind him, and before he could do anything, one of the hounds clipped him. His feet lifted off the ground, and he fell backward into the grass. His head hit the earth, his breath deflating from his chest and his weapon dislodging from his grasp. Jack played dead in an attempt to mislead his attacker, but the beast's teeth tore through the fabric of his trousers and sank into his scrawny ankle. The pain was instant and he felt his voice rise in his throat. He let out a scream, giving away his position and, like a moth to the flame, another approached, biting on his outstretched arm.

"Jack!" shouted Buck.

Jack cried again as fire coursed through his body, every inch of him feverish and achy. The hellhounds dug deeper, their sharp teeth scraping against his bones, growling with satisfaction at the taste of their latest victim, but there was something wrong with it, something unpleasant. Abruptly, the hellhounds stopped and released Jack's appendages. They let out a collective whimper and with haste scampered away.

"Oh, Jack," said Lydia, as she hovered over him. "It's a pity our time has come to its end. I see now why Creator Hades finds you a delightful adversary."

Jack slithered on his back, his fingers searching for his weapon. "Jack!"

Lydia huffed and rolled her eyes. "Don't be a fool, Stingy Jack. The Breedling can't help you. He has no real power. Let me help you. Relinquish your right to stand witness and Hades will ensure the safety of Iona's soul. In fact, once he learns her secret, he'll let you have her—whatever's left, that is."

"Not bloody likely," said Jack through gritted teeth, his fingertips finding the metallic object. "Hades would never make such a bargain, especially not with the likes of me."

Lydia crouched and reached over his brow. He jerked his head away from her touch, but she brushed the lock of hair from his face.

"You will do this, Stingy Jack. Whether by will or force, the choice is yours," said Lydia.

"Then I choose her," said Jack, firming his fingers over the cross, lifting his injured arm off the ground, and plunging the heirloom against Lydia's cheek. She screamed as her flesh blackened, steam rising from the point of contact. Jack let out a roaring cry and lifted himself off the ground.

"Get out of me sight," he growled, and in a blink, Lydia was gone.

Jack collapsed back onto the ground, out of breath. Already he felt his flesh repairing itself, no doubt branding his body with more scars. He closed his eyes to fight the raging fever inside him. The damp grass seeped through his tattered coat, doing its best to counteract the sting of the hellhounds' fierce attack. Jack did what he could to remain conscious of the pain, to focus on expelling it, but his delirious mind only offered heartache, dredging up memories he thought he had long ago laid to rest.

From the Library of the Tales Teller
The Night She Died

*I*t was night by the time Stingy Jack ran for Iona's cottage through the persisting storm. Bridges washed away in the flooding creeks as the rain saturated the lowlands in the village. He ached from his urgency, his concern for Iona paramount. He knew he should never have left her cottage, but he had done so early in the day in order to meet the local merchant and pick up the gift he had purchased. When he arrived, however, the merchant had been out, and instead of waiting, he had made himself comfortable inside the lodge. One drink had led to another, and before he knew it, he had found himself in a brawl with a drunk. It had taken four men to separate them, dragging them both out into the street and down to the jail, where they were to spend time in a cell until they sobered. Stingy Jack had hardly been drunk, but if he wanted them to release him, he had to act the part and make it look like he was sleeping off his inebriation. The only problem was in doing so he had actually fallen asleep.

That was when the rain had started its terrifying deluge.

Stingy Jack had slept the day away until a sharp pain in his chest woke him. It made him catch his breath, and in his silent *heart, he knew something was wrong. He sprang from his cot, his feet splashing into water up to his knees. He grabbed the bars of his cell and yelled for the guard, but no one came. He shook the bars to no avail as the pain in his chest worsened and real fear gripped his heart so tightly that he would never know fear like it again. With all his might, he kicked and pulled, kicked and pulled, until he grabbed the submerged cot and slammed it into the door, unhinging it. He abandoned the prison, his legs unable to move faster than his thoughts, every fiber driven to find Iona.*

Stingy Jack raced through the flashes of lightning, the booms of thunder, and the terrorizing rise of water. He was soaked to the bone when he reached her cottage, the inside aglow with welcoming light. He breathed an elated sigh and trudged to the door, letting himself in.

"Iona," he called, dripping water and mud on to the floor. He stepped further inside, finding a tall thin figure standing over the hearth.

"Ah, Jacky," said Hades as he turned to greet the Trickster.

"Where is she?" shouted Stingy Jack, reaching his hand in his pocket, prepared to fight the Devil.

"Out, I'm afraid—searching fer me, in fact," said Hades nonchalantly. "Poor lamb, pity she doesn't know how much I detest rain, such dreadful Irish weather."

"I won't ask ye again, Devil," said Stingy Jack. "What have ye done with Iona?!"

The Devil merely walked around the skin rug and stood opposite the Trickster, his stature riddled with condolence.

"I'm sorry, Jacky," said Hades. "I'm afraid yer beloved Shepherdess is not long fer this world. But not to worry, I shall take good care of her. And if ye so choose, I'll let ye join her; all ye have to do is say the word."

"Tell me where she is," demanded Stingy Jack, removing the heirloom from his pocket, the silver gleam a soft golden hue from the hot embers.

Hades grinned.

Stingy Jack lunged at his rival, but the shifty Devil vanished, reappearing behind him. He had anticipated the move and with a quick reflex swung his arm for momentum, lifted his foot, and kicked Hades in the abdomen. The Devil stepped back a few paces and then a few more as Stingy Jack continued to force Hades into a retreat. Only the Trickster's first attempt struck his adversary, but it was not his intention to hit Hades, merely put him into a position that would align him with the door. He charged Hades, barreling into his waist, and together they flew across the porch and into the mud. Stingy Jack had the Devil pinned, poised to use his weapon and send him back to Hell, but his fear returned, paralyzing him.

Hades pushed the Trickster off him and stood over Stingy Jack's crippled body.

Stingy Jack curled his body into itself and felt himself splitting in half. He screamed in utter agony as Hades lingered to watch.

"Stop," cried Stingy Jack. "Make it stop."

"All ye have to do is ask," said Hades. "And ye will never feel pain again."

"No," groaned Stingy Jack, his lips gurgling in the muddy water.

"Then stay here with yer misery," said Hades, and he vanished.

A horrendous roar built inside Stingy Jack, his heart fracturing. In his head, he heard her deafening scream and then nothing. He knew then that she was gone, that his Shepherdess lay dead somewhere in the rain. Had she been alone, or had someone been there to comfort her in the final moments? The mere thought *fueled Stingy Jack as he staggered to his feet and ran back into the cottage, unleashing his rage. He smashed and broke and tore everything he could find, dismantling the home she would never return to, but none of it helped to numb his pain. Eventually he collapsed in front of the hearth, burying his face in his hands.*

The cottage was in shambles, his madness leaving a story for others to find and interpret. They would blame him for her death and rumors of foul play and possibly witchcraft would spread, eternally branding his beloved as an outcast rather than the saintly soul she was. Stingy Jack pounded his fists on the rug, his right hand brushing against rough metal. He tilted his head and saw the iron rod lying partially in the fire, its branding end primed. Stingy Jack blinked his tears away, and without any thought of consequence, he reached for the rod and pressed it into his flesh below the wrist. His skin sizzled as it burned. The pain worth his mistake. He punished himself until he fell unconscious, the mark of his beloved Shepherdess forever on his skin.

A Breedling's Master

Jack opened his eyes as sweat beaded his forehead. He sat up, reached for the effects in his pocket, and assembled his lantern. It illuminated the immediate space around him, the fog already thinning. He inspected his ankle, noticing the shredded fabric in wake of the hounds' attack. His sock was soaked, though not by his blood but by the saliva of the hellhounds. Jack removed the shoe and sock from his foot. Instantly, he felt much cooler and his fever broke. He tossed the sock away and re-shoed his naked toes. He pulled up the torn cloth around his ankle and, as suspected, the bruised skin was already healing, the enflamed flesh revealing teeth marks. Jack rolled his pant leg and checked his arm before reaching for the turnip lantern and trying to stand. The pain was dull as he put pressure on it, and he was confident walking would not be an issue. He waited a moment to get his bearings and then lifted the light over his head.

"Buck," he called out finally.

There was a brief moment of nothing until he saw the Breedling's silhouette appear. Buck drew closer, his brown corduroys still crusted with mud from the Milwaukee train yard. In his arms was the cat, its reddish-brown fur stained with blood—at least, he thought it was blood.

"Ye hurt?" asked Jack.

"Me, no," said Buck, his voice hoarse. "You?"

"Nothing I can't handle," said Jack. "And yer friend there?" He pointed to the cat.

Buck bit his lip. "About the cat," he started.

"Ye know what, Buck, just forget it," said Jack, and he began to walk into the dissipating fog. "I'm too exhausted at the moment. Let's find a place to hold up fer a spell."

"But we should be . . ." started Buck in protest.

Jack held up his hand. "Buck, I can't do it," he said. "I may look fine because I've grown accustomed to masking any feeling, but the truth of the matter is, I can barely stand."

"All right," said Buck. "But only for a short while. We are too exposed here and to ensure no further run-ins with Rachel, Hades, or any other demon; we need to find the Ferryman."

"Sure," agreed Jack as the mist cleared to reveal the deciduous forest around them, the smell of maple and cedar in the air. They hiked through a long stretch of thick foliage, until the trees thinned. Shrubbery and seedlings filled in the gaps left in the wake of fallen trees, surrounded by a layer of white puffy seeds. He scanned the area for any signs of danger, and unable to find any, he settled on a spot.

"This should do," Jack announced, limping over to a rather misshapen oak. Its branches hung low, twisted as if by some cruel entity. He set his lantern down and hoisted himself onto a branch, which dipped out of the trunk like an elephant's trunk. He placed his hands behind his head and crossed his legs, quite content with his choice.

Buck, however, was not as eager. "Are you sure this is where you mean to rest?" he asked. "I mean, the tree looks more apt to eat us than grant us lodging."

"Don't be ridiculous," said Jack, remaining unmoved from his spot.

Buck sighed and approached the tree. He placed the cat on a bed of moss at the roots of the tree and stroked the feline's stained fur, mouthing the Apothecary's healing prayer. He repeated the words four times before letting the cat rest. He reached out for a low branch opposite Jack and pulled himself onto the wooden appendage. Buck straddled the bark and settled himself as a wave of fatigue crashed against him.

"Buck . . ." said Jack, after a while.

"Yes," said Buck, happily closing his eyes.

"Before we get to the Ferryman, there's something I've got to know," said Jack. "Why now? I mean, it's been years since Iona's death. What took ye so long?"

Buck shifted uncomfortably on the branch but managed to maintain stability. "I was detained," he offered.

"Detained? Why?"

"Because I disobeyed," said Buck, "and for argument's sake, let us keep it at that for now. I am not willing just yet to share that story. But it has taken this long, as you say, because time does not exist the same in Euxinus as it does here. And what felt like two centuries to you was an endless void to me until it was not."

"So, how did ye get away?"

"I died," Buck replied, the weight of his answer resting heavily on his chest. He watched the leaves move under the command of the breeze, animating the shadows as the sun's rays kissed his skin.

"So ye fell, then. Why?" said Jack, after a moment.

"I thought that would be obvious."

"It is, mate, but I need ye to say it."

"I fell to save Iona," said Buck. "But I knew in order to do that I needed to find you."

"I see," said Jack.

Buck turned his head, pressing his cheek against the rough bark. "Do you?" he asked.

"I see enough to know ye rebelled and fled," said Jack, keeping his attention fixed on the sky. "I know ye are all I have to do what needs to be done to save me love. But knowing all that it still doesn't make me trust ye." Jack shifted on the branch to look at Buck. "I mean ye didn't even tell me yer name."

"Of course I did," said Buck.

"No, mate, Lydia called ye Bartholomew."

"That is not my name anymore," Buck snapped.

"That doesn't make any sense," said Jack. "I haven't even gotten to the hard questions, like how did ye find me? Stop skirting around and just tell me the truth."

"It is not as simple an answer," objected Buck defensively. "To begin, you need to understand that though I may have severed all ties with the Fates, I cannot escape what I am. I am a soulcatcher, and in order to do my duty, I must be tethered to a soul. And to do that, I need someone with the power to charge me to my mission. When I escaped, or fell, as you put it, I had no idea how I would accomplish finding you without a master. My hope was to awaken in Eden, so that somehow, even without my will bound to finding you, I would at least be in the same realm as you. And I thought that maybe, just maybe, my will alone would be enough. But when I awoke, none of it mattered, for I awoke surrounded by fire."

"Ye thought ye were in Hell."

"Yes," said Buck. The phantom smell of smoke filled his nostrils. "I thought for sure I had gone to the realm of Hades— but then the unexpected happened."

"What?"

"I was saved," said Buck, in a pinched voice.

"Saved?"

"By a boy named Charlie Reese."

"Reese? Ye mean that older lad from Ziemba's Speakeasy? The one who was runnin' from Hades?" asked Jack, recalling the broad-shouldered lad with toffee eyes.

"Running from Hades? Hades was not in the speakeasy."

"Oh, I assure ye he was," said Jack. "I mean, I'm not surprised ye don't remember, as drunk as ye were, but yer mate, Charlie, was in a serious bind. On the one hand, he had Hades to deal with and on the other, there were three goons fixing to nab ye first chance they got. I think they might have been a few of Kalvis' men. Anyhow, I believe Charlie started the fight, just to get enough of a distraction to deter both of his opponents. It turned out to be quite the spectacle, if ye ask me."

"You were there," said Buck, finally making the connection. Jack must have been the Irish bloke Charlie had been referring to at the bar.

"Aye," said Jack. "I saw the whole damn mess unfold, and he whisked ye right out of there as soon as the goons were neutralized. As fer Hades, come to think of it, if ye hadn't shown up, I might not have seen the Devil as soon as I did. Funny thing, too, because I had at first thought Hades had been there for me, when really . . ." Jack laughed. "And ye really didn't know I was there?"

"No," said Buck. "At the time I had no way of knowing you were there. Not because I was impaired by vice, but because I had no means of a connection with you." He paused. "In hindsight, it was foolish of me to think my will would have been enough, but the truth was, I needed a master. I had never considered the possibility a mortal could take the place of the Fates, but as I said, when I came here, Charlie saved me. In his act of selflessness to rescue me from the fire, he not only claimed me as his responsibility, but he also gave me a new name, a new life. With one word, he could command my actions and do with me as he wished. He could charge me to find you, tether my will to your soul. But in my error, I did not see the connection right away, and so the honor went to another possessing the power of his proxy," said Buck, leaving out the part about Father Van Lewen.

"And where is he now, yer Charlie?" asked Jack.

"Gone," said Buck. "Safe, I hope." He looked down at the Chameleon, hoping the Euxian spy had news from the Apothecary. He returned his gaze to the branches overhead. "It was my fault really, I gave Charlie no choice but to run, and he had done so much for me already. How could I ask him to come with me? Besides, Euxinus is no place for a mortal. None have ever ventured across the threshold, nor is it known if one could even survive in the realm's sulfuric atmosphere." Buck closed his eyes, his mind drifting.

"Buck?" asked Jack.

"Please, Jack, no more questions."

"Just one more," said Jack, and before Buck could object, he asked, "Yer prison, is . . ."

"Is that where Iona is?" said Buck, finishing the Trickster's question. "No, Jack. The Reformatory is no place for amid souls. Instead, they are held in the heart of Hollow Mountain, beneath the trial chambers. The Reformatory is reserved primarily for spies and thieves in the guise of angels and demons. It is for the most valuable of mortal souls, known as Spirits, and for the most dangerous, the cursed Wickers. And on the rarest of occasions, the Euxian prison contains the rebellious creatures of the Fates."

"Wait," said Jack. "I thought ye just said mortal souls are not held in the prison."

"And they are not," said Buck, his sleepy calm subsiding. "Spirits are not amid souls."

"That makes no sense."

"That is because there has been little time to explain," said Buck. "But I will do the best I can. When mortals die, there are three paths of ascension: the soul, the spirit, and the Eden Wanderer. Souls are will-less and shapeless, merely an essence of energy, which as you will recall are coveted by Hades and Everlyse in their continual efforts to harvest power. Now, amid souls, or unclaimed souls, are much like claimed souls with the exception that they are put on trial to determine sense of ownership. The second path of ascension pertains to a mortal's level of enlightenment. If in life a mortal had seen through the veil and discovered things about the nature of the supernatural, in death they are able to maintain their physical appearance in essence as well as their free will, but not their physical body. Spirits have become rarer as mortals grow farther apart from their roots, forgetting they exist alongside immortals, which has made their energy all the more desirable."

"And the third is the Eden Wanderer," said Jack.

"A mortal soul made of flesh and free will, a soul that cannot be claimed."

Buck nestled his head against the rough bark scratching his scalp, awaiting the Trickster's next question, but Jack did not speak again. It left him with swirling thoughts of Charlie, Maddie, and young Danny O'Toole. Even if none of the three mortals realized it now, they would all, in some way, have a role to play in what was to come. He felt a twinge of guilt for getting them involved, although in Maddie's case, she had already been influenced by the Apothecary. Several years would pass in Eden before any return was possible. The mere thought unnerved him, and he worried not only for Charlie's safety, but for Maddie's safety as well. Would Hades seek her out? Would he have Rachel continue to act as Lydia only to steal her away?

Buck tossed, his head almost forcing his body to fall from the branch. His only consolation was that Hades did not know about young Danny. Then again, nothing was stopping the Master of Hell or Rachel from returning to Minneapolis to finish what they had started, for both had seen Danny's son in the street with his cousins. The recollection threw him into a fit of panic until he recalled the boy Colin's words. *We Irish are well-acquainted with the stories of Old Hob. Don't fret; if the Devil comes a-calling, we'll give him a fight.* He could not begin to know what protection the O'Toole family had to fend off Hades, if they had any at all, but if the mortal had spoken the truth, then the youngest O'Toole had a fighting chance.

Regardless of his newfound fondness for the mortals he cared about, he had to again set his feelings aside and trust in the governing force that was driving him forward, the charge Father Van Lewen had given him. Stingy Jack needed to stand as witness, they needed to save Iona, and the Lost Creators needed to be found.

Ferryman

A strong breeze swept through the river valley, filling every nook and cranny of the wood. It skirted across the surface of the nearby river and sent the clouds eastward to unveil the early evening sun. The leaves rustled while the branches swayed, the wind forcing the trees to move their aging limbs, some wishing that they could once again move as freely as they did in their youth. The songbirds sang their merry melodies, ushering in another strong gust, which funneled through the underbrush, disturbing the lower branches.

Jack awoke from the rocking, stirred from his unusual dreamless rest. His eyes slowly opened and in no time he was sitting up, combing his hair with the bark of the tree. Feeling resumed throughout his sleepy appendages, a tingling sensation skipping between his shoulders and fingertips to his hips and his toes. He straddled the branch—a most uncomfortable position, but he needed to maintain his balance. He removed his tattered coat and draped it across the limb. He sat for a while and looked down at his lantern, realizing he had forgotten to blow it out. The yellow hue tossed about in the warm breeze, but refused to die.

Jack smiled. Even though the wretched trinket had been a gift from Hades, he could not imagine the years since his death without it. In addition, its resilience to the elements had always astounded him. No breath, nor wind, water, or wax could douse the flame's glow. Not even dirt could extinguish it. Jack hopped off the branch, his ankle no longer plaguing him with pain, and reached for the turnip. He brought the totem to his lips and blew gently, the flame obeying his breath's command—the only force capable of extinguishing its life. He placed his effects back in his coat and then wiggled his body as he danced around in a circle. When he was through, he expected to find Buck still sleeping on the branch next to him, but to his surprise, the Breedling was not there.

"Buck!" he shouted, scanning the woods, his eyes sighting nothing but trees. His thoughts turned dark and he feared Lydia or Hades had found them. The Breedling had warned that the Master of Hell would stop at nothing to prevent him from standing as Iona's witness, obsessed with the shared secret they possessed. Jack moved around the trunk of the oak tree to survey his rear position.

"Buck!" he shouted again. The whole forest suddenly seemed to expand and an onset of dizziness clouded his brain. "Buck!"

"What?" sounded the questioning voice behind him.

Jack tripped as he stepped over the protruding roots and found Buck standing with his arms cradling his beige jacket, which was full of honeysuckle flowers. The sleeves of his shirt were rolled to his elbows, the orange ribbon no longer visible on his hand. Jack took a few strides toward the Breedling and placed his hands on Buck's shoulders. He then gripped his chin and tilted his head back, checking his neck. There were no signs of any injury. Jack tried to check the rest of him, but Buck squirmed away.

"Jack, what is wrong with you?" asked Buck, acting more surprised than irritated.

"I, er . . ." Jack tousled his hair. "I was just checking ye fer ticks. I can't stand those nasty buggers." He put a weak smile on his face and forced a laugh.

Buck smiled, clearly aware of Jack's attempt to mask his concern. "I brought these for you," he said, changing the subject. "Call it food."

Jack responded with a full grin, his expression more at ease as Buck set his jacket carefully in his arms so as not to drop any of the bell-shaped flowers.

"I know it is not much," Buck continued. "I would have brought some apples, but I forgot their flowers are in bloom this time of year."

"It's quite all right. These will be fine. I've grown quite fond of honeysuckles." Jack bit the balls of nectar from three flowers and disposed of them by throwing them on the ground. "So, in yer quest for sustenance, did ye find the river?" he asked.

"I caught a glimpse of it not far from here."

"Then lead the way," said Jack, eating the last of the honeysuckles. He handed Buck his jacket as yellow pollen sprinkled from it.

Buck wrapped it around his waist before bending down to pick up the sleeping cat.

"Still hasn't come around?" said Jack, swinging his coat over his shoulder.

"No," said Buck.

Jack stroked the feline's head and instantly its purring motor revved. "Well, it's certainly got some fight left in it," he said.

"Jack, about the cat," said Buck.

Jack lifted his hand. "I understand, Buck," he said. "This isn't no ordinary feline." He gave the cat another stroke. "I had plenty of time to think about what ye said. And, well, I ain't sorry fer doubtin' ye; however, ye haven't given me reason not to trust ye.

So, if ye say the cat is a friend, we'll leave it at that fer now."

"All right," said Buck, and he led the way through the forest, the dwindling shade giving way to the full exposure of the sun.

Jack rolled his sleeves to his elbows, exposing the brand above his wrist and numerous scars on his flesh. He caught Buck taking a curious peek at it, so he tugged his sleeve to cover it again. The tree line opened to the view of the river with a patch of beach on its bank. The murky water of the Minnesota River clashed with the rich sandy limestone, and they stood on the bank for a moment, admiring the sight. A drop of sweat rolled down Jack's cheek. Tired of the heat, he ran toward the river, dropping his coat to the ground. He lifted his knees high, prancing deeper into the water, every step growing cooler. When it was almost to his shoulders, he dove in then sprang out from under the water, his head facing the opposite bank, his legs treading.

"Buck, come join me, the water is fine!" Jack dunked his head under the water again then lifted it back up to gain the Breedling's response.

"Not a chance!" refused Buck.

"Oh, come on now," said Jack as he splashed at the water with his hands.

"No, Jack." A hint of sternness escaped Buck's lips.

"Yer loss!" shouted Jack as he pushed onto his back and floated, soaking in the rejuvenating chill.

Buck shook his head. If the Trickster wished to swim in water he could not see the bottom of, well, then that was his prerogative. He, on the other hand, had long ago acquired an aversion to murky water, the result of a most unpleasant experience.

"Still afraid of the water, Master Breedling?" purred the cat.

"Master Chameleon," said Buck, setting the feline on the ground. "You are alive."

"Thanks to you, I believe," said the tabby cat. "And to your charge." The feline's eyes looked out upon the water at the Trickster. "It appears congratulations are in order. Stingy Jack has completed the trials of the witness."

Buck knelt in the sand. "Master Chameleon, what news do you bring?" he asked, losing all focus on Jack.

"Bartholomew, you know it is unwise to speak of such matters in the open. Rachel and her hellhounds are still on your trail," said the cat.

"Yes, I know," said Buck, folding his hands together in a begging plea. "I know the risk, but in order to go forward I must know. Is Charlie safe? Do you know where he is?"

The Chameleon considered the Breedling's request. "Very, well, but I will only tell you that the charge has been given to Coyote Moon."

"The Animawalker Prince?" said Buck, surprised by the news. "But I thought the Son of Sea renounced his charge to protect mortals after the Black Tortoise disappeared."

"He did, but like Stingy Jack, the Prince of Sea does not deal in absolutes. He has been known over the centuries to relapse on his self-inflicted vow of apathy, unable, like Stingy Jack, to escape the righteous voice in his head."

"But what is to stop him from abandoning Charlie if his allegiance is broken?"

"I cannot tell you how," said the Chameleon. "But Coyote Moon is as strong a warrior as any and the Eldest has ensured the Animawalker's unbreakable word, and on this matter I shall speak no more."

Buck sighed. "My thanks," he managed, and looked out at the water again as Jack swam a figure eight. The murky water rippled from his efforts, spilling in over the sand, inching toward his feet. He shuddered.

"And there it is again, the fear," purred the cat.

"You know well of my phobia," said Buck.

The tabby cat sat back on its hind legs. "Ah, yes," said the cat. "But do you? Do you remember what happened to you that day?"

Buck closed his eyes, unwilling to answer, but by ignoring the conversation, it brought forth images he thought he had forgotten. The Fates had charged him to assist the Retrievers in the extraction of a powerful soul by the name of Alhazen. The Eden year was 1040, and he had tracked the location of the soul to the Nile River north of Cairo. He had fallen behind as the Retrievers were in pursuit. Just as he caught up, an ambush laid by both Everlyse and Hades commenced, and their combined forces outnumbered the Retrievers. His defense skills were no match against a hoard of angels and demons, so he kept his distance. As the skirmish continued, he took up the chase as Rachel tracked Alhazen to the river. Cunning in his evasion, Alhazen disappeared into the water, leaving Buck alone on the water's edge with Rachel and the angel general, Mist. It was unclear to him what happened next, but he had somehow found himself in the water, pressed beneath by an attacker. His skull felt the crushing pressure, his attacker's strength far exceeding his own. He struggled into an uncertain blackness and yet there was a sort of peace to it, a sense of letting go, sort of like dying.

Buck opened his eyes and looked at his hands. "No," he breathed.

The tabby cat stamped its paw. "Best to keep such words to yourself, Master Breedling," warned the Chameleon as hounds yowled in the distance. "Time you were off. I shall do my best to provide a suitable distraction for your pursuers." The cat nodded in a slight bow and then darted into the underbrush.

Buck simply shook his head and curled his fingers into his palms as howls moved further away from their location. He could not be certain of the truth, but if he was right, it would mean everything Maddie had told him about his gift was true and that, unbeknownst to him, the Black Tortoise had blessed him in the waters of the Nile. Buck returned his gaze to the river, searching for Jack, when he noticed movement on the opposite beach. He narrowed his eyes and saw a small boat.

"Jack!" Buck waved to the Trickster as he bobbed his head out of the water again.

Jack grunted and swam back to shore. He removed his long-sleeved shirt, revealing his pale chest, marked with scars, and wrung out as much water from the cloth as possible. He furled the shirt and pulled it over his head. It was soggy next to his skin, but he did not mind. He slid up the beach to pick up his coat, gave it a good shake, and tossed it over his shoulder before making his way over to Buck. Standing next to him, Jack placed a hand to his brow to see the small wooden boat nestled on the other side of the river. Next to it, an old man kicked sand over his fire to smother the flames.

"Ahoy!" shouted Buck, giving the old man a wave.

The old man waved back before taking four paces to his boat. With all his might, the old man pushed the boat into the water and moved with the vessel as water crept up his denim overalls to his knees before he leapt inside. The old man sat next to the outboard motor and started it by pulling on the rope. The motor revved and a puff of smoke shot out of it. The old man steered the boat to the other shore, whistling a crisp tune, the notes projecting across the water. He slowed the engine and rammed the boat into the beach.

Jack and Buck dodged out of the way.

"You boys need a ferry?" asked the old man with a German accent.

"You heading to Mankato?" asked Buck, noticing the old man was not looking at him, but rather straight ahead.

"Does the rooster cock his head at the rising sun?" asked the old man.

Jack and Buck looked at each other with questioning expressions, neither of them sure how to respond.

"The correct answer is, yes," said the old man with a chuckle. "Now, why don't you boys hop in?"

Buck climbed aboard and sat down midway in the boat. Jack took a moment longer as he waved his hands, trying to gain the old man's attention, but when he had no success, Jack pushed the boat off the beach and hopped in front. The old man turned the rudder and steered the boat into the heart of the river's current. Buck watched the old man closely, studying his face. Several crevices fell down the sides of his neck, his wrinkled skin far more aged than Mr. McGregor and more weathered by the elements. The old man's denim overalls were sunbaked, much like the skin on his arms and broad shoulders. His thick, short salt-and-pepper hair was bushy with elegant curls, but it did not cover up the nasty scar on his widow's peak, which beamed white. Jack waved his hand again, but the old man did not even flinch.

Buck rolled his eyes. "Jack," he whispered. "The man is blind."

The old man continued to ignore his new passengers and steered the boat through the water. He eased up on the rudder, and with his free hand reached into his sack and took out two tin bowls.

"You boys fancy some grub?" he asked, his face wrinkling more when he smiled.

"Yes, sir," Buck answered while Jack absentmindedly nodded.

The old man put the bowls into another sack, sitting at his feet. He scooped up its contents and stretched out his hand. Buck grabbed the bowls one by one, passing one up to Jack, who hugged it greedily. Jack looked at the strange nuts— peanuts, but they were unlike any he had seen before. The color was all wrong. He popped one into his mouth and, sure enough it tasted like a peanut, though he found its texture to be softer and saltier than usual. Buck, on the other hand, wasted no time and threw several in his mouth, his taste buds savoring every morsel.

"You boys from around these parts?" asked the old man.

"No, sir," mumbled Buck, his mouth full.

"Please, call me Goober," said the old man. "Though don't be letting mein mutter hear you say that," he added with a hearty chuckle.

"Why's that, Goober?" asked Jack, playing along, though he was sure the old man's mother was dead and gone judging by his age.

The old man laughed. "Mein mutter, God rest her soul, named me Ellis James Moldaschel and she'd be damned if anyone called me anything different. She wasn't fond of nicknames."

"If you do not mind me asking, how did you get your nickname?" asked Buck, trying to sound as curious as possible, but all he could think about was how delicious the salt on the peanuts tasted.

"I got the nickname back in the war," replied the old man. "I had been known for my craving of goober peas."

"What are goober peas?" asked Buck, tossing the last handful of nuts into his mouth.

"You ain't heard of goober peas? Well, son, you're eatin' 'em," replied the old man, his voice high-pitched with disbelief. "But I s'pose a couple of lads such as yourselves would not know such things."

"And why's that, Goober?" asked Jack, this time mumbling his words through his full mouth of boiled peanuts.

"Well, I reckon it's because you and Master Breedling here are quite beyond the simple pleasures of mere mortals." The old man smiled keenly.

Jack swallowed and began to cough violently. He turned to the front of the boat, rather embarrassed, and pounded his chest in order to dislodge the food stuck in his throat. He gasped and the bundle of peanuts slid down his gullet. He took a few breaths, while clearing the tears from his eyes before facing the rear of the boat.

"Many pardons, Master Ferryman," said Buck, dabbing his finger in the bowl to collect the remaining morsels of salt. He heard the mantra of Jimmy Reese chime in his head—*Waste not a drop.*

"Oh, it's quite all right, Master Breedling," said the old man as he began to laugh. "It's been so long since I've had company. Besides, I imagine this now poses an interesting question . . ."

"Please, Master Ferryman," addressed Buck.

"Please, Master Breedling," insisted the old man, "call me Goober."

"Goober, who told you of Jack?" asked Buck. "I was under the impression gatekeepers are uninformed about the passing of time."

"Ah, the question," said the old man. His smile faded. "While the latter is true, Master Breedling, I still have ears that can hear." The old man gave a wink. "I overheard several demons hunting for you in the woods. Nosey creatures. But that is neither here nor there, for I knew you were coming long before today. The water has whispered to me of your episodic adventure."

"But . . ."

The old man held up his hand to cut Buck short. "Master Breedling, I know you have questions, but we don't have time to entertain them all." Goober paused to maneuver around a fallen tree then killed the motor. "Now, if we could begin."

"Begin with what?" asked Jack.

"Master Jack," said the old man. "As I am sure Master Breedling has told you, to every journey into the Land of Euxinus one must first obtain a key in order to unlock an Eden Scar. What I'm sure Master Breedling has not told you is there are certain rites one must observe in order to gain this knowledge. It has become my eternal privilege to ferry those who seek such access, and it's therefore a matter of ceremony to ask a guardian to share a story. Now, Master Breedling, if you would be so kind as to begin."

"Master Ferryman," said Buck. "I come to you with a request to return to the Land of Dark Sky so that I may fulfill my charge and present this witness to the Hollow."

"And what is it you ask of me?" said the Ferryman.

"I seek the words that will grant me passage to the place that was once my home."

"Very well, Master Breedling. As you speak on your behalf, do you also speak on behalf of your charge?"

Buck glanced at Jack. He had always spoken for the souls he carried, but then again, those souls had no voices. "No," he replied, keeping his eyes on the Trickster. "Stingy Jack is no slave, nor squire, nor amid soul, and answers to no one but himself, save for the love he lost and whom awaits his witness. Therefore, he is a master unto himself, the soul that cannot be claimed, the

Eden Wanderer, and must speak on his own behalf, for to stand is his choice and his choice alone."

"As you say," said the old man, an impressed tone mingling with his words. "Master Jack . . ."

"Yes, sir," said Jack, taken aback by Buck's words.

"As Master Breedling has declined to speak for you, please, what is it you ask of me?"

"Um . . . I ask—I ask ye grant me and this Breedling safe passage to the land from whence he came, so that I may stand as witness fer the one I love."

"Well then, Master Breedling, Master Jack," continued the Ferryman. "If I were to tell you a story of a man who ate grass . . ."

"Then we would tell you the story of thirty-eight men who hung from the gallows," replied Buck, refocusing on the old man.

"And if I were to tell you such a story be true?" asked the Ferryman, lifting his finger to make an inquiry.

"Then I would say tell your story, for it will ensure our passage, on this my journey home," replied Buck. An eerie quiver slithered between his shoulder blades.

"Is your feeling the same, Master Jack?" questioned the old man.

"It is, Master Ferryman," said Jack. "Please, tell us the story of the man who ate grass."

"Then, by your request," said the old man, his eyes turning milky white. He raised his hand, casting a dark shadow around the boat. The scenery of the bluffs vanished, sweeping to the banks of the river. The boat sliced through the water, sending ripples outward, disturbing a pack of mallards, who took flight into the descending darkness. Jack and Buck both saw the large raccoon with fiery red eyes propped on the high perch of a protruding branch screaming at them, until it too disappeared. Sounds fell mute and the boat stopped swaying as though it were stationary on land. Ghostly images began to appear and as they became clear, the Ferryman spoke.

"It was the summer of 1862 . . ."

And just like that, Jack and Buck were surrounded by the setting of another time unlocked in the pages of the Ferryman's mind.

The Man Who Ate Grass *

*I*t was the summer of 1862, and the beginning of it marked the delivery of gold, a promised annuity from the government for the purchasing of land to the peoples of the Upper and Lower Sioux Agencies. It had become something upon which the Sioux depended on for survival, as hunting for wild game had become a tradition of the past. The annuity, unfortunately, never made it on its scheduled time, and forced the Sioux to resort to eating horses or dogs while others survived on roots and shriveled ears of corn. Chief Little Crow, who had long preached harmony with the settlers, began to trade weapons for food or relied on friends for meals. Times were hard, particularly because of the war between the North and the South, and things only worsened as the summer proceeded. There was talk of arms and war in the Land of Ten Thousand Lakes, but none of the chiefs wanted to start a fight with the settlers, especially one they could not hope to win. Instead, they decided to seek restitution and council before resorting to violence. And to do this, Chief Little Crow and his fellow chiefs requested an audience with Major Thomas J. Galbraith, the Indian Agent overseeing the affairs of the Agencies.

Thomas Galbraith was a detestable man, a masterful manipulator, incompetent and lacking the needed sense of humility to treat the Sioux with the respect they deserved. A month after the chiefs' initial meeting failed, five hundred destitute Sioux encamped around the storehouses, demanding food. Galbraith, feeling confident with the presence of a hundred or so soldiers from nearby Ft. Ridgley, remained regarding the procedures set in place and again refused their request. It, however, would not be the final word on the matter. For among the soldiers was twenty-five-year-old Lt. Timothy J. Sheehan of the 5th Minnesota Regiment, who, whether out of compassion or fear for his outnumbered men, persuaded the reluctant Galbraith to open the storehouses and dole out enough food to keep the Sioux from starving.

Come August 4th, after yet another month without the promised payment, an army of Sioux warriors descended on the Agency storehouses. One band eventually broke open the doors as the rest surrounded Lt. Sheehan and his men. Immensely outnumbered and out-maneuvered, Lt. Sheehan kept his men calm and, unlike Galbraith, did not underestimate their strength. As the raid continued, Lt. Sheehan noted the warriors were not out for blood, but were only interested in the collection of supplies. Quick to act, Lt. Sheehan and a detail pointed the artillery at the storehouse doors trapping the thieves inside.

Tensions escalated, but neither side wished for bloodshed. In response, Lt. Sheehan convinced Galbraith to authorize the distribution of pork and flour, on the condition that the warriors leave and send their chiefs for council the next day. The warriors agreed, taking their spoils home to awaiting hungry stomachs. The next morning, the chiefs of the Sioux Nation arrived to meet with Galbraith in the hopes an arrangement could be made. At the gathering, Galbraith had invited clerks of certain traders in the area, as well as an interpreter, and the most influential trader, Andrew Myrick.

Chief Little Crow spoke to these men on behalf of the chiefs, trying to convince them to provide food from their stores just until the annuity arrived. The interpreter translated, and Galbraith in turn put it to the clerks to decide. The clerks conversed in whispers away from the gathered chiefs in an attempt to reach a consensus and agreed to follow whichever course of action Myrick decided. Upon hearing this, Andrew Myrick rose from his chair and attempted to leave without a word. Galbraith, however, stopped him and demanded he voice his decision, to which Myrick answered, "Let them eat grass." The interpreter translated his words, and at first, the chiefs remained quiet. When the insult sank in, they rose to their feet in an uproar and left shouting.

In the days that followed, fighting and raids plagued the Minnesota River Valley, costing many lives, including Andrew Myrick, who was found dead with grass stuffed in his mouth and would forever be known as The Man Who Ate Grass.

ℰXODUS

The Ferryman reached for a tin cup at his feet as the dreamy dome began to evaporate, the ghostly shadows returning to their eternal rest. The sky appeared once more overhead, but the sun did not reappear, encased by darkening clouds. Crackles of thunder rumbled off in the distance and the air became unbearably muggy—all the makings of a cosmic storm. The bluffs reappeared with their ancient woods, stretching to the edges of the river. The water was the last thing to reemerge, its murkiness reflective. The Ferryman took a drink of his rye, quenching the dryness in the back of his throat, and started the motor, its propellers shattering the glass calm of the river as ripples protruded outward toward each bank. The old man began to whistle again as though to entertain his company, but instead, it pulled them from their trance.

"Master Jack, is there something you wish to ask?" said the old man, his eyes fixed on the front of the boat as he piloted it toward their end destination.

Buck crooked his head to look at Jack.

"I'm wonderin' where ye fit in," asked Jack, his words lethargic. "I mean, how is it ye became the gatekeeper of this Scar?"

"I can't tell you what I myself don't know, Master Jack," said the old man. "Although, be it as I don't know why, I can tell you the part I played in the overall story."

"Please, Goober," said Jack.

"Then, by your request," said the old man. "Mein mutter, God rest her soul, was a fine woman, but a little too promiscuous for her own good. She had come from a strict Christian family, and like any young woman of the time seeking the adventures of the West, she secretly rebelled against her father. First by lying with men, then by consuming liquor, and in the end, she ran away to the opening frontier. I was born sometime along the way; she never really told me when. And when I would ask her to tell me stories about my father, she would only say he had been gentle, as I was to be, and that he came from a great people.

"I never really understood her words, until she confessed to me in her last breath that I was a part of two worlds and that leaving me all alone in it was the cruelest thing she would do. It was then I realized I was a half-breed. I didn't hate her for her words. For I was able to pass myself off as a white well enough. So I wandered, making trade where I could, and found myself here in the Land of Ten Thousand Lakes."

The Ferryman paused to wipe his brow with a handkerchief and then stuffed it in the flap of his overalls. He steered the boat closer to the eastern bank along the bend in the river as puffs of factory smoke appeared in the distance.

"I ferried many years on this river," Goober continued, "acting as an independent trader. It was a solitary life, but the river accepted me, and I was grateful for that. I was returning to Fort Snelling in Minneapolis when the annuity was being prepared for shipment. I was asked by a low-ranking officer if I would be willing to provide my services and ferry the annuity to Agency headquarters. I agreed, though I had some reservations it would not all fit on my ferry, for I already had several supplies and goods to carry. The soldiers loaded the boat, and it sank. Luckily, it was tied up well enough and off the main channel, so the ferry didn't go anywhere except down. It took several days to fish out the cargo and resurface the ferry, but without some needed repairs I was unable to deliver the annuity, and as I waited, I overheard the officer arranging land transport."

"So you were the reason the annuity was late," said Jack. "Do ye think maybe that's why yer here, as punishment?"

"An interesting question, Master Jack," said the Ferryman. "But for that, I have no answer. What I know is the part I played, and it is safe for me to say further delays were not on account of me."

Goober's voice trailed off as he steered the boat to a small landing next to an ascending wooden staircase, leading up the slope of the southern bank. He killed the motor and reached for the rope at his side as the boat slipped right next to the landing. With the rope, he tied off the boat and instructed Jack to tie off the front end, securing the vessel.

"Well, lads, here we are—the river town of Mankato," announced the old man, breaking their silence. He gestured his arm and pointed out the stairs. "All you have to do is scale the bank and walk toward the train station. Your way should become clear from there."

Buck sat frozen in the boat, still slightly lost in the Ferryman's story as though he had not fully awakened from a dream.

"Come on now, ashore you go," said the Ferryman. "You don't want to be late."

"Late?" said Buck, his voice questioning, trying to gain some sense of recognition. His temples began to throb, the pain trying to tell him he had arrived at their destination. He blinked and the haze in front of his eyes lifted.

"The trial, of course," said the old man. "Best not keep Miss Iona Covington waiting."

"How . . ." started Jack.

The old man cut Jack off with a snap of his fingers. "Master Jack, you have all you need. But if there be a question lingering in the back of your noggin, then let me leave you with this," said the Ferryman, placing his hand back into his lap. "I may be spellbound in this limbo by decree of the Fates, to ferry on this river the ones who seek passage into Euxinus, but I say to you both, though I admit nothing, I have never served them. For it is this river I have always called my home."

"What does that mean?" asked Jack. "Why raise another question?"

"I am certain that when the time comes, Master Breedling will figure it out. If not, I leave it to your wit, Master Jack, to decipher the riddle." The old man smiled at their questioning faces, his eyes disappearing under the folds of his wrinkles, and he again gestured for them to leave.

Jack was the first to move, and once on the dock offered Buck his hand and lifted the Breedling out of the boat.

"A thousand pleasures to have made your acquaintance," sang Goober, stretching out his hand.

Jack shook the old man's hand, surprised by his firm grip.

"Be well, Master Jack," the old man continued. "And see well to your lass. The secret she bears is too valuable to fall into the hands of the feuding Creators or the Fates."

"I shall," said Jack weakly as a sudden weight descended upon his shoulders. He let go of the old man's hand and went to untie the rope at the front end of the boat.

Buck inched closer and reached for the Ferryman's hand.

"Keep your charge safe, Master Breedling, for too important is he to be tainted by Hades any further than he already is," said the old man as Jack threw the rope into the boat.

Buck stared at the old man, his cloudy eyes staring right back at him. He opened his mouth, tempted to ask the question, but Goober stopped him.

"Please, Master Breedling, you must keep him safe. As well as yourself, for there are many things that you still must do."

"I swear," said Buck. He reached into his pocket and placed two coins in the old man's palm. "For services rendered, Master Ferryman. And may the one you do serve look favorably upon you and keep you as you are, true and steadfast, gentle like your father, for you are from a great people."

"As to you, Master Breedling," said the old man with a smile. "May your young master see someday the quality of servitude you bring to him and honor you for it." The old man closed his fingers around the coins and brought his hand into his chest, presenting Buck a subtle salute.

Buck replied with the same amount of grace and respect.

Goober stowed the two coins in the front pouch of his overalls and untied the rope, pushing the boat away from the landing. Jack moved next to Buck, the two of them standing side by side, as they watched the Ferryman continue up the river. He gave them one last wave farewell and began to sing, his voice fading in the distance.

"Tis a sigh that is wafted across the troubled wave.

Tis a wail that is heard upon the shore.

Tis a dirge that is murmured around the lowly grave.

Oh hard times come again no more."

* * *

Atop the sloped staircase, bellows of livestock, churning factories, and dinging of church bells that rang the three o'clock hour greeted Jack and Buck. The mighty presence of the four-story red brick of Hubbard Milling Co. towered over the rail lines snaking near the river's edge. The buzz of motorized vehicles and the mingling smells of flour, oil, and coal swirled in the air. Each of them felt overwhelmed, as though it had been years since either of them had set foot amongst civilization. They passed by a water works station, heading up Washington toward Front Street, but Jack stopped on the empty tracks in recognition of a herald's voice.

"Extra, extra, read all about it! Strike escalates in Minneapolis!"

On the corner across the street, a newsboy held a bundle of papers under one of his arms and a single copy high in the air to get the attention of those passing by. At the sound of the headline, flocks of men gathered around him, buying every paper he had. The boy graciously counted his money with a delightful smile and then stashed the coins into his pockets before leaving the gathered crowd to discuss the latest news.

"Jack, what is it?" asked Buck. His eyes wandered for signs of any otherworldly spies.

"I wonder how Danny is faring," Jack admitted.

"I am sure he is fine, Jack," said Buck, giving the Trickster a sympathetic look. "Hades' main objective was to make you unfit to stand as witness, and since he has failed in this attempt, there is no need to return for Danny or his family."

"What do ye mean by unfit?" asked Jack as the crowd of man began to disperse.

"It is required of all witnesses to demonstrate three deeds of compassion, Jack, in order to be deemed worthy. One for a stranger, one for someone they know, and one for the unknown.

I did not tell you this when we first met because any knowledge of it would have influenced your actions and they needed to be genuine."

"The woman," said Jack, in realization. "You tricked me."

Buck smiled. "More like, presented you with the opportunity."

Jack laughed. "And Danny? The cat?" he asked.

"Neither of which were my doing at all," said Buck. "Those were entirely of your own accord. Iona would be proud."

Jack's face beamed with a hopeful smile, and he placed a hand on the Breedling's shoulder. "I don't know the last time I genuinely meant these words, but thank you, Buck. Thank you for getting me this far."

"And may your gratitude be rewarded," said Buck. "But I cannot accept what has not been finished and there is still more that needs to be done." He patted the Trickster's hand. "Now, let us go save your Shepherdess."

Jack sighed and rolled back his shoulders. "Aye," he said. "Then let's not keep Iona waiting."

They followed the tracks to Main Street, each of them taking in one last look at Eden as they stood waiting for traffic to let them cross the street. Buck watched an elderly man and a young boy walk over the bridge, the boy carrying two wooden sticks against his shoulder like rifles and the elderly man carrying a large bucket of fish. Jack followed the path of a black Ford Coupe as it rumbled past, stopping outside the Grand Saulpaugh Hotel, whose architecture, though unimpressive, enticed the trickster within him for one last adventure. But he easily denied that part of himself. Jack stole himself away and looked directly across the street at the six-foot-tall granite marker.

"Is that it?" he asked.

"Yes," said Buck, dashing across the street, Jack a step behind him. "The stone marks the spot."

"Buck, are ye sure we are in the right place? I don't see any gateway," said Jack further investigating the monument.

"Really? It is right in front of us." Buck pointed toward the chiseled side of the marker.

"All I see is a gravestone, Buck," said Jack. "With an engraving: *Here were hanged 38 Sioux Indians Dec. 26th 1862.*" He looked at Buck. "Are ye sure this will work?"

"Jack, do you trust me?"

"I—" Jack took a deep breath. "Aye, Buck, I trust ye."

"Then everything will be well. All you have to do is walk toward the fence."

"All right," said Jack, returning to his spot at the Breedling's side. He took a hesitant step forward, but rocked back on his heel. "Buck, I think ye should go first." His voice trembled as two rail workers walked along the tracks, their expressions leery of them.

Buck gave them a nod, but they responded by quickening their pace. "Jack, you have to go first, otherwise I cannot be sure you will follow me. I promise you, nothing will happen to you. As I said, all you need to know is where the Scar is and hear the story that unlocks it. We have heard a story, and you know where it is. There is nothing more to be said about it."

Jack stepped forward, but still he hesitated. "What's it like?"

Buck sighed. "What is what like?"

"Euxinus—what's it like?"

"It's a dark, desolate world, Jack, a skeleton of a once greater realm. The air smells of sulfur and is stale and cold, but no breeze blows in the valley anymore. It is absent of color, grace and life. A wasteland. Jack, if you are too frightened..."

"I'm nothing of the sort," huffed Jack. "It's just . . ."

Buck searched the Trickster's face, his expression mildly somber.

"Ye said that Eden Scars were created during times of tragedy and injustice."

"I did," replied Buck, his eyes catching sight of a red-winged blackbird soaring overhead and landing on the telephone wire next to the hotel.

Jack hung his head, unable to look Buck square in the eye. "When Iona died—did her death create a Scar?"

Buck's expression softened. "No, Jack," he offered. "Iona's death was far greater than the creation of any Scar. When she died, Eden itself mourned."

Jack inhaled. *Courage, me love, courage,* Iona's voice whispered, putting him at ease. "I'm coming, me love," he said under his breath, and closed his eyes. Jack took a few steps forward and suddenly all the sounds, smells, and sights of Eden evaporated and he himself was gone from the world.

Buck waited until Jack disappeared before lifting his gaze once more to the red-winged blackbird and its mate.

The birds chirped in unison, acknowledging him, but remained at a distance on their perch.

Buck nodded in reply, suddenly hesitant to follow Jack.

"They are here at the behest of the Apothecary, Master Breedling," meowed the Chameleon as the tabby cat approached.

"Why?" asked Buck, turning to the feline. "The Beloved Twins are only known to serve the interests of Heaven."

"As they do, but their loyalty solely lies with the Fallen—the Lady Vala—who, like the Prince of Sea, has given her word to assist the Apothecary and the Euxian council in the recovery of the Lost Creators," said the Chameleon.

"Who else?" asked Buck, counting to four with his fingers— *Father Van Lewen, Maddie, Coyote Moon, Lady Vala.* "Are there more than seven?"

"No," replied the cat, flicking its tail. "But you should not concern yourself with such matters. Your charge awaits."

Buck felt the tug of a memory he could not quite recall, but knew it was in regards to the number seven. *Seven what?* He tried to fish for the information, but as the Chameleon had addressed, he had no time to linger on the thought. He glanced back at the red-winged blackbirds, questioning their motives. But he again had no time to challenge the Chameleon's claim and had to trust that the Fates' spy spoke the truth about them. He looked down again at the cat, the feline's pink eyes alert.

"See you soon," he said and stepped forward.

In an instant, the beauty of Eden disappeared and he found himself in a void of darkness. He felt a tight grip squeeze his heart, coaxing him to turn back, but then his ears rang with the sound of Iona's scream and he took another step forward. Sulfur filled his nostrils as each step drew him further into the black until, at last, the eternal night sky overhead glowed with a hint of blue. He was home.

From the Library of the Tales Teller
The Shepherdess's Secret

*I*ona *lay in the mud when Bartholomew found her, her eyes swollen and her once buttery skin a sickly shade. She seemed out of strength, and though he was not fully equipped with an understanding of mortals, he knew something was wrong with her. He could feel her sorrow, but it was more than that, and somehow he empathized with her pain as her soul ripped apart. He knelt down at her side, powerless to help, but he had not come to rescue her. He came to make sure he was right about her, that she was more than what she seemed. He judged her with critical eyes, showing her no ounce of sympathy, for that was still beyond him.*

"Please," she whispered.

Bartholomew ignored her and continued his assessment.

Iona blinked the rain and tears from her eyes. She dug deep within herself for one last surge of energy and raised her arm, grabbing the stranger by the sleeve of his ruffled shirt.

"Please," she insisted. "Let him go. Let my Jack go." Her eyes widened to reveal their secret—the knowledge she possessed free for the taking in her weakened state, her body no longer able to keep it hidden.

Bartholomew barely felt her touch, but something managed to cut through the fabric to his skin and in his chest, a pinch constricted his breath. He had his answer, although it was only half of what he was seeking. Regardless, he knew the location of one of the Lost Creators and with this knowledge, it was time to return home. Bartholomew took Iona's hand and placed it tenderly on her chest. He thought for a moment to stay with her until the end, but he was not compassionate enough. He had his orders. The Fates were expecting his answer—this answer. Bartholomew rose from the earth as Iona began to cry again. She curled into a misshapen ball desperately trying to hold herself together. Her pain was more evident on her face, and it hit him in the most unexpected way, forcing him again to entertain the thought of staying. He took a step away, but not another, a phantom whisper insisting he stay. He sensed it surrounding him, but as lightning slithered across the dark sky, temporarily brightening the muddy road and the tree line, he could not find its source.

"Please," Iona whispered, "have mercy."

Bartholomew looked at the Shepherdess, uncertain if in her delirium she thought he was someone else—Hades, perhaps. But when she asked again for mercy, she directed it at him as though she knew him. The hopelessness in her eyes was more than he could bear. He turned away from her then and sprinted, slopping through the muddy road, unable to shake the mounting trepidation in his chest. Something was wrong—this was wrong. The lightning struck the ground in front of him, cratering the earth. Bartholomew pressed forward through the shower of mud inking his clothes, running as though the whole horde of Hell was chasing him. The thunder crashed with an angry rumble and over its echoes, a scream pierced the night. It struck Bartholomew, *like a sharp piece of ice jammed to the brain, and he stopped dead in his tracks. At first, he could not think or move, but then the numbness dwindled and he made the choice to go back, even though he knew it was already too late.*

Epilogue: Unexpected

Charlie awoke with a tight pinch in his heart. He stared at what should have been a star-filled sky, but his vision was dark. He let his breath settle before he blinked his eyes, trying to focus them, but still he could not see. He rotated his head to look for the flame of his dying fire, but that too was invisible to him. He rubbed his eyes, extracting the crust of sleepy sand, though it too did not help. He was blind. Charlie sensed a sudden rise of panic flutter in his chest. It was cold and empty, but the feelings were not his own. He clasped a hand over his chest as his heartbeat pulsed rapidly.

There was a sharp stream of agony, followed by a wave of numbness that spread to every inch of his body. He was unable to muster any rational thought, and the pressure weighed on his chest, crushing him against the ground. His breath shallowed, and his ears rang with the scream of a woman. The elements of his paralysis built, stripping him of every ounce of self—then nothing. The scream stopped. His breath ceased. His heart slowed to a crawl, and for a brief second, it was as though he lay dead in the dirt.

Charlie gasped before coughing, his heart resuming its normal rhythm. His ears heard the sounds of the wood around him again.

Charlie blinked. His eyes saw the stars and the hue of the fire casting shadows upward amongst the trees. His body felt as it should. He rotated his head, alerted by a rustle in the underbrush. The fire was too bright for him to see clearly, but with a moment to adjust, he became aware of the yellow eyes watching him. The image of a snout and a furry head with large pointed ears began to sharpen, giving form to a coyote. It stood in a crouch, its head low to the ground, ready to spring at a hint of movement. Charlie slowly slid his hand from his chest to his head, inching ever so slightly above it. His fingers touched the barrel of his shotgun and he wondered if he was as fast as he used to be—hell of a time to find out.

The coyote's crouch intensified. It was only a matter of who would spring first.

Charlie breathed deeply—*count to three, move with purpose, and your aim will be true*. He gripped the gun tightly and popped to his knees. His movement was not graceful, but his footing was sound, at the ready to shoot. He waited, anticipating the attack. Charlie lifted himself from his low position, keeping the gun level with his line of sight. His eyes gazed over the flames but did not meet with those of the coyote. He darted his eyes along the ground in both directions, but the animal was nowhere to be found.

Charlie maintained his guard, not trusting to chance the creature had truly retreated. He listened carefully.

A twig snapped.

Charlie spun around, but it was too late. The coyote leapt, its large paws jabbing him in the chest and forcing him back to the ground. The sudden jolt dislodged the gun from his hands. Charlie sized up the beast, taking note of its uncharacteristically large size, more wolf-like than a scrawny dog. Its paws pressed hard and commandingly into his breasts. Charlie did not struggle.

He had not the strength to try.

Do it . . . end it . . . do it quickly.

The coyote lowered its head, its nose nearly touching his face. It sniffed.

That's right, do it. Do it now!

The coyote's pale eyes fixed on the smooth toffee in Charlie's eyes.

Charlie returned the stare. He did not want to blink for fear of missing his own death, but noticed the coyote's eyes were not full of madness. Instead, they were calm. Charlie did not want to believe it, but it was hard to deny the creature meant him no harm.

"Don't stare at me!" cried Charlie. "Do what it is you came here to do. Take my life!"

The coyote's ears fell back, saddened by his words. It moved its nose to touch his, the intensity of its stare consuming him. The coyote's warm breath trickled down his neck.

This is it. Now it will be done—but, much to his dismay, nothing transpired.

Charlie shifted his eyes, searching for meaning. The flames reflected in the coyote's left eye and there it gleamed—a message. Charlie knew who the message was from, the one whose name he refused to speak. He was grateful that the Breedling was all right, but hated the feeling that sat like a rock in the pit of his gut. He understood then the reason why he had lain dead for a brief moment, why he felt cold, empty, and alone. The Breedling had gone back to his world. Charlie shook his head. He did not want to believe it. He did not want to think of the responsibility he left behind, the tagalong whose truth he could not bear to know. He fluttered his eyes to acknowledge he understood—his death would have to wait.

The coyote rose its head and bellowed. Its volume filled the vastness around them and lingered until it faded. The coyote let out another cry. This time an answer arose in the distance and without another look at Charlie, it disappeared into the underbrush.

Charlie rolled onto his side, bringing his knees up to his chest. His eyes were on the fire again, the glow no longer comforting but rather a reminder of what he had lost. The tears came more easily since he had left Chicago, his mind and heart unable to forget, unable to forgive. He wrapped himself tighter, hoping this time he could fend off the misery. How he wished the coyote had released him from it.

"I'm sorry," he sobbed, his voice lost in the night air, unable to speak either of their names. The one he could not save and the one he had.

Acknowledgments

Book Two would not be possible without the support of my family, friends and fans. I write for me, but also with you in mind. Thank you for letting Buck, Jack, Charlie, Hades, and all the others into your imagination. I am eternally grateful for your fandom and my characters sincerely look forward to more adventures with you.

To my Lord and Lady Patrons: my dearest friends Erin and Billy Ellis; my sister Mary; my Desert Phoenix, Inger Erickson; and Luanne Petron. Thank you kindly for your generosity.

As always, my creative team at Wise Ink Creative Publishing: Laura Zats; my designer, Steve Meyer-Rassow; my editor, Amanda Rutter; my proofreader, Patrick Maloney; and Roseanne Cheng. Collaborating with each of you is always a fantastic and pleasurable adventure.

To my bohemian sister, Terri Hansen, and my fifth mom, Patti Mueller; your excitement, feedback, and support have been a godsend, and I appreciate you both for believing in me.

To the Recreation, Parks, & Leisure Services Department at Minnesota State University, Mankato: You let me be creative when English would not. You made me a better writer and researcher. Thank you Joy, Ron, Jim, and Pete for your tutelage.

Finally, thank you to the following organizations, businesses, authors, and creators who gave me inspiration and knowledge and kept the writer's block at bay:

- Winona Public Library
- Milwaukee Road Historic Association
- Wisconsin Historical Society
- Milwaukee Public Library Digital Collections
- University of Wisconsin Milwaukee Library Archives & Digital Sanborn Maps
- Minnesota Historical Society Visual Resources Database
- Mplswarehouse.com
- Hennepin County Library Digital Sanborn Maps Collection
- Minnesota Historical Preservation Office
- "Minneapolis Warehouse District Designation Study" by City of MPLS Community Planning & Economic Development Planning Division—2009
- Blue Earth County Historic Society
- *Over the Earth I Come: The Great Sioux Uprising of 1862* by Duane Schultz—Chapter 2: "Let Them Eat Grass," pgs. 7-29 (*The Man Who Ate Grass*)
- "City of Mankato Historic Context Study" by Thomas R. Zahn & Associates LLC—2009-2010 (http://www.mankato-mn. gov/upload/images/Mankato%20FINAL%20Context%20 Study%20mid-res.pdf)
- *Who Framed Roger Rabbit* screenplay by Jeffrey Price & Peter Seaman (Touchstone) 1988

- HistoryChannel.com "The Legend of the Jack O' Lantern"
- Google Maps Street View; Wikipedia.com
- Hilton Milwaukee City Center and Renaissance Minneapolis Depot

Kimberlee Ann Bastian is the author of the *Element Odysseys* series, starting with her debut novel *The Breedling and the City in the Garden,* and its sequel *The Breedling and the Trickster.*

Kimberlee has a unique love affair with all things vintage, historic architecture, and magic. When she is not in her writer's room or consuming other literary worlds, she enjoys time with family and cycling around the bluffs of your Southeastern MN home.